Fawcett Crest and Gold Medal Books
by Jack Higgins:

EAST OF DESOLATION

HELL IS TOO CROWDED

IN THE HOUR BEFORE MIDNIGHT

THE IRON TIGER

THE KEYS OF HELL

THE LAST PLACE GOD MADE

NIGHT JUDGEMENT AT SINOS

PASSAGE BY NIGHT

A PRAYER FOR THE DYING

THE SAVAGE DAY

TOLL FOR THE BRAVE

WRATH OF THE LION

THE VALHALLA EXCHANGE

a novel by

Harry Patterson

A FAWCETT CREST BOOK

Fawcett Books, Greenwich, Connecticut

THE VALHALLA EXCHANGE

THIS BOOK CONTAINS THE COMPLETE TEXT OF
THE ORIGINAL HARDCOVER EDITION.

Published by Fawcett Crest Books, CBS Publications, CBS
Consumer Publishing, a Division of CBS Inc., by arrangement with Stein and Day.

ISBN: 0-449-23449-5

Alternate Selection of the Book-of-the-Month Club, June 1977

Printed in the United States of America

10 9 8 7 6 5 4 3 2 1

*For my mother and father, who helped
more than a little with this one*

Whether Martin Bormann survived the holocaust that was Berlin at the end of the Second World War may be arguable, but it is a matter of record that Russian radar reported a light aircraft leaving the vicinity of the Tiergarten in Berlin on the morning of April 30, the very day on which Adolf Hitler committed suicide. As for the remainder of this story, only the more astonishing parts are true—the rest is fiction.

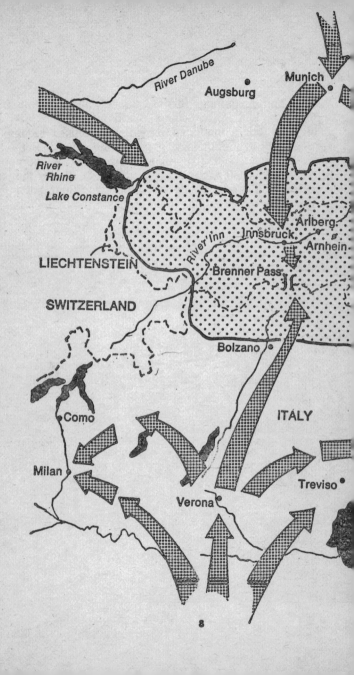

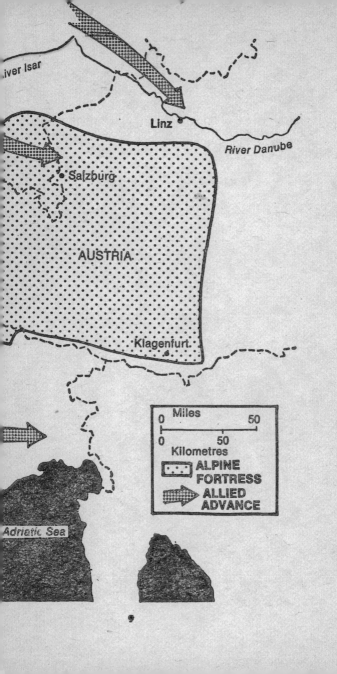

River Isar

Linz

River Danube

Salzburg

AUSTRIA

Klagenfurt

Miles
0   50

0   50
Kilometres

ALPINE
FORTRESS

ALLIED
ADVANCE

Adriatic Sea

9

One

ON the Day of the Dead in Bolivia, children take food and presents to the cemetery to leave on the graves of the departed. An interesting blend of the pagan and Christian traditions, and highly appropriate the way things turned out. But even the most superstitious of Bolivian peasants would hardly expect the dead to get up and walk on such an occasion. I did.

La Huerta was a mining town of five or six thousand people, lost in the peaks of the high Andes. The back of beyond. There was no direct passenger flight from Peru, so I'd flown in from Lima in an old DC-3 that was doing some kind of cargo run to an American mining company.

It was raining hard when I arrived, but by some dispensation or other there was a cab standing outside the small terminal building. The driver was a cheerful Indian with a heavy moustache. He wore a yellow oilskin coat and a straw hat and seemed surprised and gratified at the sight of a customer.

"The hotel, *señor?*" he asked as he seized my valise.

"The Excelsior," I said.

"But that is the hotel, *señor.*" His teeth gleamed in the lamplight. "The only one."

The interior of the cab stank, the roof leaked, and as we started down the hill to the lights of the town, I felt unaccountably depressed. Why the hell was I here, doing the same thing I'd done so many times before? Chasing my tail for a story that probably didn't exist in the first place. And La Huerta itself didn't help as we turned into a maze of narrow streets, each one with the usual open sewer running down the center, decaying, flat-roofed houses crowding in, poverty and squalor on every side.

We emerged into a central plaza a few minutes later. There was a large and rather interesting baroque fountain in the center—some relic of colonial days, water gushing forth from the mouths and nostrils of a score of nymphs and dryads. The fact that it was working at all seemed a small miracle. The hotel was on the far side. As I got out I noticed a number of people sheltering under a colonnade to my right. Some of them were in carnival costume, and there was the smell of smoke on the damp air.

"What's all that?" I asked.

"All Saints' Day, *señor*. A time of festival."

"They don't look as if they're enjoying themselves too much."

"The rain." He shrugged. "It makes it difficult for the fireworks. But then this is a solemn occasion with us. Soon they will go in procession to the cemetery to greet their loved ones. The Day of the Dead, we call it. You have heard of this, *señor?*"

"They have the same thing in Mexico."

I paid him off, went up the steps, and entered the hotel. Like everything else in La Huerta, it had seen better days, but now its pink stucco walls were peeling and there were damp patches on the ceiling. The desk clerk put down his newspaper hurriedly, as amazed as the cabdriver had been at the prospect of custom.

"I'd like a room."

"But of course, *señor*. For how long?"

"One night. I'm flying back to Peru in the morning."

I passed my papers across so that he could go through the usual rigmarole the government insists on where foreigners are concerned.

As he filled in the register he said, "You have business here, *señor?* With the mining company, perhaps?"

I opened my wallet and extracted an American ten-dollar bill, which I placed carefully on the counter beside the register. He stopped writing, the eyes dark, watchful.

"It was reported in one of the Lima newspapers that a man died here Monday. Dropped dead in the plaza, right outside your front door. It rated a mention because the police found fifty thousand dollars in cash in his suitcase and passports in three different names."

"Ah, yes, *Señor* Bauer. You are a friend of his, *señor?*"

"No, but I might know him if I see him."

"He is with the local undertaker. In such cases

they keep the body for a week while relatives are sought."

"So I was informed."

"Lieutenant Gómez is chief of police in charge of the affair, and police headquarters are on the other side of the plaza."

"I never find the police too helpful in these affairs." I laid another ten-dollar bill beside the first. "I'm a journalist. There could be a story in this for me. It's as simple as that."

"Ah, I see now. A newspaperman." His eyes lightened. "How may I help you?"

"Bauer—what can you tell me about him?"

"Very little, *señor*. He arrived last week from Sucre. Said he expected a friend to join him."

"And did anyone?"

"Not that I know of."

"What did he look like? Describe him."

"Sixty-five, maybe older. Yes, he could have been older, but it's difficult to say. He was one of those men who give an impression of vitality at all times. A bull of a man."

"Why do you say that?"

"Powerfully built. Not tall, you understand me, but with broad shoulders." He stretched his arms. "A thick, powerful neck."

"A fat man?"

"No, I don't remember him that way. More the power of the man, an impression of strength. He spoke good Spanish, with a German accent."

"You can recognize it?"

"Oh, yes, *señor*. Many German engineers come here."

"Can I see the entry in the register?"

He turned it around to show me. It was on the line above mine. There were the details from his passport entered by the clerk, and beside it Bauer's signature—a trifle spidery, but firm—and the date beside it, using a crossed seven, continental style.

I nodded and pushed the two bills across. "Thank you."

"*Señor.*" He snapped up the twenty dollars and tucked it into his breast pocket. "I'll show you your room."

I glanced at my watch. It was just after eleven. "Too late to visit the undertaker now."

"Oh, no, *señor,* there is a porter on duty all night. It is the custom here for the dead to be in waiting for three days, during which time they are watched over both night and day in case. . . ." Here, he hesitated.

"Of a mistake?" I suggested.

"Exactly, *señor.*" He smiled sadly. "Death is a very final affair, so one wants to be sure. Take the first street on the left. You will find the undertaker's at the far end. You can't miss it. There's a blue light above the door. The watchman's name is Hugo. Tell him Rafael Mareno sent you."

"My thanks," I said formally.

"At your orders, *señor.* And if you would care to eat on your return, something could be managed. I am on duty all night."

He picked up his newspaper, and I retraced my steps across the hall and went outside. The procession had formed up and started across the square as I paused at the top of the steps. It was much as I had seen in Mexico. There were a couple of characters in front, blazing torches in hand, dressed to represent the lords of death and hell. Next came the children, clutching guttering candles, some already extinguished in the heavy rain, the adults following on behind with baskets of bread and fruit. Someone started to play a flute, low and plaintive, and a finger drum joined in. Otherwise, they moved in complete silence.

We seemed to be going the same way, and I joined on at the tail of the procession, turning up the collar of my trenchcoat against the heavy rain. The undertaker's was plain enough, the subdued blue light above the door as Mareno had indicated. I paused, watching the procession continue, the sound of that flute and drum strangely haunting, and only when they had turned into another alley and moved out of sight did I pull the bell chain.

There was silence for quite some time, only the rain. I was about to reach for the chain again when I became aware of a movement inside, dragging footsteps approaching. A grille opened at eye level, a face peered out, pale in the darkness.

"Hugo?"

"What is it you want, *señor?*" The voice was the merest whisper.

"I would like to see the body of *Señor* Ricardo Bauer."

"Perhaps in the morning, *señor.*"

"Rafael Mareno sent me."

There was a pause, then the grille was closed. There was the sound of bolts being withdrawn; the door creaked open. He stood there, an oil lamp in one hand, very old, very frail, almost as if one of his own charges had decided to get up and walk. I slipped inside; he closed the door.

"You will follow me, please?"

He led the way along a short passage and opened an oaken door, and I could smell death instantly, the cloying sweetness of it heavy on the cold air. I hesitated, then followed him through.

The room into which I entered was a place of shadows, a single oil lamp suspended from a chain in the center supplying the only light. It was a waiting mortuary of a type I had seen a couple of times before in Palermo and Vienna, although the Viennese version had been considerably more elaborate. There were perhaps a dozen coffins on the other side of the room, but first he led me up some steps to a small platform on which stood a desk and chair.

I gazed down into the shadows in fascination. Each coffin was open, a corpse clearly visible inside, the stiff fingers firmly entwined in one end of a string that went up over a pulley arrangement and across to the desk, where the other end was fastened to an old-fashioned bell that hung from a wall bracket.

He put down his lamp. I said, "Has anyone ever rung that thing?"

"The bell?" I saw now that he was very old, eighty at least, the face desiccated, the eyes moist. "Once, *señor,* ten years ago. A young girl. But she died again three days later. Her father refused to acknowledge the fact. He kept her with him for a month. Finally the police had to intervene."

"I can see how they would have to."

He opened a ledger and dipped a pen in an inkwell. "Your relationship to *Señor* Bauer, *señor?* I must enter it in the official record."

I took out my wallet and produced another of those ten-dollar bills. "Nothing so formal, my friend. I'm just a newspaperman passing through. I heard the story and thought I might recognize him."

He hesitated, then laid down the pen. "As you say, *señor*." He picked up the lamp. "This way."

It was the end coffin in the back row, and I received something of a shock as the old man raised his lamp to reveal red lips, a gleam of teeth, full, rounded cheeks. And then I realized, of course, that the undertaker had been going to work on him. It was as if a wax tailor's dummy had been laid out for my inspection, a totally unreal face heavy with makeup, resembling no photo that I had ever seen. But how could he hope to, thirty years later? A big, big difference between forty-five and seventy-five.

When the bell jangled I almost jumped out of my skin, and then realized it had sounded from outside. Hugo said, "You will excuse me, *señor*. There is someone at the door."

He shuffled off, leaving me there beside Bauer's coffin. If there had been rings, they'd taken them off, and the powerful fingers were intertwined on his chest, the string between them. They'd dressed him in a neat blue suit, white collar, dark tie. It really was rather remarkable.

I became aware of the voices outside in the corridor, one unmistakably American. "You speak English? No?"

Then the same voice continuing in bad Spanish. "I must see the body of the man Bauer. I've come a long way, and my time is limited."

Hugo tried to protest, *"Señor*—it is late," but he was obviously brushed aside.

"Where is the body? In here?"

For some reason, some sixth sense operating if you like, I moved back into the darkness of the corner. A moment later I was glad that I had.

He stepped into the room and paused, white hair gleaming in the lamplight, rain glistening on his military raincoat, shoulders firm, the figure still militarily erect, only the whiteness of the hair and the clipped moustache hinting at his seventy-five years.

I don't think I've ever been so totally astonished, for I was looking at a legend in his own time, General Hamilton Canning, Congressional Medal of Honor, DSC, Silver Star, Médaille Militaire, the Philippines, D-Day, Korea, even Vietnam in the early days. A piece of walking history, one of the most respected of living Americans.

He had a harsh, distinctive voice, not unpleasant, but it carried with it the authority of a man who'd been used to getting his own way for most of his life.

"Which one?"

Hugo limped past him, lamp held high, and I crouched back in the corner. "Here, *señor*."

Canning's face seemed calm enough, but in the eyes I saw the turbulence, a blazing intensity, and also a kind of hope as he stood at the end of the coffin and looked down at the waxen face. And then hope died, the light went out in the eyes— something. The shoulders sagged, and for the first time he looked his age.

He turned wearily and nodded to Hugo. "I won't trouble you any further."

"This is not the person you were seeking, *señor?*"

Canning shook his head. "No, my friend, I don't think so. Good night to you."

He seemed to take a deep breath, all the old vigor returning, and strode from the room. I came out of the shadows quickly.

"*Señor.*" Hugo started to speak.

I motioned him to silence and moved to the entrance. As Canning opened the door, I saw the cab from the airstrip outside, the driver waiting in the rain.

The general said, "You can take me to the hotel now," and closed the door behind him.

Hugo tugged at my sleeve. "*Señor,* what passes here?"

"Exactly what I was wondering, Hugo," I said softly, and I went along the passage quickly and let myself out.

■

The cab was parked outside the hotel. As I approached, a man in a leather flying jacket and peaked cap hurried down the steps and got in. The cab drove away through the rain. I watched it go for a moment, unable to see if Canning was inside.

Rafael wasn't behind the desk, but as I paused, shaking the rain from my coat, a door on my left opened and he emerged.

He smiled. "Were you successful, *señor?*"

"Not really," I said. "Did I see the cab driving away just now?"

"Ah, yes, that was the pilot of Mr. Smith, an American gentleman who has just checked in. He was on his way to La Paz in his private airplane, but they had to put down here because of the weather."

"I see. Mr. Smith, you say?"

"That is correct, *señor*. I've just given him a drink in the bar. Could I perhaps get you something?"

"Well, now," I said. "A large brandy might be a sensible idea, considering the state I'm in."

I followed him, unbuttoning my trenchcoat. It was a pleasant enough room, rough stone walls, a well-stocked bar at one side. Canning was seated in an armchair in front of a blazing log fire, a glass in one hand. He looked up sharply.

"Company, *señor*," Rafael said cheerfully. "A fellow guest. *Señor* O'Hagan—*Señor* Smith. I'll just get your brandy now," he added and moved away.

"Not a night for even an old tomcat to be out," I said, throwing my coat over a chair. "As my old grannie used to say."

He smiled up at me, the famous Canning charm well in evidence, and stuck out his hand. "English, Mr. O'Hagan?"

"By way of Ulster," I said. "But we won't get into that, General."

The smile stayed firmly in place—only the eyes changed, cold, hard—and the hand tightened on mine with a grip of surprising strength, considering his age.

It was Rafael who broke the spell, arriving with my brandy on a tray. "Can I get you another one, *señor?*" he asked.

Canning smiled, all charm again. "Later, my friend. Later."

"*Señores.*"

Rafael departed. Canning leaned back, watching me, then swallowed a little Scotch. He didn't waste time trying to tell me how mistaken I was, but said simply, "We've met before, presumably?"

"About fifteen minutes ago, up the street at the mortuary," I said. "I was standing in the shadows, I should explain, so I had you at something of a disadvantage. Oh, I've seen you before at press conferences over the years, that sort of thing, but then one couldn't really specialize in writing about politics and military affairs without knowing Hamilton Canning."

"O'Hagan," he said. "The one who writes for the *Times?*"

"I'm afraid so, General."

"You've a good mind, son, but remind me to put you straight on China. You've been way out of line in that area lately."

"You're the expert." I took out a cigarette. "What about Bauer, General?"

"What about him?" He leaned back, legs sprawled, all negligent ease.

I laughed. "All right, let's try it another way. You ask *me* why a reasonably well-known correspondent for *The Times of London* takes the trouble to haul himself all the way from Lima to a pesthole like this just to look at the body of a man called Ricardo Bauer who dropped dead in the street here on Monday."

"All right, son," he said lazily. "You tell me. I'm all ears."

"Ricardo Bauer," I said, "as more than one expert will tell you, is one of the aliases used by Martin Bormann in Brazil, Argentina, Chile, and Paraguay on many occasions during the past thirty years."

"Martin Bormann?" he said.

"Oh, come off it, General. *Reichsleiter* Martin Bormann, head of the Nazi Party Chancellery and secretary to the *Führer*. The one member of Hitler's top table unaccounted for since the war."

"Bormann's dead," he said softly. "He was killed attempting to break out of Berlin. Blown up crossing the Weidendammer Bridge on the night of May 1, 1945."

"Early hours of May second, General," I said. "Let's get it right. Bormann left the bunker at one-thirty A.M. It was Erich Kempka, Hitler's chauffeur, who saw him come under artillery fire on that bridge. Unfortunately for that story, the Hitler Youth leader, Artur Axmann, crossed the Spree River on a railway bridge as part of a group led by Bormann, and that was considerably later."

He nodded. "But Axmann asserted also that he'd seen Bormann and Hitler's doctor, Stumpfegger, lying dead near Lehrter Station."

"And no one else to confirm the story," I said. "Very convenient."

He put down his glass, took out a pipe, and started to fill it from a leather pouch. "So you believe he's alive. Wouldn't you say that's kind of crazy?"

"It would certainly put me in pretty mixed company," I said. "Starting with Stalin and lesser mortals like Jacob Glas, Bormann's chauffeur, who saw him in Munich after the war. Then there was Eich-mann—when the Israelis picked him up in 1960, he told them Bormann was alive. Now why would he do that if it wasn't true?"

"A neat point. Go on."

"Simon Wiesenthal, the Nazi-hunter, always insisted he was alive, maintained he had regular reports on him. Farago said he actually interviewed him. Since 1964, the West German authorities have had a hundred thousand marks on his head, and he was found guilty of war crimes at Nuremberg and sentenced to death *in absentia*." I leaned forward. "What more do you want, General? Would you like to hear the one about the Spaniard who maintains he traveled to Argentina from Spain with Bormann in a U-boat in 1945?"

He smiled, leaning over to put another log on the fire. "Yes, I interviewed him soon after he came out with that story. But if Bormann's been alive all these years, what's he been doing?"

"The *Kameradenwerk*," I said. "'Action for comrades.' The organization they set up to take care of the movement after the war, with hundreds of millions in gold salted away to pay for it."

"Possible." He nodded, staring into the fire. "Possible."

"One thing is sure," I said. "That isn't him lying up there at the mortuary. At least you don't think so."

He glanced up at me. "Why do you say that?"

"I saw your face."

He nodded. "No, it wasn't Bormann."

"How did you know about him? Bauer, I mean.

Events in La Huerta hardly make front-page news in *The New York Times*."

"I employ an agent in Brazil who has a list of certain names. Any mention of any of them anywhere in South America and he informs me. I flew straight down."

"Now that I find truly remarkable."

"What do you want to know, son? What he looked like? Will that do? Five feet six inches, bull neck, prominent cheekbones, broad, rather brutal face. You could lose him in any crowd because he looked so damned ordinary. Just another working stiff off the waterfront or whatever. He was virtually unknown to the German public and press. Honors, medals meant nothing to him. Power was all." It was as if he were talking to himself as he sat there staring into the fire. "He was the most powerful man in Germany, and nobody appreciated it until after the war."

"A butcher," I said, "who condoned the Final Solution and the deaths of millions of Jews."

"Who also sent war orphans to his wife in Bavaria to look after," Canning said. "You know what Göring said at Nuremberg when they asked him if he knew where Bormann was? He said, 'I hope he's frying in hell, but I don't know.'"

He heaved himself out of the chair, went behind the bar, and reached for a bottle of Scotch. "Can I get you another?"

"Why not?" I got up and sat on one of the bar stools. "Brandy."

As he poured some into my glass he said, "I was once a prisoner of war, did you know that?"

"That's a reasonably well-known fact, General," I said. "You were captured in Korea. The Chinese had you for two years in Manchuria. Isn't that why Nixon hauled you out of retirement the other year to go to Peking with him?"

"No, I mean way, way back. I was a prisoner once before. Toward the end of the Second World War, the Germans had me. At Schloss Arlberg in Bavaria. A special setup for prominent prisoners."

And I genuinely hadn't known, although it was so far back it was hardly surprising—and then his really enduring fame had been gained in Korea, after all.

I said, "I didn't know that, General."

He dropped ice into his glass, and poured a very large measure of whisky. "Yes, I was there right to the bitter end. In the area erroneously known as the Alpine Redoubt. One of Dr. Goebbels's smarter pieces of propaganda. He actually had the Allies believing there was such a place. It meant the troops were very cautious about probing into that area at first, which made it a safe resting place for big Nazis on the run from Berlin in those last few days."

"Hitler could have gone, but didn't."

"That's right."

"And Bormann?"

"What do you mean?"

"The one thing that's never made any sense to me," I said. "He was a brilliant man. Too clever by half to leave his chances of survival to a mad scramble at the final end of things. If he'd really wanted to escape, he'd have gone to Berchtesgaden when he had the chance, instead of staying in the bunker till the end. He'd have had a plan."

"Oh, but he did, son." Canning nodded slowly. "You can bet your sweet life on that."

"And how would you know, General?" I asked softly.

And at that he exploded, came apart at the seams.

"Because I saw him, damn you," he cried harshly. "Because I stood as close to him as I am to you, traded shots with him, had my hands on his throat, do you understand?" He paused, hands held out, looking at them in a kind of wonder. "And lost him," he whispered.

He leaned on the bar, head down. There was a long, long moment in which I couldn't think of a thing to say, but waited, my stomach hollow with excitement. When he finally raised his head, he was calm again.

"You know what's so strange, O'Hagan? So bloody incredible? I kept it to myself all these years. Never mentioned it to a soul until now."

Two

I T began, if it may be said to have begun anywhere, on the morning of Wednesday, April 25, 1945, a few miles north of Innsbruck.

When Jack Howard emerged from the truck at the rear of the column just after first light, it was bitterly cold, a powdering of dry snow on the ground, for the valley in which they had halted for the night was high in the Bavarian Alps, although he couldn't see much of the mountains because of the heavy clinging mist which had settled among the trees. It reminded him too much of the Ardennes for comfort. He stamped his feet to induce a little warmth, and lit a cigarette.

Sergeant Hoover had started a wood fire, and the men—only five of them now—crouched beside it. Anderson, O'Grady, Garland, and Finebaum—who'd once played clarinet for Glenn Miller and never let anyone forget it. Just now he was on his face trying to blow fresh life into the flames. He was the first to notice Howard.

"Hey, the captain's up, and he don't look too good."

"Why don't you try a mirror?" Garland inquired. "You think you look like a daisy or something?"

"Stinkweed—that's the only flower he ever resembled," O'Grady said.

"That's it, hotshot," Finebaum told him. "You're out. From here on in, you find your own beans." He turned to Hoover. "I ask you, Sarge. I appeal to your better nature. Is that the best these mothers can offer after all I've done for them?"

"That's a truly lousy act, Finebaum, did I ever tell you that?" Hoover poured coffee into an aluminum cup. "You're going to need plenty of practice, boy, if you're ever going to get back into vaudeville."

"Well, I'll tell you," Finebaum said. "I've had kind of a special problem lately. I ran out of audience. Most of them died on me."

Hoover took the coffee across to the truck and gave it to Howard without a word. Somewhere thunder rumbled on the horizon.

Eighty-eights?" the captain said.

Hoover nodded. "Don't they ever give up? It don't make any kind of sense to me. Every time we turn on the radio, they tell us this war's as good as finished."

"Maybe they forgot to tell the Germans."

"That makes sense. Any chance of submitting it through channels?"

Howard shook his head. "It wouldn't do any good, Harry. Those Krauts don't intend to give in until they get you. That's what it's all about."

Hoover grunted. "Those mothers better be quick, or they're going to miss out, that's all I can say. You want to eat now? We still got plenty of K-rations, and Finebaum traded some smokes last night for half a dozen cans of beans from some of those Limey tank guys up the column."

"The coffee's just fine, Harry," Howard said. "Maybe later."

The sergeant moved back to the fire, and Howard paced up and down beside the truck, stamping his feet and clutching the hot cup tightly in mittened fingers. He was twenty-three years of age, young to be a captain in the Rangers, but that was a circumstance of war. He wore a crumpled mackinaw coat, wool-knit muffler at his throat, and a knitted cap. There were times when he could have passed for nineteen, but this was not one of them, not with the four-day growth of dark beard on his chin, the sunken eyes.

But once he had been nineteen, an Ohio farmer's son with some pretensions to being a poet and the desire to write for a living which had sent him to Columbia to study journalism. That was a long time ago—before the Flood. Before the further circumstance of war which had brought him to his present situation in charge of the reconnaissance element for a column of the British Seventh Armored Division, probing into Bavaria toward Berchtesgaden.

Hoover squatted beside the fire. Finebaum passed him a plate of beans. "The captain not eating?"

"Not right now."

31

"Jesus," Finebaum said. "What kind of a way is that to carry on?"

"Respect, Finebaum." Hoover prodded him with his knife. "Just a little more respect when you speak about him."

"Sure, I respect him," Finebaum said. "I respect him like crazy, and I know how you and he went in at Salerno together, and how those Krauts jumped you outside Anzio with those machine guns zeroed in and took out three-quarters of the battalion, and how our gracious captain saved the rest. So he's God's gift to the army—so he should eat occasionally. He ain't swallowed more than a couple of mouthfuls since Sunday."

"Sunday he lost `nine men," Hoover said. "Maybe you're forgetting."

"Those guys are dead—so they're dead, right? He don't keep his strength up, he might lose a few more, including me. I mean, look at him! He's got so skinny, that stinking coat he wears is two sizes too big for him. He looks like some fresh kid in his first year at college."

"I know," Hoover said. "The kind they give the Silver Star with Oak Leaf Cluster to."

The others laughed, and Finebaum managed to look injured. 'Okay, okay. I've come this far. I just figure it would look kind of silly to die now."

"Everybody dies," Hoover said. "Sooner or later. Even you."

"Okay—but not here. Not now. I mean, after surviving D-Day, Omaha, Saint-Lô, the Ardennes, and a few interesting stop-offs in between, it would look kind of stupid to buy it here, playing wet nurse to a bunch of Limeys."

"We've been on the same side for nearly four years now," Hoover said. "Or hadn't you noticed?"

"How can I help it with guys going around dressed like that?" Finebaum nodded to where the commanding officer of the column, a lieutenant colonel named Denning, was approaching, his adjutant at his side. They were Highlanders and wore rather dashing Glengarry bonnets.

"'Morning, Howard," Denning said as he got close. "Damn cold night. Winter's hung on late up here this year."

"I guess so, Colonel."

"Let's have a look at the map, Miller." The adjutant spread it against the side of the truck, and the colonel ran a finger along the center. "Here's Innsbruck, and here we are. Another five miles to the head of this valley and we hit a junction with the main road to Salzburg. We could have trouble there, wouldn't you say so?"

"Very possibly, Colonel."

"Good. We'll move out in thirty minutes. I suggest you take the lead and send your other jeep on ahead to scout out the land."

"As you say, sir."

Denning and the adjutant moved away, and Howard turned to Hoover and the rest of the men, who had all edged in close enough to hear. "You got that, Harry?"

"I think so, sir."

"Good. You take Finebaum and O'Grady. Garland and Anderson stay with me. Report in over your radio every five minutes without fail. Now get moving."

As they swung into action, Finebaum said plaintively, "Holy Mary, Mother of God, I'm only a Jewish boy, but pray for us sinners in the hour of our need."

■

On the radio, the news was good. The Russians had finally encircled Berlin and had made contact with American troops on the Elbe River seventy-five miles south of the capital, cutting Germany in half.

"The only way in and out of Berlin now is by air, sir," Anderson said to Howard. "They can't keep going any longer—they've got to give in. It's the only logical thing to do."

"Oh, I don't know," Howard said. "I'd say that if your name was Hitler or Goebbels or Himmler and the only prospect offered was a short trial and a long rope, you might think it worthwhile to go down taking as many of the other side with you as you possibly could."

Anderson, who had the wheel, looked worried, as well he might, for, unlike Garland, he was married, with two children, a girl of five and a boy aged six. He gripped the wheel so tightly that the knuckles on his hands turned white.

You shouldn't have joined, old buddy, Howard thought. You should have found an easier way. Plenty did.

Strange how callous he had become where the suffering of others was concerned, but that was the war. It had left him indifferent where death was concerned, even to its uglier aspects. The time when a body had an emotional effect was long since gone. He had seen too many of them. The fact of death was all that mattered.

The radio crackled into life. Hoover's voice sounded clearly. "Sugar Nan Two to Sugar Nan One. Are you receiving me?"

"Strength nine," Howard said. "Where are you, Harry?"

"We've reached the road junction, sir. Not a Kraut in sight. What do we do now?"

Howard checked his watch. "Stay there. We'll be with you in twenty minutes. Over and out."

He replaced the handmike and turned to Garland. "Strange—I would have expected something from them up there. A good place to put up a fight. Still . . ."

There was a sudden roaring in his ears, and a great wind seemed to pick him up and carry him away. The world moved in and out and then somehow he was lying in a ditch, Garland beside him, minus his helmet and most of the top of his skull. The jeep or what was left of it, was on its side, the Cromwell tank behind blazing furiously, its ammunition exploding like a fireworks display. One of the crew scrambled out of the turret, his uniform on fire, and fell to the ground.

There was no reality to it at all—none. And then Howard realized why. He couldn't hear a damn thing. Something to do with the explosion, probably. Things seemed to be happening in slow motion, as if under water—no noise, not even the whisper of a sound. There was blood on his hands, but he got his field glasses up to his eyes and traversed the trees on the hillside on the other side of the road. Almost immediately a Tiger tank jumped into view, a young man with a pale face in the black uniform of a *Sturmbannführer* of SS panzer troops standing in the gun turret, quite exposed. As Howard watched helplessly, he saw the microphone raised. The lips moved, and then the Tiger's 88 belched flame and smoke.

■

The man whom Howard had seen in the turret of the lead Tiger was SS Major Karl Ritter, of the Third Company, 502nd SS Heavy Tank Battalion, and what was to take place during the ensuing five minutes was probably the single most devastating Tiger action of the Second World War.

Ritter was a Tiger ace, with 120 claimed victories on the Russian Front, a man who had learned his business the hard way and knew exactly what he was doing. With only two operational Tigers on the hillside with him, he was hopelessly outnumbered—a fact which a reconnaissance on foot had indicated to him that morning—and it was obvious that Denning would expect trouble at the junction with the Salzburg road. Therefore, an earlier attack had seemed essential—indeed, there was no alternative.

It succeeded magnificently, for on the particular stretch of forest track he had chosen there was no room for any vehicle to reverse or change direction. The first shell from his Tiger's 88 narrowly missed direct contact with the lead jeep, turning it over and putting Howard and his men into the ditch. The second shell, seconds later, brewed up the leading Cromwell tank. Ritter was already transmitting orders to his gunner, Sergeant Major Erich Hoffer. The 88 traversed again, and a moment later scored a direct hit on a Bren-gun carrier bringing up the rear.

The entire column was now at a standstill, hopelessly trapped, unable to move forward or back. Ritter made a hand signal, the other two Tigers moved out of the woods on either side, and the carnage began.

In the five minutes which followed, their three 88s and six machine guns left thirty armored vehicles ablaze, including eight Cromwell tanks.

■

The front reconnaissance jeep was out of sight among the trees at the junction with the road to Salzburg. O'Grady was sitting behind the wheel, Hoover beside him lighting a cigarette. Finebaum was a few yards away, directly above the road, squatting against a tree, his M1 across his knees, eating beans from a can with a knife.

O'Grady was eighteen and a replacement of only a few weeks' standing. He said, "He's disgusting, you know that, Sarge? He not only acts like a pig, he eats like one. And the way he goes on, never stopping talking, making out everything's some kind of bad joke."

"Maybe it is as far as he's concerned," Hoover said. "When we landed at Omaha, there were a hundred and twenty-three guys in the outfit. Now there are six, including you, and you don't count worth a shit. And don't ever let Finebaum fool you. He's got a pocketful of medals somewhere, just for the dead men he's left around."

There was the sudden dull thunder of heavy

gunfire down in the valley below, the rattle of a machine gun.

Finebaum hurried toward the jeep, rifle in hand. "Hey, Harry, that don't sound too good to me. What do you make of it?"

"I think maybe somebody just made a bad mistake." Hoover slapped O'Grady on the shoulder. "Okay, kid, let's get the hell out of here."

Finebaum scrambled into the rear and positioned himself behind the Browning heavy machine gun as O'Grady reversed quickly and started back down the track to the valley road. The sound of firing was continuous now, interspersed with one heavy explosion after another, and then they rounded a bend and found a Tiger tank moving up the road toward them.

Finebaum's hands tightened on the handles of the machine gun, but they were too close for any positive action and there was nowhere to run, the pine trees pressing in on either side of the road at that point.

O'Grady screamed, at the last moment releasing the wheel and flinging up his arms as if to protect himself, and then they were close enough for Finebaum to see the death's-head badge on the cap of the SS major in the turret of the Tiger. A moment later the collision took place, and he was thrown headfirst into the brush. The Tiger moved on relentlessly, crushing the jeep beneath it, and disappeared around the bend in the road.

■

Howard had lost consciousness for a while and came back to life to the sound of repeated explosions from the ammunition in another burning

Cromwell. It was a scene from hell—smoke everywhere, the cries of the dying, the stench of burning flesh. He could see Colonel Denning lying in the middle of the road on his back a few yards away, revolver still clutched firmly in one hand, and, beyond him, a Bren-gun carrier was tilted on its side against a tree, bodies spilling out, tumbled one on top of another.

He tried to get to his feet, started to fall, and was caught as he went down. Hoover said, "Easy, sir. I've got you."

Howard turned in a daze and found Finebaum there, also. "You all right, Harry?"

"We lost O'Grady. Ran head-on into a Tiger up the road. Where are you hit?"

"Nothing serious. Most of the blood's Garland's. He and Anderson bought it."

Finebaum stood holding his M1 ready. "Hey, this must have been a real turkey shoot."

"I just met Death," Howard said dully. "A nice-looking guy in a black uniform, with a silver skull-and-crossbones in his cap."

"Is that so?" Finebaum said. "I think maybe we had a brush with the same guy." He stuck a cigarette in his mouth and shook his head. "This is bad. Bad. I mean to say, the way I had it figured, this stinking war was over, and here some bastards are still trying to get me."

■

The 502nd SS Heavy Tank Battalion, or what was left of it, had temporary headquarters in the village of Lindorf, just off the main Salzburg road, and the battalion commander, *Standartenführer*

Max Jager, had set up his command post in the local inn.

Karl Ritter had been lucky enough to get possession of one of the first-floor bedrooms and was sleeping, for the first time in thirty-six hours, the sleep of total exhaustion. He lay on top of the bed in full uniform, having been too tired even to remove his boots.

At three o'clock in the afternoon he came awake to a hand on his shoulder and found Hoffer bending over him. Ritter sat up instantly. "Yes, what is it?"

"The colonel wants you, sir. They say it's urgent."

"More work for the undertakers." Ritter ran his hands over his fair hair and stood up. "So—did you manage to snatch a little sleep, Erich?"

Hoffer, a thin, wiry young man of twenty-seven, wore a black Panzer sidecap and one-piece overalls camouflaged to look like autumn foliage. He was an innkeeper's son from the Harz Mountains, had been with Ritter for four years, and was totally devoted to him.

"A couple of hours."

Ritter pulled on his service cap and adjusted the angle to his liking. "You're a terrible liar—you know that, don't you, Erich? There's oil on your hands. You've been at those engines again."

"Somebody has to," Hoffer said. "No more spares."

"Not even for the SS." Ritter smiled sardonically. "Things must really be in a mess. Look, see if you can rustle up a little coffee and something to eat. And a glass of schnapps wouldn't come amiss. I shouldn't imagine this will take long."

He went downstairs quickly and was directed by an orderly to a room at the back of the inn where he found Colonel Jager and two of the other company commanders examining a map which lay open on the table.

Jager turned and came forward, hand outstretched. "My dear Karl, I can't tell you how delighted I am. A great, great honor, not only for you, but for the entire battalion."

Ritter looked bewildered. "I'm afraid I don't understand."

"But of course. How could you?" Jager picked up a signal flimsy. "I naturally passed full details of this morning's astonishing exploit straight to Division. It appears they radioed Berlin. I've just received this. Special orders, Karl, for you and *Sturmscharführer* Hoffer. As you can see, you're to leave at once."

■

Hoffer had indeed managed to obtain a little coffee—the real stuff, too—and some cold meat and black bread. He was just arranging it on the small night table in the bedroom when the door opened and Ritter entered.

Hoffer knew something was up at once, for he had never seen the major look so pale, a remarkable fact when one considered that he usually had no color at all.

Ritter tossed his service cap onto the bed and adjusted the Knight's Cross with Oak Leaves that hung at the neck of his black tunic. "Is that coffee I smell, Erich? Real coffee? Who did you have to kill? Schnapps, too?"

"Steinhager, Major." Hoffer picked up the stone bottle. "Best I could do."

"Well, then, you'd better find a couple of glasses, hadn't you? They tell me we've got something to celebrate."

"Celebrate, sir?"

"Yes, Erich. How would you like a trip to Berlin?"

"Berlin, Major?" Hoffer looked bewildered. "But Berlin is surrounded. It was on the radio."

"Still possible to fly to Templehof or Gatow if you're important enough, and we are, Erich. Come on, man, fill the glasses."

And suddenly Ritter was angry, the face paler than ever, the hand shaking as he held out a glass to the sergeant major.

"Important, sir? Us?"

"My dear Erich, you've just been awarded the Knight's Cross—long overdue, I might add. And I am to receive the Swords, but now comes the best part. From the *Führer* himself, Erich. Isn't it rich? Germany on the brink of total disaster, and he can find a plane to fly us in specially—with *Luftwaffe* fighter escort, if you please." He laughed wildly. "The poor sod must think we've just won the war for him or something."

Three

ON the morning of April 26, two JU-52s loaded with tank ammunition managed to land in the center of Berlin, in the vicinity of the Siegessäule, on a runway hastily constructed from a road in that area.

Karl Ritter and Erich Hoffer were the only two passengers, and they clambered out of the hatch into a scene of indescribable confusion, followed by their pilot, a young Luftwaffe captain named Rösch.

There was considerable panic among the soldiers who immediately started to unload the ammunition. Hardly surprising, for Russian heavy artillery was pounding the city hard, and every so often a shell whistled overhead to explode among the ruined buildings to the rear of them. The air was filled with sulfur smoke and dust, and a heavy pall blanketed everything.

Rösch, Ritter, and Hoffer ran to the shelter of a nearby wall and crouched. The young pilot offered them cigarettes. "Welcome to the City of the Dead," he said. "Dante's new Inferno."

"You've done this before?" Ritter asked.

"No, this is a new development. We can still get into Templehof and Gatow by air, but it's impossible to get from there to here on the ground. The Ivans have infiltrated all over the place." He smiled sardonically. "Still, we'll throw them back—given time, needless to say. After all, there's an army of veterans to call on. *Volkssturm* units, average age sixty. And a few thousand Hitler Youth at the other end, mostly around fourteen. Nothing much in between, except the *Führer*, whom God preserve, naturally. He should be worth a few divisions, wouldn't you say?"

An uncomfortable conversation which was cut short by the sudden arrival of a field car with an SS military police driver and sergeant. The sergeant's uniform was immaculate; the *Feldgendarmerie* gorget around his neck sparkled.

"*Sturmbannführer* Ritter?"

"That's right."

The sergeant's heels clicked together; his arm flashed briefly in a perfect party salute. "General Fegelein's compliments. We're here to escort you to the *Führer*'s headquarters."

"We'll be with you in a minute." The sergeant trotted away, and Ritter turned to Rösch. "A strange game we play."

"Here at the end of things, you mean?" Rösch smiled. "At least I'm getting out. My orders are to turn around as soon as possible and take fifty wounded with me from the Charité Hospital, but

44

you, my friend—you, I fear, will find it rather more difficult to leave Berlin."

"My grandmother was a good Catholic. She taught me to believe in miracles." Ritter held out his hand. "Good luck."

"And to you." Rösch ducked instinctively as another of the heavy 17.5 shells screamed overhead. "You'll need it."

■

The field car turned out of the Wilhelmplatz and into Vosstrasse, and the bulk of the Reich Chancellery rose before them. It was a sorry sight, battered and defaced by the bombardment, and every so often another shell at random screamed in to further the work of destruction. The streets were deserted, piled high with rubble, so that the driver had to pick his way with care.

"Good God," Hoffer said. "No one could function in such a shambles. It's impossible."

"Underneath," the police sergeant told him. "Thirty meters of concrete between those Russian shells and the *Führer*'s bunker. Nothing can reach him down there."

Nothing? Ritter thought. Can it truly be possible this clown realizes what he is saying, or is he as touched by madness as his masters?

The car ramp was wrecked, but there was still room to take the field car inside. As they stopped, an SS sentry moved out of the gloom. The sergeant waved him away and turned to Ritter. "If you will follow me, please. First we must report to Major General Mohnke."

Ritter removed his leather military greatcoat and

handed it to Hoffer. Underneath, the black panzer uniform was immaculate, the decorations gleamed. He adjusted his gloves. The sergeant was considerably impressed and drew himself stiffly to attention as if aware that this was a game they shared and eager to play his part.

"If the *Sturmbannführer* is ready?"

Ritter nodded, the sergeant moved off briskly, and they followed him down through a dark passage with concrete walls that sweated moisture in the dim light. Soldiers crouched in every available inch of space, many of them sleeping—mainly SS, from the look of things. Some glanced up with weary, lackluster eyes that showed no surprise, even at Ritter's bandbox appearance.

When they talked, their voices were low and subdued, and the main sound seemed to be the monotonous hum of the dynamos and the whirring of the electric fans in the ventilation system. Occasionally there was the faintest of tremors as the earth shook high above them, and the air was musty and unpleasant, tainted with sulfur.

Major General Mohnke's office was as uninviting as everything else Ritter had seen on his way down through the labyrinth of passageways. Small and Spartan, with the usual concrete walls, too small even for the desk and chair and half a dozen officers it contained when they arrived. Mohnke was an SS *Brigadeführer* who was now commander of the Adolf Hitler Volunteer Corps, a force of two thousand supposedly handpicked men who were to form the final ring of defense around the Chancellery.

He paused in full flight as the immaculate Ritter entered the room. Everyone turned; the sergeant saluted and placed Ritter's orders on the desk. Mohnke looked at them briefly, his eyes lit up, and he leaned across the table, hand outstretched.

"My dear Ritter, what a pleasure to meet you." He reached for the telephone and said to the others, "*Sturmbannführer* Ritter, gentlemen, hero of that incredible exploit near Innsbruck that I was telling you about."

Most of them made appropriate noises, one or two shook hands, others reached out to touch him as if for good luck. It was a slightly unnerving experience, and he was glad when Mohnke replaced the receiver and said, "General Fegelein tells me the *Führer* wishes to see you without delay." His arm swung up dramatically in a full party salute. "Your comrades of the SS are proud of you, *Sturmbannführer*. Your victory is ours."

"Am I mad, or are they, Erich?" Ritter whispered as they followed the sergeant ever deeper into the bunker.

"For God's sake, Major." Hoffer put a hand briefly on his arm. "If someone overhears that kind of remark . . ."

"All right, I'll be good," Ritter said soothingly. "Lead on, Erich. I can't wait to see what happens in the next act."

They descended now to the lower levels of the *Führerbunker* itself. A section which, although Ritter did not know it then, housed most of the *Führer*'s personal staff, as well as Goebbels and his

47

family, Bormann, and Dr. Ludwig Stumpfegger, the *Führer*'s personal physician. General Fegelein had a room adjacent to Bormann's.

It was similar to Mohnke's—small, with damp concrete walls, and furnished with a desk, a couple of chairs, and a filing cabinet. The desk was covered with military maps which the general was studying closely when the sergeant opened the door and stood to one side.

Fegelein looked up, his face serious, but when he saw Ritter he laughed excitedly and rushed around the desk to greet him. "My dear Ritter, what an honor—for all of us. The *Führer* can hardly wait, I assure you."

Such enthusiasm was a little too much, considering that Ritter had never clapped eyes on the man before. A onetime commander of SS cavalry—he knew that—awarded the Knight's Cross, so he was no coward, but the handshake lacked firmness and there was sweat on the brow, particularly along the thinning hairline. This was a badly frightened man, a breed with which Ritter had become only too familiar over the past few months.

"An exaggeration, I'm sure, General."

"And you, too, *Sturmscharführer*." Fegelein did not take Hoffer's hand, but nodded briefly. "A magnificent performance."

"Indeed," Ritter said dryly. "His was, after all, the finger on the trigger."

"Of course, my dear Ritter, we all acknowledge that fact. On the other hand . . ."

Before he could take the conversation any further, the door opened and a broad, rather squat man entered the room. He wore a nondescript uniform. His only decoration was the Order of Blood, a much-coveted Nazi medal specially struck for those who had served prison sentences for political crimes under the old Weimar Republic. He carried a sheaf of papers in one hand.

"Ah, Martin," Fegelein said. "Was it important? I have the *Führer*'s orders to escort this gentleman to him the instant he arrives. *Sturmbannführer* Ritter, hero of Wednesday's incredible exploit on the Innsbruck road. You of course know *Reichsleiter* Bormann, Major."

But Ritter did not, because—as he was for most Germans—Martin Bormann was only a name to him, a face that was occasionally to be found in a group photo of party dignitaries, with nothing memorable about it. Not a Goebbels or a Himmler— once seen, never forgotten.

And yet here he was, the most powerful man in Germany, particularly now that Himmler had run off. *Reichsleiter* Martin Bormann, head of the Nazi Party Chancellery and secretary to the *Führer*.

"A great pleasure, Major." His handshake was firm, with a hint of even greater strength there if necessary.

He had a harsh, yet strangely soft, voice, a broad, brutal face with Slavic cheekbones, a prominent nose. The impression was of a big man, although Ritter found he had to look down at him.

"Reichsleiter."

"And this is your gunner, Hoffer." Bormann turned to the sergeant major. "Quite a marksman, but then I sometimes think you Harz Mountain men cut your teeth on a shotgun barrel."

It was the first sign from anyone that Hoffer was

more than a cipher—an acknowledgment of his existence as a human being—and could not fail to impress Ritter, however reluctantly.

Bormann opened the door and turned to Fegelein. "My business can wait. I'll see you downstairs, anyway. I, too, have business with the *Führer.*"

He went out, and Fegelein turned to the two men—Ritter magnificent in the black uniform, Hoffer somehow complimenting the show with his one-piece camouflage suit, sleeves rolled up to the elbow. It couldn't be better. Just the sort of fillip the *Führer* needed.

■

Bormann's sleeping quarters were in the Chancellery bunker, but his office, close to Fegelein's, was strategically situated so that he was able to keep the closest of contact with Hitler. One door opened into the telephone exchange and general communications center, the other to Goebbels's personal office. Nothing, therefore, could go into the *Führer* or out again without the *Reichsleiter*'s knowledge, which was exactly as he had arranged the situation.

When he entered his office directly after leaving Fegelein, he found SS Colonel Willi Rattenhuber, whose services he had utilized as an additional aide to Zander since March 30, leaning over a map on the desk.

"Any further word on Himmler?" Bormann asked.

"Not as yet, *Reichsleiter.*"

"The bastard is up to something—you may depend on it—and so is Fegelein. Watch him, Willi—watch him closely."

"Yes, *Reichsleiter*."

"And there's something else I want you to do, Willi. There's a *Sturmbannführer* named Ritter, of the 502nd SS Heavy Tank Battalion, on his way down now to receive the Swords from the *Führer*. When you get a moment, I want his records—everything you can find on him."

"*Reichsleiter*."

"That's what I like about you, Willi. You never ask questions." Bormann clapped him on the arm. "And now we'll go down to the garden bunker, and I'll show him to you. I think you'll approve. In fact, I have a happy feeling that he may serve my purpose very well indeed."

■

In the garden bunker was the *Führer's* study, a bedroom, two living rooms, and a bathroom. Close by was the map room used for all high-level conferences. The hall outside served as an anteroom, and it was there that Ritter and Hoffer waited.

Bormann paused at the bottom of the steps and held Rattenhuber back in the shadows. "He looks good, Willi, don't you agree? Quite magnificent in that pretty uniform, with the medals gleaming, the pale face, the blond hair. Uncle Heini would have been proud of him—all that's fairest in the Aryan race. Not like us at all, Willi. He will undoubtedly prove a shot in the arm for the *Führer*. And notice the slight, sardonic smile on his mouth. I tell you there's hope for this boy, Willi. A young man of parts."

Rattenhuber said hastily, "The *Führer* comes now, *Reichsleiter*."

Ritter, standing at the end of a line of half a

dozen young boys in the uniform of the Hitler Youth, felt curiously detached. It was rather like one of those dreams in which everything has an appearance of reality, yet events are past belief. The children on his right hand, for instance. Twelve or thirteen, here to be decorated for bravery. The boy next to him had a bandage around his forehead, under the heavy man's helmet. Blood seeped through steadily, and occasionally the child shifted his feet as if to prevent himself from falling.

"Shoulders back," Ritter said softly. "Not long now." And then the door opened. Hitler moved out, flanked by Fegelein, Jodl, Keitel, and Krebs, the new chief of the General Staff.

Ritter had seen the *Führer* on several occasions in his life. Speaking at Nuremberg rallies, Paris in 1940, on a visit to the Eastern Front in 1942. His recollection of Hitler had been of an inspired leader of men, a man of magical rhetoric whose spell could not fail to touch anyone within hearing.

But the man who shuffled into the anteroom now might have been a totally different person. This was a sick old man, shoulders hunched under the uniform jacket that seemed a size too large, pale, hollow-cheeked, no sparkle in the lackluster eyes; and when he turned to take the first Iron Cross Second Class, from the box Jodl held, his hand trembled.

He worked his way along the line, muttering a word or two of some sort of encouragement here and there, patting an occasional cheek, and then reached Ritter and Hoffer.

Fegelein said, "*Sturmbannführer* Karl Ritter and *Sturmscharführer* Erich Hoffer of the Five Hundred and Second SS Heavy Tank Battalion." He started to read the citation, "Shortly after dawn on the morning of Wednesday, April twenty-fifth—" but the *Führer* cut him off with a chopping motion of one hand.

There was fire in the dark eyes, a sudden energy as he snapped his fingers impatiently for Jodl to pass the decoration. Ritter stared impassively ahead, aware of the hands touching him lightly, and then, for the briefest of moments, they tightened on his arm.

He looked directly into the eyes, aware of the power, the burning intensity, there again if only for a moment, the hoarse voice saying, "Your *Führer* thanks you, on behalf of the German people."

Hitler turned. "Are you aware of this officer's achievement, gentlemen? Assisted by only two other tanks, he wiped out an entire British column of the Seventh Armored Division. Thirty armored vehicles left blazing. Can you hear that and still tell me that we cannot win this war? If one man can do so much, what could fifty like him accomplish?"

They all shifted uncomfortably. Krebs said, "But of course, my *Führer*. Under your inspired leadership, anything is possible."

"Goebbels must have written that line for him," Bormann whispered to Rattenhuber. "You know, Willi, I'm enjoying this—and look at our proud young *Sturmbannführer*. He looks like Death himself with that pale face and black uniform, come to remind us all of what waits outside these walls. Have you ever read 'Masque of the Red Death,' by the American writer Poe?"

"No, I can't say that I have, *Reichsleiter*."

"You should, Willi. An interesting parable of the impossibility of locking out reality for long."

An orderly clattered down the steps, brushed past Bormann and Rattenhuber, and hesitated on seeing what was taking place. Krebs, who obviously recognized the man, moved to one side and snapped his fingers. The orderly passed him a signal flimsy, which Krebs quickly scanned.

Hitler moved forward eagerly. "Is it news of Wenck?" he demanded.

He was still convinced that the Twelfth Army, under General Wenck, was going to break through to the relief of Berlin at any moment.

Krebs hesitated, and the *Führer* said, "Read it, man! Read it!"

Krebs swallowed hard, then said, "No possibility of Wenck and the Ninth Army joining. Await further instruction."

The *Führer* exploded with rage. "The same story as Sunday. I gave the Eleventh Panzer Army, and all available personnel in his area, to SS General Steiner, with orders to attack. And what happened?"

The fact that the army in question had existed on paper only, a figment of someone's imagination, was not the point, for no one would have had the courage to tell him.

"So even my SS let me down—betray me in my hour of need. Well, it won't do, gentlemen." He was almost hysterical now. "I have a way of dealing with traitors. Remember the July plot? Remember the films I ordered you to watch of the executions?"

He turned, stumbled back into the map room, followed by Jodl, Keitel, and Krebs. The door closed. Fegelein, moving as a man in a dream, signaled to one of the SS orderlies, who took the children away.

There was silence, then Ritter said, "What now, General?"

Fegelein started. "What did you say?"

"What do we do now?"

"Oh, go to the canteen. Food will be provided. Have a drink. Relax." He forced a smile and clapped Ritter on the shoulder. "Take it easy for a while, Major. I'll send for you soon. Fresh fields to conquer, I promise."

He nodded to an orderly, who led the way. Ritter and Hoffer followed him up the steps. Bormann and Rattenhuber were no longer there.

At the top, Ritter said softly, "What do you think of that, then, Erich? Little children and old men led by a raving madman. So now we start paying the bill, I think—all of us."

■

When he reached his office, Fegelein closed the door, went behind his desk, and sat down. He opened a cupboard, took out a bottle of brandy, removed the cork, and swallowed deeply. He had been a frightened man for some time, but this latest display had finished him off.

He was exactly the same as dozens of other men who had risen to power in the Nazi party. A man of no background and little education. A onetime groom and jockey who had risen through the ranks of the SS and, after being appointed Himmler's aide at *Führer* headquarters, had consolidated his position by marrying Eva Braun's sister Gretl.

But now even Himmler had cleared off, had refused every attempt aimed at returning him to the death trap which Berlin had become. It occurred to Fegelein that perhaps the time had come for some definite action on his own part. He took another quick pull on the brandy bottle, got up, took down his cap from behind the door, and went out.

＊

It was seven o'clock that evening, and Ritter and Hoffer were sitting together in the canteen, talking softly, a bottle of Moselle between them, when a sudden hubbub broke out. There were cries outside in the corridor, laughter, and then the door burst open and two young officers ran in.

Ritter grabbed at one of them as he went by. "Hey, what's all the excitement?"

"*Luftwaffe* General Ritter von Greim has just arrived from Munich with the air ace, Hannah Reitsch. They landed at Gatow and came on in a Fieseler Storch."

"The general himself flew," the other young officer said. "When he was hit, Reitsch took over the controls and landed the aircraft in the street near the *Brandenburger Tor*. What a woman!"

They moved away. Another voice said, "A day for heroes, it would seem."

Ritter looked up and found Bormann standing there. "*Reichsleiter.*" He started to rise.

Bormann pushed him down. "Yes, a remarkable business. What they omitted to tell you was that they were escorted by fifty fighter planes from Munich. Apparently over forty were shot down. On the other hand, it was essential General von Greim get here. You see, the *Führer* intends to promote him to commander-in-chief of the *Luftwaffe*, with the rank of *Feldmarschall,* Göring having finally proved a broken reed. Naturally he wished to tell General von Greim of this himself. Signal flimsies are so impersonal, don't you think?"

He moved away. Hoffer said in a kind of awe, "Over forty planes—forty, and for what?"

"To tell him in person what he could have told him over the telephone," Ritter said. "A remarkable man, our *Führer,* Erich."

"For God's sake, Major." Hoffer put out a hand, for the first time real anger showing through. "Keep talking like that and they might take you out and hang you. Me, too. Is that what you want?"

■

When Bormann went into his office, Rattenhuber was waiting for him.

"Did you find General Fegelein?" the *Reichsleiter* inquired.

"He left the bunker five hours ago." Rattenhuber checked his notes. "According to my information he is at present at his home in Charlottenburg—wearing civilian clothes, I might add."

Bormann nodded calmly. "How very interesting."

"Do we inform the *Führer?*"

"I don't think so, Willi. Give a man enough

57

rope—you know the old saying. I'll ask where Fegelein is in the *Führer*'s hearing later on tonight. Allow him to make this very unpleasant discovery for himself. Now, Willi, we have something far more important to discuss. The question of the prominent prisoners in our hands. You have the files I asked for?"

"Certainly, *Reichsleiter.*" Rattenhuber placed several manila folders on the desk. "There is a problem here. The *Führer* has very pronounced ideas on what should happen to them. It seems that he was visited by *Obergruppenführer* Berger, head of the Prisoner-of-War Administration. Berger tried to discuss the fate of several important British, French, and American prisoners, as well as of Schuschnigg, the Austrian chancellor, and Halder and Schacht. It seems the *Führer* told him to shoot them all."

"Conspicuous consumption, I would have thought, Willi. In other words, a great waste." Bormann tapped the files. "But it's these ladies and gentlemen who interest me. The prisoners at Arlberg."

"I'm afraid several have already been moved since my visit, on your instructions, two months ago. Orders of the *Reichsführer*," Rattenhuber told him.

"Yes, for once Uncle Heini moved a little faster than I had expected," Bormann said dryly. "What are we left with?"

"Just five. Three men, two women."

"Good," Bormann said. "A nice round number. We'll start with the ladies first, shall we? Refresh my memory."

"Madame Claire de Beauville, *Reichsleiter*. Age, thirty. Nationality, French. Her father made a great deal of money in canned foods. She married Etienne de Beauville. A fine old family. They were thought to be typical socialites flirting with their new masters. In fact, her husband was working with French Resistance units in Paris. He was picked up in June last year on information received and taken to *Sicherheitsdienst* headquarters on the Avénue Foch in Paris. He was shot trying to escape."

"The French," Bormann said. "So romantic."

"The wife was thought to be involved. There was a radio at the house. She insisted she knew nothing about it, but Security was convinced she could well have been working as a 'pianist.' "

He looked up, bewildered, and Bormann smiled. "Typical English schoolboy humor. This is apparently the British Special Operations Executive term for a radio operator."

"Oh, I see." Rattenhuber returned to the file. "Through marriage, she is related to most of the great French families."

"Which is why she is at Arlberg. So—who's next?"

"Madame Claudine Chevalier."

"The concert pianist?"

"That's right, *Reichsleiter*."

"She must be seventy, at least."

"Seventy-five."

"A national institution. In 1940 she made a trip to Berlin to give a concert at the *Führer*'s special request. It made her very unpopular in Paris at the time."

"A very clever front to mask her real activities, *Reichsleiter*. She was one of a group of influential people who organized an escape line which succeeded in spiriting several well-known Jews from Paris to Vichy."

"So—an astute old lady with nerve and courage. Does that dispose of the French?"

"No, *Reichsleiter*. There is Paul Gaillard to consider."

"Ah, the onetime cabinet minister."

"That is so, *Reichsleiter*. Aged sixty. At one time a physician and surgeon. He has, of course, an international reputation as an author. Dabbled in politics a little before the war. Minister for internal affairs in the Vichy government, who turned out to be signing releases of known political offenders. He was also suspected of being in touch with de Gaulle. Member of the French Academy."

"Anything else?"

"Something of a romantic, according to the Security report. Joined the French Army as a private in 1915, as some sort of public gesture against the government of the day. It seems he thought they were making a botch of the war. Flirted with communism in the twenties, but a visit to Russia in 1927 cured him of that disease."

"What about his weaknesses?"

"Weaknesses, *Reichsleiter?*"

"Come now, Willi, we all have them. Some men like women, others play cards all night—or drink, perhaps. What about Gaillard?"

"None, *Reichsleiter,* and the Security report is

really most thorough. There is one extraordinary thing about him, however."

"What's that?"

"He's had a great love of skiing all his life. In 1924, when they held the first Winter Olympics at Chamonix, he took a gold medal. A remarkable achievement. You see, he was, at the time, thirty-nine years of age, *Reichsleiter*."

"Interesting," Bormann said softly. "Now that really does say something about his character. What about the Englishman?"

"I'm not too certain that's an accurate description, *Reichsleiter*. Justin Fitzgerald Birr, fifteenth earl of Dundrum, an Irish title, and Ireland is the place of his birth. He is also tenth Baron Felversham. The title is, of course, English, and an estate goes with it in Yorkshire."

"The English and the Irish really can't make up their minds about each other, can they, Willi? As soon as there's a war, thousands of Irishmen seem to join the British Army with alacrity. Very confusing."

"Exactly, *Reichsleiter*. Lord Dundrum, which is how people address him, had an uncle who was a major of infantry in the First World War. An excellent record—decorated and so on—then, in 1919, he went home, joined the IRA, and became commander of a flying column during their fight for independence. It apparently caused a considerable scandal."

"And the earl? What of his war record?"

"Aged thirty. DSO and Military Cross. At the beginning of the war he was a lieutenant in the

Irish Guards. Two years later, a lieutenant colonel in the Special Air Service. In its brief existence his unit destroyed one hundred and thirteen aircraft on the ground behind Rommel's lines. He was captured in Sicily. Made five attempts to escape, including two from Colditz. It was then they decided that his special circumstances merited his transfer to Arlberg as a *prominenti*."

"Which explains the last and most important point concerning the good earl of Dundrum."

"Exactly, *Reichsleiter*. It would seem the gentleman is, through his mother, second cousin to King George."

"Which certainly makes him prominent, Willi. Very prominent, indeed. And now—the best saved till last. What about our American friend?"

"Brigadier General Hamilton Canning, aged forty-five."

"The same as me," Bormann said.

"Almost exactly. You, *Reichsleiter,* I believe, were born on the seventeenth of June. General Canning on the twenty-seventh of July. He would seem typical of a certain kind of American—a man in a perpetual hurry to get somewhere."

"I know his record," Bormann said. "But go through it again for me."

"Very well, *Reichsleiter.* In 1917 he joined the French Foreign Legion as a private. Transferred to the American Army the following year, with the rank of second lieutenant. Between the wars he didn't fit in too well. A troublemaker who was much disliked at the Pentagon."

"In other words, he was too clever for them,

read too many books, spoke too many languages," Bormann said. "Just like the High Command we know and love, Willi. But carry on."

"He was a military attaché in Berlin for three years—1934 to 1937. Apparently became very friendly with Rommel."

"That damn traitor." Bormann's usually equable poise deserted him. "He would."

"He saw action on a limited scale in Shanghai against the Japanese in 1939, but he was still only a major by 1940. He was then commanding a small force in the Philippines. Fought a brilliant defensive action against the Japanese in Mindanao. He was given up for dead, but turned up in a Moro junk at Darwin in Australia. The magazines made something of a hero of him, so they had to promote him then. He spent almost a year in the hospital. Then they sent him to England. Some sort of headquarters job, but he managed to get into Combined Operations."

"And then?"

"Dropped into the Dordogne just after D-Day with British SAS units and Rangers to work with French partisans. Surrounded on a plateau in the Auvergne Mountains by SS paratroopers in July last year. Jumped from a train taking him to Germany, and broke a leg. Tried to escape from the hospital. They tried him at Colditz for a while, but that didn't work."

"And then Arlberg."

"It was decided, I believe, by the *Reichsführer* himself, that he was an obvious candidate to be a *prominenti*."

"And who do we have in charge of things at Schloss Arlberg, Willi?"

"*Oberstleutnant* Max Hesser, of the Panzer Grenadiers. Gained his Knight's Cross at Leningrad, where he lost his left arm. A professional soldier of the old school."

"I know, Willi, don't tell me. Held together by guts and piano wire. And who does he have with him now?"

"Only twenty men, *Reichsleiter*. Anyone capable of frontline action has been taken from him in the past few weeks. *Oberleutnant* Schenck, now his second-in-command, is fifty-five, a reservist. *Sturmscharführer* Schneider is a good man. Iron Cross Second and First Class, but he has a silver plate in his head. The rest are reservists, mostly in their fifties or cripples."

He closed the last file. Bormann leaned back in his chair, fingertips together. It was quiet now, except for the faintest rumblings far above them as the Russian artillery continued to pound Berlin.

"Listen to that," Bormann said. "Closer by the hour. Do you ever wonder what comes after?"

"*Reichsleiter?*" Rattenhuber looked faintly alarmed.

"One has plans, of course, but sometimes things go wrong, Willi. Some unexpected snag that turns the whole thing on its head. In such an eventuality one needs what I believe the Americans term an 'ace-in-the-hole.' "

"The *prominenti, Reichsleiter?* But are they important enough?"

"Who knows, Willi? Excellent bargaining counters in an emergency, no more than that. Madame Chevalier and Gaillard are almost national institutions, and Madame de Beauville's connections embrace some of the most influential families in France. The English love a lord at the best of times—doubly so when he's related to the king himself."

"And Canning?"

"The Americans are notoriously sentimental about their heroes."

He sat staring into space for a moment.

"So, what do we do with them?" Rattenhuber said. "What does the *Reichsleiter* have in mind?"

"Oh, I'll think of something, Willi," Bormann smiled. "I think you may depend on it."

Four

AND at Schloss Arlberg, on the Inn River, 450 miles south of Berlin and 55 miles northwest of Innsbruck, Lieutenant Colonel Justin Birr, fifteenth earl of Dundrum, leaned out the narrow window at the top of the north tower and peered down into the darkness of the garden, 80 feet below.

He could feel the plaited rope stir beneath his hands, and behind him in the gloom Paul Gaillard said, "Is he there?"

"No, not yet." A moment later the rope slackened, there was a sudden flash of light below, then darkness again. "That's it," Birr said. "Now me, if I can get through this damned window. Hamilton certainly can pick them."

He stood on a stool, turned to support himself on Gaillard's shoulders, and eased his legs into space. He stayed there for a moment, hands on the rope. "Sure you won't change your mind, Paul?"

"My dear Justin, I wouldn't get halfway down before my arms gave out."

"All right," Birr said. "You know what to do.

When I get down—or perhaps I should say *if* I do—we'll flash you a signal. You haul the rope up, stick it in that cubbyhole under the floorboards, then get the hell out of there."

"You may rely on me."

"I know. Give my regards to the ladies."

"*Bon chance,* my friend."

Birr let himself slide and was suddenly alone in the darkness, swaying slightly in the wind, his hands slipping from knot to knot. Homemade rope and eighty feet to the garden. I must be mad, he thought.

It was raining slightly, not a single star to be seen anywhere, and already his arms were beginning to ache. He let himself slide faster, his feet banging against the wall, scratching his knuckles, at one point twirling around madly in circles. Quite suddenly, the rope parted.

My God, that's it! he thought, clamping his jaws together in the moment of death to stop himself from crying out, then hit the ground after falling no more than ten feet, and rolled over in the wet grass, winded.

There was a hand at his elbow, helping him to his feet. "You all right?" Canning said.

"I think so." Birr flexed his arms. "A damn close thing, Hamilton, but then it usually is when you're around."

"We aim to please." Canning shined his flashlight upward briefly. "Okay, let's get moving. The entrance to the sewer I told you about is in the lily pond on the lower terrace."

They moved down through the darkness cautiously, negotiated a flight of steps, and skirted the fountain at the bottom. The ornamental lily pond was on the other side of a short stretch of lawn. There was a wall at the rear of it, water gushing from the mouth of a bronze lion's head, rattling into the pool below. Birr had seen it often enough during exercise. "Okay, here we go."

Canning sat down and lowered himself into the water, knee deep. He waded forward. Birr followed him and found the American crouched beside the lion's head in the darkness.

"You can feel the grille here, half under the water," Canning whispered. "If we can get that off, we're straight into the main drainage system. One tunnel after the other, all the way down to the river."

"And if not?" Birr inquired.

"Short rations again and a stone cell, but that, as they say, is problematical. Right now we've got about ten minutes before Schneider and that damned Alsatian of his come by on garden patrol."

He produced a short length of steel bar from his pocket, inserted it on one side of the bronze grille, and levered. There was an audible crack, the metal, corroded by the years, snapping instantly. He pulled hard, and the entire grille came away in his hands.

"You see how it is, Justin. All you have to do is live right. After you."

Birr crouched down on his hands and knees in the water, switching on his flashlight, and crawled through into a narrow brick tunnel. Canning moved in behind him, pulling the grille back into place.

"Don't you think you're getting a little old for the Boy Scouts, Hamilton?" Birr whispered over his shoulder.

"Shut up and get moving," Canning told him. "If we can reach the river and find a boat by midnight, we'll have six or seven hours to play with before they find out we're gone."

Birr moved on, crawling on his hands and knees through a couple of feet of water, the flashlight in his teeth. He emerged, after a few yards, into a tunnel that was a good five feet in diameter, so that he could actually walk if he crouched a little.

The water was only about a foot deep here, for the tunnel sloped downward steeply, and the smell was not unpleasant—like old leaves and autumn on the river in a punt.

"Keep going," Canning said. "From what I found out from that gardener, we emerge into the main sewer pretty quickly. From there, it's a straight run down to the Inn."

"I can smell it already," Birr told him.

A few minutes later the tunnel did indeed empty into the main sewer in a miniature waterfall. Birr pointed his flashlight at the brown, foam-flecked waters which rushed by several feet below.

"My God, just smell it, Hamilton. This really is beyond a joke."

"Oh, get in there, for Christ's sake." Canning gave him a shove, and Birr dropped down, losing his balance, and disappeared beneath the surface. He was on his feet in an instant and stood there cursing, still clutching his flashlight. "It's liquid shit, Hamilton. Liquid shit."

"You can have a wash when we get to the river," Canning said as he lowered himself down to join him. "Now let's make time."

He started down the tunnel, flashlight extended

before him, and Birr followed for perhaps sixty or seventy yards, and then the tunnel petered out in a blank wall.

"That's it, then," Birr said. "And a bloody good job, too, as far as I'm concerned. We'll have to go back."

"Not on your sweet life. The water's got to go somewhere." Canning slipped his flashlight into his pocket, took a deep breath, and crouched. He surfaced at once. "As I thought. The tunnel continues on a lower level. I'm going through."

Birr said, "And what if it's twenty or thirty yards long, you idiot—or longer? You'll not have time to turn and come back. You'll drown."

"So, I'll take that chance, Justin." Canning was tying one end of the rope about his waist now. "I want out—you understand? I've no intention of sitting on my ass up there in the castle waiting for the *Reichsführer*'s hired assassins to come and finish me off." He held out the other end of the rope. "Fasten that around your waist if you want to come, too. If I get through, I'll give it a pull."

"And if not?"

"Winter roses on my grave. Scarlet ones like those Claire cultivated in the conservatory." He grinned once, took a deep breath, and disappeared beneath the surface of the water.

Justin Birr waited. The flashlight gave only minimal illumination, barely sufficient to pick out the slime on the ancient stone walls or the occasional rat that swam past in the dark water. The stench was frightful—really most unpleasant—and by now the cold had cut through to his very bones, or so it seemed.

He was aware of a sudden tug and hesitated, wondering for a moment whether it was simply his imagination. There was another tug; more insistent this time: "All right, damn you," he said and extinguished the flashlight and put it into his breast pocket. His hands felt under the water for the edge of the arched roof. He took a deep breath and went down.

His feet banged against the stonework, but he kicked desperately; aware of the rope tugging at his waist, and then, just when he was convinced he couldn't keep going any longer, he saw a faint light ahead and surfaced, gasping for breath.

Canning, crouching out of the water at the side of a larger tunnel, reached down to pull him up. "Easy does it."

"Really, Hamilton, this particular small jaunt of yours is getting out of hand. I smell like a lavatory gone wrong, and I'm frozen into the bargain."

Canning ignored him. "Listen—I can hear the river. Can't be far now."

He set off at a fast pace, slipping and sliding on the slope of the tunnel, and Birr got to his feet wearily and went after him. And then Canning was laughing excitedly and running, splashing knee-deep in the brown water.

"I can see it. We're there."

"Indeed you are, gentlemen. Indeed you are."

A brilliant spot was turned on, flooding the tunnel with light. Birr hesitated, then went forward and dropped on his hands and knees beside Canning, who crouched at the large circular grille which blocked the end of the tunnel. Schneider knelt on one knee on the other side, several armed men behind him.

"We've been waiting for you, gentlemen. Magda was growing impatient."

His Alsatian bitch whined eagerly, pushing her muzzle between the bars. Canning tugged at her ears. "You wouldn't hurt me, you silly old bitch, would you?"

"All right, Sergeant Major," Justin Birr said. "We'll come quietly."

■

Oberstleutnant Max Hesser leaned back in his chair, got out his cigarette case, and opened it one-handed with a skill born of long practice. *Oberleutnant* Schenck waited at the other side of the desk. He was dressed for duty, a pistol at his belt.

"Extraordinary," the colonel said. "What on earth will Canning be up to next?"

"God knows, *Herr Oberst*."

"And the note you received telling you that the escape attempt was to take place. You say it was unsigned?"

"As you may see for yourself, *Herr Oberst*."

He passed a slip of paper across, and Hesser examined it. " 'Canning and Birr escaping through the main sewer tonight.' Crudely done in pencil and block capitals but perfect German." He sighed. "So—there is a traitor in the camp. One of their friends betrays them."

"Not necessarily, *Herr Oberst*, if I might make a suggestion."

"But of course, man. Carry on."

"The general's knowledge of the sewer and

drainage system must have been gained from somewhere. One of the soldiers or a servant, perhaps."

"Ah, I see your point," Hesser said. "Someone who took a bribe, then slipped you that anonymous note to make sure the escape attempt would prove abortive." He shook his head. "I don't like it, Schenck. It leaves a bad taste." He sighed. "Anyway, I suppose I'd better have them in."

Schenck withdrew, and Hesser stood up and moved to the liquor cabinet. He was a handsome man in spite of the deep scar which bisected his forehead, curving into the right eye which was now glass, and the uniform was trim and well-fitting, the empty left sleeve tucked into the belt.

He was pouring himself a brandy when the door opened behind him. He turned as Schenck ushered Canning and Birr into the room, Schneider behind them.

"Good God in heaven," Hesser said.

They presented a sorry sight indeed—barefoot, covered with filth, water dripping onto the carpet. Hesser hurriedly filled two more glasses.

"From the looks of you, I'd say you needed it."

Canning and Birr slopped forward. "Very civil of you," Birr said.

Canning grinned and raised his glass. *"Prosit."*

"And now to business." Hesser went back to his desk and sat down. "This nonsense, gentlemen. It must stop."

"It is the duty of an officer to make every attempt to achieve his liberty and rejoin his unit," Canning said. "You know that."

"Yes. Under other circumstances I would agree

with you, but not now. Not on April 26, 1945. Gentlemen, after five and a half years, the war draws to a close. It's almost over—any day now. All we have to do is wait."

"What for—an SS execution squad?" Canning said. "We know what the *Führer* told Berger when he asked about the *prominenti*. He said, Shoot them. Shoot all of them. Last I heard, Himmler agreed with him."

"You are in my charge, gentlemen. I have tried to make this plain many times before."

"Great," Canning said. "And what happens if they drive up to the front door with a directive from the *Führer*. Will you pull up the drawbridge, or order us to be shot? You took the soldier's oath, didn't you, just like everyone else in the German armed forces?"

Hesser stared up at him, very white, the great scar glowing angrily. Birr said gently, "He does have a point, Colonel."

Hesser said, "I could put you gentlemen on short rations and confine you to your cells, but I won't. Under the circumstances and considering the point in time at which we all stand, I shall have you returned to the prisoners' section and your friends. I hope you will respond in kind to this gesture."

Schenck placed a hand on Canning's arm, and the general pulled himself free. "For God's sake, Max." He leaned across the desk, voice urgent. "There's only one way out for you. Send Schenck here in search of an Allied unit while there's still time. Someone you can surrender to legally, saving your own honor and our skins."

Hesser stared at him for a long moment, then said, "Have the general and Lord Dundrum returned to their quarters now, Schenck."

"*Herr Oberst.*" Schenck clicked his heels and turned to the two men. "General?"

"Oh, go to hell," Canning told him, turned, and walked out.

Birr paused. For a moment it was as if he intended to say something. Instead, he shrugged and followed. Schenck and Schneider went after them. Hesser went back to the cabinet and poured himself another drink. As he was replacing the bottle, there was a knock on the door and Schenck came back in.

"Would you care for one?" Hesser asked.

"No, thank you, *Herr Oberst.* My stomach takes kindly only to beer these days."

He waited patiently. Hesser walked across to the fire. "You think he's right, don't you?" Schenck hesitated, and Hesser said, "Come on, man. Speak your mind."

"Very well, *Herr Oberst.* Yes, I must say I do. Let's get it over and done with, that's my attitude. If we don't, then I greatly fear that something terrible may take place here, the results of which may drag us all down."

"You know something?" Hesser kicked a log that had rolled forward back into place in a shower of sparks. "I'm inclined to agree with you."

■

Canning and Birr—followed by Schneider, two soldiers with Schmeissers, and Magda—crossed the main hall and mounted the staircase, so wide that a company of soldiers could have marched up, line abreast.

"I was once shown around the MGM studios by Clark Gable," Birr said. "This place often reminds me of Stage Six. Did I ever tell you that?"

"Frequently," Canning told him.

They crossed the smaller, upper landing and paused at an iron-bound oak door, outside of which stood an armed sentry. Schneider produced a key about a foot long, inserted it in the massive lock, and turned. He pushed open the door and stood back.

"Gentlemen." As they moved in, he added, "Oh, by the way, the upper section of the north tower is out of bounds, and in the future there will be two guards in the water garden at all times."

"That's really very considerate of you," Birr said. "Don't you agree, General?"

"You can play that vaudeville act all night, but I've had it," Canning said and started up the dark stone stairway.

Birr followed him, and the door clanged shut behind them. They were now in the north tower, the central keep of the castle, that portion to which, in the old days, the defenders had always retreated in the last resort. It was completely isolated from the rest of Schloss Arlberg, the lowest window fifty feet from the ground and heavily barred. It made a relatively secure prisoners' section under most circumstances and meant that Hesser was able to allow the inmates a certain freedom, at least within the confines of the walls.

Madame Chevalier was playing the piano—they

could hear her clearly—a Bach prelude, crisp and ice-cold, all technique, no heart. The kind of thing she liked to play to combat the arthritis in her fingers. Canning opened the door of the dining hall.

It was a magnificent room, with a high, arched ceiling festooned with battle standards from other times, and a magnificent selection of fifteenth- and sixteenth-century armor on the walls. The fireplace was of baronial proportions. Gaillard and Claire de Beauville sat beside the log fire, smoking and talking quietly. Madame Chevalier was at the Bechstein.

At the sight of Canning and Birr, she stopped playing, gave a howl of laughter, and started the "Dead March from Saul."

"Very, very humorous," Canning told her. "I'm splitting my sides laughing."

Claire and Paul Gaillard stood up. "But what happened?" Gaillard said. "The first I knew that there was anything amiss was when men arrived to lock the upper tower door. I'd just come down after securing the rope."

"They were waiting for us, that's what happened," Birr said. "Dear old Schneider, and Magda panting eagerly over Hamilton as usual. He's become the great love of her life."

"But how could they have known?" Claire demanded.

"That's what I'd like to know," Canning said.

"I should have thought it obvious." Birr crossed to the sideboard and helped himself to a brandy. "That gardener, Schmidt. The one you got the information about the drainage system from. Maybe a hundred cigarettes weren't enough."

"The bastard," Canning said. "I'll kill him."

"But after you've had a bath, Hamilton—please." Claire waved a hand delicately in front of her nose. "You really do smell a little high."

"Camembert—out of season," said Gaillard.

There was general laughter. Canning said grimly, "The crackling of thorns under a pot, isn't that what the Good Book says? I hope you're still laughing, all of you, when the *Reichsführer*'s thugs march you out to the nearest wall." He walked out angrily during the silence that followed.

Birr emptied his glass. "Strange, but I can't think of a single funny thing to say, so, if you'll excuse me. . . ."

After he'd gone, Gaillard said, "He's right, of course. It isn't good. Now if Hamilton or Lord Dundrum had got away and reached American or British troops, they could have brought help."

"Nonsense, this whole business." Claire sat down again. "Hesser would never stand by and see us treated like that. It isn't in his nature."

"I'm afraid Colonel Hesser would have very little to do with it," Gaillard said. "He's a soldier, and soldiers have a terrible habit of doing what they're told, my dear."

There was a knock at the door, it opened, and Hesser came in. He smiled, his slight half-bow extending to the three of them, then turned to Madame Chevalier.

"Chess?"

"Why not?" She was playing a Schubert nocturne now, full of passion and meaning. "But first settle an argument for us, Max. Paul here believes that if the SS come to shoot us, you'll let them. Claire doesn't believe you could stand by and do nothing. What do you think?"

"I have the strangest of feelings that I will beat you in seven moves tonight."

"A soldier's answer, I see. Ah, well."

She stood up, came around the piano, and moved to the chess table. Hesser sat opposite her. She made the first move. Claire picked up a book and started to read. Gaillard sat staring into the fire, smoking his pipe. It was very quiet.

After a while the door opened and Canning came in wearing a brown battledress blouse and cream slacks. Claire de Beauvoir said, "That's better, Hamilton. Actually you really look rather handsome tonight. Crawling through sewers must be good for you."

Hesser said, without looking up, "Ah, General, I was hoping you'd put in an appearance."

"I'd have thought we'd seen enough of each other for one night," Canning told him.

"Perhaps, but the point you were making earlier—I think your argument may have some merit. Perhaps we could discuss it in the morning. Let's say directly after breakfast?"

"Now you're damn well talking," Canning said.

Hesser ignored him, leaned forward, moved a bishop. "Checkmate, I think."

Madame Chevalier examined the board and

sighed. "Seven moves, you told me. You've done it in five."

Max Hesser smiled. "My dear Madame, one must always try to be ahead of the game. The first rule of good soldiering."

And in Berlin, just after midnight, Bormann still sat in his office, for the *Führer* himself worked through the night these days, seldom going to bed before seven A.M., and Bormann liked to remain close. Close enough to keep others away.

There was a knock at the door and Rattenhuber entered, a sealed envelope in his hand. "For you, *Reichsleiter.*"

"Who from, Willi?"

"I don't know, *Reichsleiter.* I found it on my desk, marked 'priority seven.'"

Which was a code reference for communications of the most secret sort, intended for Bormann's eyes alone.

Bormann opened the envelope, then looked up, no expression in his eyes. "Willi, the Fieseler Storch in which *Feldmarschall* von Greim and Hannah Reitsch flew into Berlin has been destroyed. Get on the phone to Gatow at once. Tell them they must send another plane by morning, one capable of flying directly out of the city."

"Very well, *Reichsleiter.*"

Bormann held up the envelope. "Know what's in here, Willi? Some very interesting news. It would appear that our beloved *Reichsführer*, dear Uncle Heini, has offered to surrender to the British and Americans."

"My God," Rattenhuber exclaimed.

"But what will the *Führer* say, Willi? That's the most interesting thing." Bormann pushed back his chair and stood up. "Let's go and find out, shall we?"

Five

FROM his window, Hesser could see out across the courtyard and outer walls to the road winding steeply down the valley to the river below. Beyond the trees was the tiny village of Arlberg, looking rather like something out of a fairy tale by the Brothers Grimm, the pine trees on the lower slopes of the mountain behind it green against the snow. In fact it was snowing again now, only slightly, but for a moment it seemed to make the world a cleaner, more shining place. Some throwback to childhood, probably.

The door opened behind him, and Schenck entered. Hesser said, "Snowing again. It's hanging on this year."

"True, *Herr Oberst*," Schenck said. "When I passed through the village early this morning, I noticed the woodcutters' children from the outlying districts skiing to school."

Hesser moved to the liquor cabinet and poured himself a brandy. Schenck tried to stay suitably impassive, and Hesser said, "I know, the road to ruin, but it's bad this morning. Worse than usual, and this helps a damn sight more than those pills."

He could feel his left arm in every detail within the empty sleeve, every wire inside his broken body, and the glass eye was sheer torture.

"What does it matter, anyway? The same roads all lead to hell in the end. But never mind that now. Did you try Berlin again this morning?"

"Yes, *Herr Oberst*, but we're just not succeeding in getting through."

"And the radio?"

"*Kaput, Herr Oberst*. Stern found a couple of valves gone."

"Can't he replace them?"

"When he opened the box of spares, they had all suffered damage in transit, from the look of things."

"Are you trying to tell me we've no kind of communication at all with anyone?"

"For the moment I am afraid that is true, *Herr Oberst*, but with luck we should still get through to Berlin if we keep trying, and Stern is out in a field car now, touring the district to see if he can find the spares he needs."

"Very well. Is there anything else?"

"General Canning and Colonel Birr are here."

"All right, show them in. And Schenck," he added as the old lieutenant moved to the door.

"*Herr Oberst*."

"You stay, too."

Canning wore a sidecap and olive-drab officer's trenchcoat. Birr was in a reversible camouflage-and-white winter uniform parka with a hood of a type issued generally in the German Army on the Eastern Front.

Hesser said, "Ready for exercise, I see, gentlemen."

"Never mind that," Canning said brusquely. "What have you decided?"

Hesser raised a hand defensively. "You go too fast, General. There is a great deal to consider here."

"For Christ's sake," Canning said. "Here we go again. Are you going to do something positive, or aren't you?"

"We've been trying to get through to Prisoner-of-War Administration headquarters in Berlin since last night, without success."

"Berlin?" Canning said. "You must be joking. The Russians are walking all over it."

"Not quite," Hesser said evenly. "The *Führer*, you may be dismayed to know, still lives, and there are considerable German forces in the capital."

"Four hundred and fifty miles away," Canning said urgently. "This is here, Max. What are *you* going to do *here*, that's what I want to know."

"Or to put it another way," Birr said, "have you thought any more about sending Lieutenant Schenck to look for a British or American unit, perhaps in company with one of us?"

"No." Hesser slammed his good hand against the desk. "That I will not permit. That would be going too far. I am a German officer, gentlemen, you must not forget that. I serve my country the best way I can."

"So what the hell is that supposed to mean?" Canning demanded.

Hesser frowned, thinking for a moment, then nodded. "For today, I will still keep trying to reach Berlin. I must know what their definite orders are in this matter." Canning started to protest, but Hesser cut him short. "No, this is the way I intend to handle things. You must make up your mind to it. First—to use a phrase you are fond of—we try channels."

"And then?" Birr asked.

"If we are no further forward by this time tomorrow, I shall consider sending *Oberleutnant* Schenck out into the wide world to see what he can find. Always supposing he is willing to take his chances." He turned to Schenck. "I will not make this an order, you understand?"

Schenck smiled bleakly. "I shall be happy to do as the *Herr Oberst* sees fit."

"Why waste another day?" Canning began, but Hesser simply stood up.

"That is all I have to say, gentlemen. Good morning." He nodded to Schenck. "You will take the general and Colonel Birr to exercise now."

•

It was cold in the water garden, snow flying every which way in the wind. The guards on each gate wore parkas, and Schneider trailed along with Magda behind Canning and Birr. Canning turned at one point and snapped his fingers. The Alsatian strained at her lead and whined.

"Oh, let her go, man," he snapped at Schneider in German.

Schneider slipped her chain reluctantly, and the

bitch ran to Canning and licked his hand. He knelt and fondled her ears and said to Birr, "Well, what do you think?"

"More than I'd hoped for. Hesser's a Prussian, remember. A professional soldier of the old school, God and the Fatherland branded on his backbone. You're asking him to throw in his hand. Not only to string up the white flag, but to go running around, trying to attract somebody's attention with it. That's expecting a hell of a lot. I'd settle for what you've got if I were you."

"Yes, maybe you're right." Canning stood up as Paul Gaillard and Madame Chevalier appeared from the lower water garden, walking briskly. She wore a German military greatcoat and a head scarf, and Gaillard had on a black beret and overcoat.

"How did you get on?" the Frenchman demanded as they approached.

"Oh, you tell them, Justin," Canning said. "I've had enough for one day."

He moved away, Magda at his knee, went down the steps past the lily pond, and entered the conservatory. Schneider followed but stayed on the porch.

It was warm and humid in there, plants everywhere, palms and vines heavy with grapes. He followed the black-and-white mosaic of the path and came to the center fountain, where he found Claire de Beauville tending the scarlet winter roses that were her special pride.

Canning paused for a moment, watching her. She was really beautiful, the dark hair pulled back to the nape of the neck, exposing the oval triangle of the face. The high cheekbones, the wide, quiet eyes, the generous mouth. He was conscious of the old familiar stirring and the slight feeling of anger that went with it.

Orphaned at an early age and supported by an uncle in the shipping business in Shanghai whom he never saw, he had spent most of his youth at boarding schools of one kind or another before he finally entered West Point. From that moment he had given his all to the army, sacrificed everything to the demands of military life with single-minded devotion. He had never felt the need for wife or family. There had been women, of course, but only in the most basic way. Now everything had changed. For the first time in his life another human being could touch him, and that was not a concept that fitted comfortably into his scheme of things.

Claire turned, gardening fork in one hand, and smiled. "There you are. What happened?"

"Oh, we have to wait another twenty-four hours. Max wants to make one last attempt to get in touch with Prisoner-of-War Administration headquarters in Berlin. The correct Junker officer, right to the bitter end."

"And you, Hamilton, what do you want?"

"To be free now," he said, his voice suddenly urgent. "It's been too long, Claire, don't you see?"

"And you've missed too much, isn't that it?" He frowned, and she carried on. "The war, Hamilton. Your precious war. Bugles faintly on the wind, the smoke of battle. Meat and drink to you, what your soul craves. And who knows, if you were free now, there might still be the chance to get involved. Have one last, glorious fling."

"That's a hell of a thing to say."

"But true. And what can I offer as a substitute? Only winter roses."

She smiled slightly. He caught her then, pulling her into his arms, his mouth fastening hungrily on hers.

■

Ritter, seated at the piano in the canteen, was playing a Chopin etude, a particular favorite of his. It was a piece which comforted him, in spite of the fact that this present instrument was distinctly out of tune. It reminded him of other days. Of his father and mother and the small country estate in Prussia where he had been raised.

The Russians were shelling constantly now, the sound of the explosions audible even at that depth, the concrete walls trembling. There was that pervasive smell of sulfur, dust everywhere.

A drunken SS lieutenant lurched against the piano, slopping beer over the keys. "We've had enough of that rubbish. What about something rousing? Something to lift the heart. A chorus of 'Horst Wessel,' perhaps?"

Ritter stopped playing and looked up at him. "You're speaking to me, I presume?" His voice was very quiet, yet infinitely dangerous, the white face burning, the eyes dark.

The lieutenant took in the Knight's Cross, the Oak Leaves, the Swords, the insignia of rank, and tried to draw himself together. "I'm sorry, *Sturmbannführer*. My mistake."

"So it would appear. Go away."

The lieutenant moved off to join a noisy, jostling throng as drunk as himself. A young nurse in service uniform was passing by. One of them pulled her across his knee. Another slipped a hand up her skirt. She laughed and reached up to kiss a third hungrily.

Ritter, totally disgusted, helped himself to a bottle of Steinhager at the bar, filled a glass, and sat at an empty table. After a while, Hoffer entered. He looked around the canteen, then came across quickly, his face pale with excitement.

"I saw a hell of a thing a little while ago, Major."

"And what would that be?"

"General Fegelein being marched along the corridor by two of the escort guard, minus his epaulettes and insignia. He looked frightened to death."

"The fortunes of war, Erich. Get yourself a glass."

"Good God, Major, a general of the SS. A Knight's Cross holder."

"And like all of us in the end, clay of the most common variety, my friend—or at least his feet were."

"We shouldn't have come here to this place." Hoffer glanced about him, his face working. "We're never going to get out. We're going to die here like rats, and in bad company."

"I don't think so."

There was an immediate expression of hope on Hoffer's face. "You've heard something?"

"No, but all my instincts tell me that I shall. Now

get yourself a glass and bring that chessboard over here."

■

Bormann and Rattenhuber, watching from a doorway at the rear of the room, had observed the entire scene. Rattenhuber said, "His mother was a really big aristocrat. One of those families that go all the way back to Frederick."

"Look at him," Bormann said. "Did you see the way he handled that drunken swine? And I'll tell you something, Willi. A hundred marks says he hasn't raised his arm and said *Heil Hitler* for at least two years. I know his kind. They salute like a British Guards officer—a finger to the peak of the cap. And the men, Willi. Shall I tell you what they think, even the men of the SS? Would you imagine they'd still follow old peasants like you and me?"

"They follow." Rattenhuber hesitated. "They follow their officers, *Reichsleiter*. They have discipline, the *Waffen*-SS. The finest in the world."

"But Ritter, Willi. A man like him they'll follow into the jaws of hell, and you know why? Because men like him don't give a damn. They're what they are. Themselves alone."

"And what would that be, *Reichsleiter?*"

"In his case, a very gentle perfect knight. You see, Willi? All that reading I do—even English literature. They think me Bormann the boor, Goebbels and company, but I know more than they do— about everything. Don't you agree?"

"But of course, *Reichsleiter.*"

"And Ritter—fine Aryan stock, like one of those idealized paintings the *Führer* loves so much. A standard impossible for the rest of us to attain.

Forget the nasty things, Willi. The rapes, the burnings, the camps, the executions. Just think of the ideal. The finest soldier you've ever known. Decent, honorable, chivalrous, and totally without fear. What every soldier in the *Waffen*-SS would like to imagine himself to be, that's what Ritter *is*."

"And you think these Finnish barbarians we discussed earlier would concur?"

"The Knight's Cross, Willi, with Oak Leaves *and* Swords? What do you think?"

Rattenhuber nodded. "I think that perhaps the *Reichsleiter* would like me to bring him to the office now."

"Later, Willi. Now I must go to the *Führer*. The news of Himmler's defection and Fegelein's cowardice has considerably angered him. He needs me. You speak to Ritter, Willi, when he's had a drink or two. Judge if it's changed him. I'll see him later. After midnight."

The shelling increased in intensity, the thunder overhead continuous now, so that the walls shook constantly and, in the canteen, behavior deteriorated considerably. The place was crowded with a noisy, jostling throng, here and there a drunk lying under the table.

When Rattenhuber returned a couple of hours later, Ritter and Hoffer were still at the table at the rear of the room, playing chess.

Rattenhuber said, "May I join you?"

Ritter glanced up. "Why not?"

Rattenhuber winced as a particularly thunderous explosion shook the entire room. "I didn't like the sound of that. Do you think we're safe here, Major?"

Ritter looked at Hoffer. "Erich?"

Hoffer shrugged. "Seventeen-point-five caliber is the heaviest they've got. Nothing that could get down this far."

"A comforting thought." Rattenhuber offered them both cigarettes.

Ritter said, "Hoffer saw a strange sight some hours ago. General Fegelein being led along the corridor under escort, minus epaulettes and insignia."

"Yes, very sad. A disgrace to all of us," Rattenhuber said. "He cleared off yesterday. When the *Führer* found he was missing, he sent a detachment out looking for him. The fool was actually at his own house in Charlottenburg in civilian clothes and with a woman. They took him outside and shot him half an hour ago."

Ritter showed no emotion whatsoever. "If what you say is so, then there could be no other penalty."

"No, we can't just leave the war by taking off our uniform and putting on a raincoat, not at this stage," Rattenhuber said. "Not any of us." He lit another cigarette. "By the way, Major, the *Reichsleiter* would like to see you a little later on. I'd be obliged if you'd hold yourself in readiness."

"Naturally," Ritter said. "I'm at the *Reichsleiter*'s orders." The slight, sardonic smile that touched his mouth had an edge of contempt to it. "Was there anything else?"

Rattenhuber felt in some curious way as if he

were being dismissed. "No," he said hurriedly. "I'll look for you here."

An SS orderly entered the room, gazed around quickly, then bore down on them. He clicked his heels and offered a message to Rattenhuber. Rattenhuber read it, his face broke into a delighted smile, and he waved the orderly away.

"Excellent news. The Fieseler Storch in which *Feldmarschall* von Greim and Hannah Reitsch flew into Berlin on the twenty-sixth was destroyed this morning by artillery fire."

"So the *Feldmarschall* is also a permanent guest here?" Ritter said. "Bad luck."

"No, he got away this evening in a replacement plane, an Arado trainer piloted by Hannah Reitsch after she'd made two unsuccessful attempts. They took off near the *Brandenburger Tor*." He stood up. "You must excuse me. The *Reichsleiter* has been waiting for such news, and the *Führer*, also." He went out.

Hoffer said, "But what does he want you for?"

"I expect I'll find that out when he sees me," Ritter said. He nodded at the chessboard. "And now, if you don't mind, it's your move."

■

Just before midnight, Walter Wagner, a city councilor and minor official of the propaganda ministry, was hustled into the bunker under armed guard. Totally bewildered and still not quite believing what was happening to him, at approximately one o'clock in the morning he married Adolf Hitler and Eva Braun. The only other two people present were the witnesses, Martin Bormann and Joseph Goebbels, Reich minister for propaganda.

A wedding breakfast was served immediately afterward, at which champagne was available in copious quantities. At approximately two o'clock, the *Führer* went into an adjoining room to dictate his will and final political testament to one of his two secretaries, Frau Junge. Bormann, who had been waiting for an appropriate moment, seized his chance and left, also.

Rattenhuber was waiting for him in the corridor. "And now we've got that out of the way, I'll see Ritter," the *Reichsleiter* said. "Bring him to me, Willi."

When Rattenhuber ushered Ritter into the office, there was a particularly intense bombardment taking place. The *Reichsleiter* looked up as smoke and dust drifted from the ventilator. "If that hadn't been happening for some days now, I'd be alarmed."

"Not pleasant," Ritter said.

"No place to be at the moment—Berlin—if it can be avoided."

Rattenhuber took up his position beside the door. There was a long silence during which Bormann gazed up at the young SS officer calmly. Finally he said, "You would like to leave Berlin, *Sturmbannführer?*"

Ritter actually smiled. "I think you may say that I would dearly love to, *Reichsleiter,* but I would not have thought it a possibility now."

"Oh, all things are possible to men who are willing to dare anything. I had formed the opinion that you were of that breed. Am I right?"

"If you say so."

"Good, we must see if we can accommodate

you, then. This man of yours—Hoffer. He is to be trusted?"

"With my life—yes," Ritter said. "I would not depend too much on his loyalty to any political idea, however—not at this stage."

"In other words, a man of sound sense and judgment. I like that." Bormann turned to the map which lay before him. "You know this area here, northwest of Innsbruck, on the Inn River?"

"I know where it is," Ritter said. "Let's put it that way. My unit was in that general area when I left. Perhaps fifty miles away."

"Not now," Bormann said. "What was left of them was wiped out by tanks of the American Sixth Army a hundred miles or more from there yesterday morning."

For a moment his voice seemed to fade for Ritter as he thought of the regiment, old comrades, Colonel Jager. He came back to reality to hear Bormann saying, "I'm sorry—a bad shock for you."

"No matter," Ritter said. "An old and tired story, repeated many times. Please continue."

"Very well. This entire area—the triangle between Innsbruck, Salzburg, and Klagenfurt—is still in our hands, but the situation is very fluid. The enemy are probing in with great care because they believe the stories they've heard of an Alpine Fortress where we can hold out for years. Once they appreciate the truth of the situation, they'll be through to Berchtesgaden like a hot knife into butter."

"And this could happen at any time?"

"Undoubtedly. So, to accomplish what I seek, we must move fast."

"And what would that be, *Reichsleiter?*"

Bormann picked up a pencil and drew a circle around Arlberg. "Here at Schloss Arlberg, on the Inn, you will find five important prisoners. What we call *prominenti*. One of them is the American general, Canning. Who the others are needn't concern you at the moment. It's enough to know that they are all people held in special regard by their individual nations. You can read the files later."

"A moment," Ritter said. "You speak as if you expect me to go there in person. As if it is an accomplished fact. But this would first mean leaving Berlin."

"Naturally."

"But how can this be?"

"You may have heard that the Fieseler Storch in which *Feldmarschall* von Greim and Hannah Reitsch flew into Berlin was destroyed yesterday."

"Yes, I know that. They flew out last night in a replacement, an Arado training plane." And then, with a sudden flash of insight, Ritter saw it all. "Ah, I see now. The Fieseler Storch . . ."

". . . is in a garage at the back of an automobile showroom just off the main avenue near the *Brandenburger Tor.* I'll give you the address before you leave. You will fly out tonight, or probably just after midnight tomorrow, the best time to evade the Russian antiaircraft. About ten miles from Arlberg, here at Arnheim, there's an airstrip. Used for mountain rescue operations before the war. No one there now. You should arrive by breakfast time."

"Then what?"

"You'll find transport. It's all arranged. Even

my enemies admit I'm an organizer." Bormann smiled. "You will proceed from there to Arlberg, where you will take charge of the five prisoners I have mentioned and bring them back to Arnheim with you. They'll be picked up from there by transport plane later in the day. Any questions?"

"Several. The purpose of this operation?"

"The prisoners, you mean?" Bormann waved a hand. "Put out of your mind any wild rumors you may have heard about the execution of prominent persons. I abhor waste, Major, believe me. These people will be useful bargaining counters when we reach the situation of having to sit down and discuss peace terms with our enemies."

"Hostages might be a better word."

"If you like."

"All right," Ritter said, "but what about the situation at the castle? Who's in charge?"

"Soldiers of the *Wehrmacht,* but only just. A Colonel Hesser—a good man, but crippled, and nineteen or twenty old men. Reservists. Nothing to worry about."

"And I'll have a piece of paper, I suppose, ordering him to hand them over?"

"Signed by the *Führer* himself."

"What if he refuses, not that I'm trying to be difficult, you understand. It's just that after six years of service I've got accustomed to the fact that in war anything can happen, especially when one expects the opposite. I like to take care of all eventualities."

"And so you shall." Bormann indicated the map again, tapping with his pencil. "At this very moment, no more than ten miles west of Arnheim you'll find an SS unit, or what's left of it. Thirty or forty men, according to my information."

"These days, as the *Reichsleiter* knows, the term 'SS' can cover a multitude of sins. Are they German?"

"No, but firstrate troops. Finns, who were with Wiking Division in Russia, operating mainly as ski troops."

"Mercenaries?" Ritter said.

"Soldiers of the *Waffen*-SS whose contract does not expire until nine A.M. on the first of May. You will hold them to their contract and bend them to your purpose until you have secured your prisoners. Do you understand me?"

"I believe so."

"Good." Bormann handed him a small folder. "Everything you need is in there, including the address of the garage where you'll find the Stork. The pilot's name is Berger. He's SS, too, so you see it's all being kept in the family. Oh, and there's just one other rather important thing."

"What's that, *Reichsleiter?*"

"Someone will be going along with you, as my personal representative, just to see that everything goes all right. A Herr Strasser. I hope I can rely on you to offer him every courtesy."

Ritter stood looking down at the folder which he gripped tightly in both hands. "Is there something worrying you, Major?" Martin Bormann asked gently.

"The prisoners," Ritter said and looked up. "I want your assurance, your personal word on your honor, that no harm will come to them. That the situation will be exactly as you have stated."

"My dear Ritter." Bormann came around the desk and put a hand on his shoulder. "Anything else would simply be stupid, and I'm not that, believe me."

Ritter nodded slowly. "As you say, *Reichsleiter.*"

"Good," Bormann said. "Excellent. I'd get some sleep now if I were you. Rattenhuber here will see that you and Hoffer get a pass that will get you out of here sometime tomorrow afternoon. I may not see you again before you go, although I'll try. If not, good luck."

He held out his hand. Ritter hesitated, then took it briefly. Rattenhuber held the door open for him. As he closed it, Bormann went around the desk. When he turned, there was a strange expression on his face.

"My honor, Willi. He asked me to swear on my honor. Did you ever hear of such a thing, with almost everyone else I know doubting its very existence for the past twenty years or more?"

■

Hoffer was waiting in the canteen and leaned over excitedly as Ritter sat down. "What was it all about?"

"I'm not sure, Erich," Ritter said. "You see, there was what he told me and what he left out. Still, for what it's worth . . ."

He leaned forward, his hands on the folder, and started to talk.

Six

AT Schloss Arlberg it was still snowing when Schenck knocked at the door and entered Hesser's office. The colonel was standing at the window, looking out across the valley. He turned and walked to the desk.

"So, the situation is still the same?"

"I'm afraid so, *Herr Oberst*. We are still unable to get through to Berlin."

"And the radio?"

"Stern has visited every village in these parts, without success. There are certain to be radios in the area, of course, that may well use the right type of valve, but as the *Herr Oberst* knows, their possession in this district has been declared illegal for more than a year now. Those individuals guilty of breaking the law are unlikely to admit to the fact at this stage."

"Understandable in the circumstances." Hesser sat down. "The time for a definite decision has come."

"So it would appear, *Herr Oberst*."

Hesser sat for a moment, plucking at his empty sleeve. "As I said yesterday, I will not make an order of this business. I would be failing in my duty if I didn't point out that it could be extremely hazardous. In the fluid state of the front line in this area, any enemy unit you run into may be inclined to shoot first and ask questions afterward. You understand this?"

"Perfectly."

"And you're still willing to take a chance?"

"Herr Oberst," Schenck said, "I'm an old man by military standards, perhaps too old for this sort of game. I last saw action on the Western Front in 1918, but it would be quite out of the question for you to go, sir, and certainly improper to send one of the other ranks on such a mission. As I am the only other available officer, it would seem to me that we have little choice in the matter."

"Who would you take with you?"

"Schmidt, I think. He's my own age, but an excellent driver. We'll take one of the field cars."

"Very well," Hesser said. "It would seem, as you say, that there is no other choice. Please bring General Canning and Colonel Birr, and I'll inform them of my decision."

"They are outside now, *Herr Oberst.*"

Schenck moved to the door, and Hesser said, "Schenck?"

"Herr Oberst."

"I appreciate this. You're a brave man."

"No, *Herr Oberst,* anything but that. A very frightened man." Schenck smiled. "But I do have a wife and two daughters I'm more than anxious to see again. What I do now, I'm doing for them. The best thing for all of us, believe me."

"Yes, perhaps you're right."

Schenck went out and returned a few moments later with Canning and Birr. The general came forward eagerly. "Well, have you come to a decision?"

Hesser nodded. *"Oberleutnant* Schenck will be leaving"—here he glanced at his watch—"at noon, precisely. He'll take a field car and one driver with him, and he will search for an Allied unit somewhere in the general direction of Innsbruck. You agree, Schenck?"

"Whatever you say, *Herr Oberst*."

"Thank God you've come to your senses," Canning said. "Can we go now and tell the others?"

"I don't see why not."

Canning and Birr turned to the door, and Hesser stood up. "One thing before you go."

"What's that?" Canning turned impatiently.

"Oberleutnant Schenck and *Korporal* Schmidt will be running a considerable personal risk in this business. I hope you appreciate that."

Canning frowned, and it was Birr who held out his hand to Schenck. "We certainly do, and I for one would like to thank you now on behalf of all of us."

"I will do my best, *Herr Oberst*"—Schenck smiled briefly—"to stay alive for all our sakes."

■

Paul Gaillard and Claire were sitting at the window in the dining hall when Canning and Birr entered; Madame Chevalier was at her daily practice at the piano. She stopped playing at once.

Gaillard stood up. "What happened?"

"We go," Canning said excitedly. "Or at least Schenck does. He leaves at noon." He stood in front of the fire, hands behind his back. "Do you folks realize that with any kind of luck he could be back here in a matter of hours? That by this evening we could be free?"

Birr lit a cigarette. "On the other hand, if he runs into the wrong sort of trigger-happy bunch, he could also be dead by then. Have you considered that?"

"Nonsense," Canning said. "Schenck spent four years on the Western Front in the First World War. Wounded three times. He's too old a bird to get knocked off now."

"But if he does, Hamilton." Claire walked to the fire and sat down. "What do we do?"

"Then it may be necessary for us to take more positive action ourselves." Canning crossed to the door and opened it. He turned. "I know one thing. If anybody tries to take me out of here, SS or whoever, they're going to have to do it the hard way."

He went out, closing the door behind him.

■

When Rattenhuber went into Bormann's office, the *Reichsleiter* was writing at his desk. "I'll only be a moment, Willi. I missed my diary entry last night. I was with the *Führer* for hours." After a while he put down his pen and closed the book. "So, Willi, and how are things going out there? How's morale?"

Rattenhuber looked uncomfortable. "Morale, *Reichsleiter?*"

"Come on, man. No need to beat about the bush at this stage of the game."

"Very well, *Reichsleiter*. If you must know, it's a total disgrace. I've never seen so many drunks in uniform in all my life. The canteen is full of them. And the women aren't behaving any better. Everything seems to be going to pieces."

"What do you expect, Willi? You know why the Russian artillery has stopped? Because they were killing their own people as their tanks and infantry pushed toward Wilhelmplatz. According to the latest reports, they've come to a halt no more than sixteen hundred feet from the Chancellery. There's heavy fighting in Belle-Allianceplatz and in the Potsdamerstrasse, though I understand our troops are holding their own near Bismarckstrasse."

"But what about Wenck's army?"

"Still maintaining its link with Reimann's corps, but that's no use to us, Willi. We're finished."

Rattenhuber looked shocked. "Finished, *Reichsleiter?*"

"Oh, for quite some time now, didn't you know? When Steiner's counterattack failed to materialize on the twenty-second, the *Führer* announced that the war was lost. That he intended to die in Berlin. Did you know that at his wedding breakfast he actually talked of suicide?"

"My God!" Rattenhuber said in horror.

"Perhaps the greatest service he could render the German people."

He seemed to be waiting for some kind of comment. Rattenhuber licked dry lips nervously. *"Reichsleiter?"*

"An interesting thought. To die for the cause, if you are the right person, can sometimes be more important than to live." He smiled gently, contriving to look even more sinister than usual. "But for lesser mortals, such excesses are not always necessary. You, for instance, Willi."

"Me, *Reichsleiter?* I don't understand."

"Your destiny is to live, Willi. To put it simply, you are to leave this evening."

Rattenhuber stared at him in astonishment. "Leave Berlin, you mean?"

"Together with the *Führer*'s army adjutant, Johannmeier, Lorenz from the propaganda ministry, and Zander. His task is to take a copy of the *Führer*'s political testament and will to Admiral Dönitz. I suggested sending you as well, and the *Führer* agreed."

"I—I am honored," Rattenhuber stammered.

"I'm sure you are, Willi," Bormann said dryly. "But whether you reach Dönitz or not is problematical and of no particular consequence. There are other tasks for you now of more importance."

Rattenhuber's face was pale. "The *Kameradenwerk?* It begins?"

"Of course, Willi. Did I not always say it would? In my end is my beginning. I read that once somewhere. Highly appropriate."

There was a tremendous explosion somewhere close by, the walls of the bunker shook, a cloud of dust filtered in through the ventilator.

Bormann glanced up, showing absolutely no sign of fear. "There goes the Ivan artillery again. You know, in some ways it reminds me of the Twilight of the Gods. All the forces of evil are in league against them, and then suddenly a new citadel arises, more beautiful than ever, and Baldur lives again." He turned, his face grave. "It will be so for us, Willi, for Germany. This I promise you."

And Rattenhuber, in spite of the noise of the shells landing without cease thirty yards above his head, the sulfurous stench, the dust which threatened to choke him, straightened his shoulders.

"I, too, believe, *Reichsleiter*. Have never ceased to believe in the destiny of the German people."

"Good, Willi. Excellent." Bormann took a letter from his desk and shook the dust from it. "This is the reason it is so important you get out of Berlin, and that clown Dönitz has nothing to do with it."

At Schloss Arlberg, in the main courtyard, Schenck was preparing to leave. He stood beside the field car, the collar of his greatcoat turned up against the snow, and waited as Corporal Schmidt made a final check on the engine.

"Everything all right?" Schenck asked.

"As far as I can see, *Herr Leutnant*."

"Good man."

As he turned, Hesser, Canning, and Birr came down the steps of the main entrance and moved across the courtyard.

"All set, Schenck?" Hesser demanded.

"Yes, *Herr Oberst*."

"Good. General Canning has something for you."

Canning held out an envelope. "This is a letter I've written, explaining the situation here. Hand it to the first British or American officer you come to. I think it should do the trick."

"My thanks, General." Schenck put the envelope in his pocket, then unfastened the service belt that carried the holstered Walther automatic pistol at his waist. He held it out to Hesser. "Under the circumstances, I shan't be needing this." He reached inside the field car and picked up Corporal Schmidt's Schmeisser from the rear seat. "Or this."

Hesser hesitated, then took them. "Perhaps the wiser course."

"I think so, sir." Schenck nodded to Schmidt, who started the engine. The *Oberleutnant* drew himself together and delivered a punctilious military salute. *"Herr Oberst,* gentlemen."

They all saluted in return; he climbed into the passenger seat and nodded. Schmidt drove away, out of the main entrance across the drawbridge, and they disappeared around the first bend in the road.

As the sound of the engine faded, Birr said, "You know, I've just thought of something."

"What's that?" Canning asked.

"That if Schenck runs into a German unit, and they find that letter on him, it isn't going to do him a great deal of good."

"I know," Canning said harshly. "I thought of that when I was writing the damn thing, but at this stage of the game he must just take his chances—

like the rest of us," he added and turned and walked back across the courtyard.

At approximately four o'clock in the afternoon, Rattenhuber conducted Ritter and Hoffer to the bunker exit leading onto Hermann-Göringstrasse. They each had a small field pack loaded with provisions for the journey and wore camouflaged ponchos and steel helmets. They were armed with Schmeisser machine pistols, and in true SS fashion carried two stick grenades in the top of each boot.

The artillery barrage was still as relentless as ever, and there was the sound of heavy fighting up near Potsdamerplatz.

Rattenhuber put a hand on Ritter's shoulder. "What can I say, except good luck and God go with you."

God? Ritter thought. Is He on my side, too? He smiled ironically, tapped Hoffer on the shoulder, and moved out. There was a burst of machine-gun fire, and Rattenhuber watched them flatten themselves on the ground. A moment later they were up and running and safely into the ruined buildings opposite.

Bormann moved out of the shadows behind him. "So, they are on their way, Willi."

"Yes, *Reichsleiter*."

Bormann glanced at his watch. "I can afford to be away from the bunker for perhaps three hours at the most. In any case, you, too, must be back by then to make your own departure on schedule. We must move fast."

"Yes, *Reichsleiter*."

Rattenhuber hurried away into the darkness of

the vehicle ramp. A moment later there was the sound of an engine starting, and he drove out of the shadows at the wheel of a field car. There was an MG34 machine gun in the back, and Bormann mounted it on the windshield swivel and got in. Rattenhuber put on a steel helmet and offered the *Reichsleiter* another.

Bormann shook his head. "If there's a bullet for me, that won't save me. I haven't worn one since my field artillery days in 1918. Now, let's get moving. We haven't got time to waste."

Rattenhuber accelerated away, driving very fast, and they turned out of Hermann-Göringstrasse and moved in the general direction of Potsdamerplatz.

*

Once past the Tiergarten, Ritter and Hoffer moved fast through the blocks of apartment houses. A continuous mortar barrage fell around them, and after a while a squadron of Russian fighter-bombers came in low over the rooftops, spraying everything in sight with cannon fire.

They dodged into a doorway beside a sandbagged gun emplacement from which Hitler Youth fired light machine guns ineffectually into the sky.

"My God," Hoffer said in disgust. "Children playing soldiers, and for all the good they're doing, they might as well be firing Christmas toys."

"But willing to die, Erich," Ritter said. "They still believe."

He was examining the rough map which Rattenhuber had given him. Hoffer tugged at his sleeve. "And us, Major. What about us? What in hell are we doing here? What's the point?"

"Survival, Erich," Ritter said. "A game we've been playing for quite some time now, you and I. We might as well see it through. Who knows? It could prove interesting."

"That's all it's ever been to you, isn't it?" Hoffer said. "Some kind of black joke. That's why you can only smile with that curl to your lips."

"And it will still be there when you fold my hands on my chest, Erich," Ritter told him. "I promise you. Now let's get moving. We've about a quarter of a mile to go."

They moved from street to street, from one mortar crater to the next, through the charnel house that was Berlin, passing on the way groups of terrified civilians, mostly women and children, and the soldiers of the *Volkssturm*, mainly tired old men, most of them already walking corpses.

Finally, they reached the East–West Avenue, saw the Victory Column in the distance. There were few people here now, and for some reason the bombardment seemed to have faded and the avenue was strangely quiet and deserted.

"Over here," Ritter said and darted toward the side street opposite. The showrooms on the corner were shattered, plate-glass windows gaping. The sign above the main entrance said "Burgdorf Autos."

Ritter led the way along the pavement and paused outside the garage doors at the rear. They were closed. "This is it," he said. There was a judas gate to one side. He turned to Hoffer and grinned lightly. "I'll lead, you cover."

Hoffer cocked the Schmeisser and flattened himself against the wall. Ritter tried the handle of the gate gingerly. It opened to his touch. He paused, then shoved the door open and went in fast, going down hard. There was a burst of machine-gun fire, a pause, then Hoffer fired an answering burst around the door.

In the silence, as the echoes died, Ritter called, "Friends. We're looking for *Obersturmführer* Heini Berger."

It was very quiet, the garage a place of shadows in the evening light. A voice called softly, "Identify yourselves."

"Valhalla Exchange," Ritter called.

He could see the Fieseler Storch now, over to one side, and then a boot scraped and a young, dark-haired SS officer in camouflage uniform moved out of the shadows. His old-style field cap was tilted at a rakish angle and he carried an American Thompson submachine gun in one hand.

"Nice to see you," he said. "For a moment there, I thought you might be a bunch of Ivans smelling out foxes."

Ritter nodded toward the Thompson, which carried a round, hundred-drum magazine. "They'd have been in for a nasty surprise."

Berger grinned lazily. "Yes, a little item I picked up in the Ardennes. I always did like to overdo things." He put a cigarette in his mouth and flicked a lighter made from a Russian rifle bullet.

"What about Herr Strasser?" Ritter said, looking around.

"Oh, he isn't due for a while yet." Berger sat down on a packing case, putting the Thompson on the floor. "No rush—we're not due out of here until midnight."

"I see." Ritter sat down beside him, and Hoffer wandered over to the Stork. "This man Strasser—you know him?"

Berger hesitated perceptibly. "Don't you?"

"Never met him in my life before."

"Neither have I. I'm just the bloody bus driver on this show."

Ritter nodded toward the Stork. "We're not going to make the Bavarian Alps in one hop in that."

"No, we're scheduled to put down halfway, at an airstrip in the Thuringian Forest, west of Plauen. Always supposing it's still in our hands."

"And if it isn't?"

"An interesting thought."

"You think we'll make it? Out of Berlin, I mean?"

"I don't see why not. Hannah Reitsch made it with Greim, didn't she?"

"Not in total darkness, which it will be when we take off."

"Yes, I was aware of that fact," Berger said. "On the other hand, it does mean that the Russians won't be expecting us. They aren't likely to have any fighters up. No need now they've taken Templehof and Gatow. With any kind of luck, we could be away before they know what's happening."

"But you would still have to take off along the avenue in the dark," Ritter said, "and the Victory Column. . . ."

"I know. Very large and very solid. Still, I expect I'll manage to think of something." There were a couple of old sacks on the floor, and he lay down on them, cradling the Thompson in his arms. "I think I'll get a little shut-eye. Something tells me I'm going to need it. If you wouldn't mind watching the front door and give me a push when Strasser comes . . ."

He pulled the peak of his service cap over his eyes. Ritter smiled slightly and turned to Hoffer, who looked bewildered. "What's going on, Major? What's he playing at?"

"He's sleeping, Erich. Very sensible under the circumstances. Now do you want to take the first watch, or shall I?"

■

It was toward evening when *Oberleutnant* Schenck and *Korporal* Schmidt drove into the village of Graz, on the road to Innsbruck. It was completely deserted, not a soul in sight. They had traveled a distance of approximately forty miles since leaving Arlberg, had lost nearly three hours on the way due to a fault in the field car's fuel system. It had taken Schmidt that length of time to diagnose what was wrong and put it right.

They hadn't seen a single soldier, of either side, and there had also been a total absence of refugees on the road. But that made sense. Typical peasants, these mountain people. They would stick with their land, whatever happened. No running away for them. Nowhere to go.

A curtain moved at a ground-floor window of a house opposite. Schenck got out of the field car, crossed the street, and knocked at the door. There was no response, so he kicked impatiently. "Come on, for God's sake!" he called. "I'm Austrian like you. I'm not here to cause trouble."

After a while, the bolts were drawn and the door opened. An old, white-haired man with a bristling white moustache stood there, a young woman cowering behind him, holding a baby.

"Herr Leutnant," he said, civilly enough.

"Where is everybody?"

"They stay inside."

"Waiting for the Americans to come?"

"Or the British or the French." He managed a smile. "As long as it isn't the Russians."

"Are there any German units left in this area?"

"No—there were some panzers, but they pulled out two days ago."

"And the other side? Have you seen anything of them?" The old man hesitated, and Schenck said, "Come on. It's important."

"This morning I visited my son's farm, just to see if everything was all right. He's away in the army, and his wife here is staying with me. It's three miles down the road from here. There were English troops camped in the meadow and using the farm buildings, so I came away."

"What kind of troops? Tanks? Infantry?"

The old man shook his head. "They'd put up a great many tents—large tents—and there were ambulances coming in and out all the time. All their vehicles carried the red cross."

"Good." Schenck felt a surge of excitement. "I won't bother you any more."

He hurried back to the field car and climbed in. "Three miles down the road, Schmidt. A British Army field hospital, from the sound of it."

It's going to work, he thought. It's going to be all right. It couldn't be better. Schmidt accelerated out of the square, bouncing over the cobbles between the old medieval houses that leaned out, almost touching each other, so that there was room for only one vehicle along the narrow street.

They came around a corner and entered another, smaller square and found a British Army field ambulance bearing down on them. Schmidt spun the wheel desperately, skidded on the light powdering of snow. For a single frozen moment in time, Schenck was aware of the sergeant in the leather jerkin, the young private in a tin hat sitting beside him, and then they collided with the ambulance's front offside wheel and bounced to one side, mounting the low parapet of the fountain in the center of the square and turning over.

Schmidt had been thrown clear and started to get up. Schenck, who was still inside the field car, saw the young private in the tin hat jump out of the ambulance, a Sten gun in his hand. He fired a short burst that drove Schmidt back across the parapet, into the fountain.

Schenck managed to get to his feet and waved his arms. "No!" he shouted. "No!"

The boy fired again, the bullets ricocheting from the cobbles. Schenck felt a violent blow in his right shoulder and arm and was thrown back against the field car.

He was aware of voices—raised voices. The sergeant was swinging the boy around and wrenching the Sten gun away from him. A moment later, he was kneeling over Schenck.

Schenck's mouth worked desperately as he felt himself slipping away. He managed to get the letter from his pocket, held it up in one bloodstained hand. "Your commanding officer—take me to him," he said hoarsely in English. "A matter of life and death." And then he fainted.

■

Major Roger Mullholland of the 173rd Field Hospital had been operating since eight o'clock that morning. A long day by any standards, and a succession of cases any one of which would have been a candidate for major surgery under the finest hospital conditions. All he had were tents and field equipment. He did his best, as did the men under his command, as he'd been doing his best for weeks now, but it wasn't enough.

He turned from his last case, which had necessitated the amputation of a young field gunner's legs below the knees, and found Schenck laid out on the next operating table, still in his army greatcoat.

"Who the hell is this?"

His sergeant major, a burly Glaswegian named Grant, said, "Some Jerry officer driving through Graz in a field car. They collided with one of the ambulances. There was a shoot-out, sir."

"How bad is he?"

"Two rounds in the shoulder. Another in the upper arm. He asked to be taken to the CO. Kept brandishing this in his hand."

He held up the bloodstained letter. Mullholland said, "All right, get him ready. Come one, come all."

He opened the envelope, took out the letter, and started to read. A moment later he said, "Dear God Almighty, as if I didn't have enough to take care of."

Seven

AT a stage in the war when it had become apparent to him that Germany was almost certain to lose, Adolf Eichmann, head of the Jewish Office of the Gestapo, had ordered a shelter to be constructed, according to the most stringent specifications, under his headquarters at 116 Kurfürstenstrasse. It had its own generating plant and ventilating system and was self-sufficient in every respect.

The entire project was carried out under conditions of total secrecy, but in the Third Reich nothing was secret from Martin Bormann for long. On making the happy discovery, and needing a discreet establishment for purposes of his own, he had announced his intention of moving in, and Eichmann, too terrified to argue, agreed, putting up with the inconvenience of the arrangement until March, when he'd decided to make a run for it.

When Bormann and Rattenhuber arrived, the place seemed deserted. The front door hung crazily on its hinges, the windows gaped, and the roof had been extensively damaged by shelling. Rattenhuber drove along the alley at one side, wheels crunching over broken glass, and pulled into the courtyard at the rear of the building.

For the moment, the artillery bombardment had faded, and most of the shooting that was taking place was some little way off. Bormann got out and walked down a sloping concrete ramp to a couple of gray-painted, steel doors. He hammered with the toe of his boot. A grille was opened. The man who peered through had SS decals on his steel helmet. Bormann didn't say a word. The grille slammed shut, and a moment later the doors opened electronically.

Rattenhuber drove down the ramp, pausing for Bormann to get back in, and they entered a dark tunnel, passing two SS guards, and finally came to a halt in a brightly lit concrete garage.

There were two more SS guards and a young, hard-faced *Hauptsturmführer*. Like his men, he wore a sleeveband on his left arm that carried the legend "RFSS." *Reichsführer der SS.* The cuff-title of Himmler's personal staff, a device of Bormann's to deter the curious.

"So, Schultz, how goes it?" Bormann asked.

"No problems, *Reichsleiter*." Schultz delivered a perfect party salute. "Are you going up?"

"Yes, I think so."

Schultz led the way toward a steel elevator and pressed the button. He stood back. "At your orders, *Reichsleiter*."

Bormann and Rattenhuber moved inside, the colonel pressed the button to ascend, and the doors closed. He carried his Schmeisser, and there was a stick grenade tucked into his belt.

"Not long now, Willi," Bormann said. "The culmination of many months of hard work. You were surprised, I think, when I brought you into this affair?"

"No—an honor, *Reichsleiter,* I assure you," Rattenhuber said. "A great honor to be asked to assist with such a task."

"No more than you deserve, Willi. Zander was not to be trusted. I needed someone of intelligence and discretion. Someone I could trust. This business is of primary importance, Willi, I think you know that. Essential if the *Kameradenwerk* is to succeed."

"You may rely on me, *Reichsleiter,*" Rattenhuber said emotionally. "To the death."

Bormann placed an arm about his shoulders. "I know I can, Willi. I know I can." The elevator stopped; the door opened. A young man in thick-lensed glasses and a white doctor's coat stood waiting. "Good evening, *Reichsleiter,*" he said politely.

"Ah, Scheel, Professor Wiedler is expecting me, I trust?"

"Of course, *Reichsleiter.* This way."

The only sound was the hum of the generators as they walked along the carpeted corridor. Scheel opened the door at the end and ushered them through into a working laboratory furnished mainly with electronic equipment. The man who sat in front of a massive recording machine in headphones was attired, like Scheel, in a white coat. He had an intelligent, anxious face and wore gold-rimmed, half-moon reading spectacles. He glanced around, took off the glasses, and got up hastily.

"My dear Professor." Bormann shook hands affably. "How goes it?"

"Excellently, *Reichsleiter*. I think I may say it couldn't have gone any better."

Fritz Wiedler was a doctor of medicine of the universities of Heidelberg and Cambridge. A fervent supporter of National Socialism from its earliest days, a Nobel prizewinner for his researches in cell structure, and one of the youngest professors the University of Berlin had ever known, he had a reputation as one of the greatest plastic surgeons in Europe.

He was a supreme example of a certain kind of scientist, a man totally dedicated to the pursuit of his profession, with a fervor that could only be described as criminal. For Wiedler, the end totally justified the means, and when his Nazi masters had come to power, he had prospered mightily.

He had worked with Rascher on low-pressure research for the *Luftwaffe*, using live prisoners as guinea pigs. Then he had tried spare-parts surgery, using the limbs of prisoners where necessary, at Gebhardt's sanatorium near Ravensbruck, where Himmler often went in search of cures for his chronic stomach complaint.

But it was as a member of the SS Institute for the Research and Study of Heredity that he really came into his own, working with Mengele at Auschwitz on the study of twins, first alive and later dead, all for the greater glory of science and the Third Reich.

And then Bormann had recruited him. Had offered him the chance of the ultimate experiment. In a sense, to create life itself. A challenge that no scientist worth his salt could possibly have turned down.

"Where are the rest of the staff?" Bormann asked.

"Having their evening meal."

"Five nurses—three females, two male, am I right?"

"That is correct, *Reichsleiter*. Is there anything wrong?"

"Not at all," Bormann said tranquilly. "It's just that in these difficult times people tend to panic and make a run for it. I just wanted to make sure none of your people had."

Wiedler looked shocked. "None of them would think of such a thing, *Reichsleiter*, and besides, they'd never get past the guards."

"True," Bormann said. "So it goes well, you say. Are we ready yet?"

"I think so, *Reichsleiter*. You must judge for yourself."

"Let's get on with it, then."

Wiedler took a bunch of keys from his pocket, selected one, and moved to a door at the other end of the laboratory. Bormann, Rattenhuber, and Scheel followed. Wiedler inserted the key in the lock; the door swung open.

Music was playing, Schubert's Seventh Symphony, slow, majestic, the sound of it filling the room. Wiedler led the way in. They followed.

A man in flannel slacks and brown shirt was sitting at a table under a harsh white light, reading a book, his back toward them.

Wiedler said, "Good evening, Herr Strasser."

The man called Strasser pushed back his chair, got to his feet, and turned, and Martin Bormann gazed upon the mirror image of himself.

■

Rattenhuber's startled gasp had something of horror in it. "My God!" he whispered.

"Yes, Willi, now you know," Bormann said and held out his hand. "Strasser, how are you?"

"Never better, *Reichsleiter.*"

The voice was identical, and Bormann shook his head slowly. "Not that I can tell with certainty. I mean, who knows how he speaks, exactly, but it seems all right to me."

"All right," Scheel said indignantly. *"Reichsleiter,* it's perfect, I assure you. Three months we've worked, day and night, using the very latest in recording devices, using tape instead of wire. Here, we'll demonstrate. When I switch on the microphone, say something, *Reichsleiter.* Anything you like."

Bormann hesitated, then said, "My name is Martin Bormann. I was born on June the seventeenth, in Halberstadt, in Lower Saxony."

Scheel ran the tape back, then played it. The reproduction was excellent. Then he nodded to Strasser. "Now you."

"My name is Martin Bormann," Strasser said, "I was born on June the seventeenth, in Halberstadt, in Lower Saxony."

"There, you see?" Scheel said triumphantly.

"Yes, I must agree." Bormann tilted Strasser's chin. "I might as well be looking into the mirror."

"Not quite, *Reichsleiter,*" Wiedler said. "If you stand side by side, a close examination does indicate certain features as not being quite the same, but that doesn't matter. The important thing is that no one will be able to tell you apart. And there are scars—not many, it's true—but I've arranged it so they appear to be creases in the skin, the natural product of age."

"I can't see them," Bormann said.

"Yes, I don't think I've ever worked better with a knife, though I do say it myself."

Bormann nodded. "Excellent. And now I would have a word with Herr Strasser alone."

"Certainly, *Reichsleiter,*" Wiedler said.

He and Scheel moved out, and Bormann pulled Rattenhuber back. "The question of the staff, Willi. You know what to do."

"Of course, *Reichsleiter.*"

He went out, and Bormann closed the door and turned to face himself. "So Strasser, the day is finally here."

"So it would appear, *Reichsleiter*. The *Kameradenwerk*—it begins?"

"It begins, my friend," said Martin Bormann, and he started to unbutton his tunic.

■

Wiedler and the other man waited patiently in the laboratory. It was perhaps twenty minutes later that the door opened and Bormann and Strasser appeared. The *Reichsleiter* was in uniform.

Strasser wore a slouch hat and a black leather coat.

"And now, *Reichsleiter*," Professor Wiedler began.

"It remains only to say good-bye," Martin Bormann said.

He nodded to Rattenhuber, who was standing by the door. The colonel's Schmeisser bucked in his hands, a stream of bullets knocking Wiedler and Scheel back against the wall. Rattenhuber emptied the magazine and replaced it with a fresh one.

He turned to Bormann, face pale. "The staff?" Bormann inquired.

"I locked them in."

Bormann nodded approvingly. "Good—finish it."

Rattenhuber went outside. A moment later, there was the rattle of the Schmeisser sounding continuously above a chorus of screams. The Russian artillery had started again; the building shook violently far above their heads.

Rattenhuber came back in, walking slowly. "It is done, *Reichsleiter*."

Bormann nodded. "Good—finish off here now, and we'll go downstairs."

He walked out into the corridor, followed by Strasser. Rattenhuber took the stick grenade from his belt and tossed it in through the door of the laboratory. As the reverberations died away, there was the angry crackling of flames as chemicals ignited.

Smoke drifted out into the corridor as Bormann and Strasser reached the elevator and Rattenhuber ran toward them. "No need to panic," Bormann said. "Plenty of time."

The elevator doors opened. They stepped inside and started down.

■

When the doors opened at the bottom, Schultz was waiting, a Walther in his hand, his two SS guards behind him, Schmeissers ready.

"No need to worry," Bormann said. "Everything's under control."

"As you say, *Reichsleiter*," Schultz said, and then he looked at Strasser and his mouth opened in amazement.

"We are leaving now, Schultz, all of us," Bormann said gently. "Bring in the rest of your men."

Schultz turned, walked a few paces, and whistled, fingers in teeth. A moment later, the two guards from the garage door ran down the ramp.

"If you'd line them up, I'd just like to say a word about the situation we're going to find outside," Bormann said.

"*Reichsleiter*." Schultz barked orders at his men, they lined up, and he stood in front of them.

"You have done good work. Excellent work." Behind Bormann, Rattenhuber was climbing into the field car behind the MG34. "But now, my friends, the time has come to part."

In the final moment, Schultz realized what was happening. His mouth opened in a soundless cry, but by then Rattenhuber was working the machine gun, driving Schultz and his men back in a mad dance of death across the concrete.

When he finally stopped, a couple of them were still twitching. "Finish it," Bormann ordered.

Rattenhuber picked up his Schmeisser, walked across to the guards, and fired a short burst into the skull of one who still moved. He moved back hastily as blood and brains sprayed his boots, and in the same moment became aware of a harsh metallic click as the MG34 was cocked again.

He swung around to find Strasser standing in the field car behind the machine gun. "To the death, Willi, isn't that what you said?"

His fingers squeezed, the face beneath the brim of the slouch hat totally lacking in any kind of emotion. It was the last thing Willi Rattenhuber saw before he died.

Strasser stopped firing and jumped down. "It's time I was away. I'll take Schultz's Mercedes."

"And me?"

"I suggest you wait here till eleven o'clock. Start back to the bunker then. You should arrive around midnight, allowing for the state of the streets."

"Dangerous times," Bormann said. "An artillery shell, a piece of shrapnel, a stray bullet, not to mention the possibility of running into a Russian patrol."

"Like the *Führer,* I walk with the certainty of a sleepwalker," Strasser said. "I wear invisible armor, believing completely that nothing will happen to me—to either of us. A great deal depends on us, my friend. The future of many people."

"I know."

Strasser smiled. "I must go now."

He crossed to the open Mercedes touring car

and climbed behind the wheel. As he started the engine, Bormann picked up a Schmeisser and hurried across to him. "Take this."

"No, thanks, I won't need it," Strasser said, and he drove away up into the darkness of the ramp.

■

Ritter was squatting on the ground, his back against the wall, Schmeisser across his knees. His eyes were closed, but he wasn't really asleep and heard the sound of the approaching vehicle as soon as Hoffer, who was on guard.

"Major!" Hoffer called.

"I know," Ritter said.

He stood beside the sergeant major, listening, and Berger joined them. "It isn't a tank, anyway."

"No, some sort of car," Ritter said.

It braked to a halt outside, and steps approached.

The three men waited quietly in the darkness; there was a pause, a slight, eerie creaking, and then the judas gate opened. Ritter and Berger pointed their flashlights at the same moment and picked Strasser out of the darkness.

"Herr Strasser," Berger said cheerfully. "We were just getting ready to go into blazing action. Why can't you whistle a few bars of 'Deutschland Über Alles' or something?"

"If you could get the doors open, I have a Mercedes outside that would probably be better under cover. We don't want to attract any unwelcome attention."

Hoffer said, "My God, it's the. . . ."

Strasser turned toward them. He looked directly at Ritter and said calmly, "Strasser—the

name is Heinrich Strasser. I'm here to act on behalf of the head of the Party Chancellery in the
matter you already know of. You were expecting
me, Major?"

"Oh, yes," Ritter said. "You were expected."
He turned to Hoffer as Berger opened the garage
doors. "Bring in Herr Strasser's car for him,
Erich."

Strasser put an arm around Berger's shoulders.
"Have we got any chance of getting away with
this thing?"

"I don't see why not," Berger told him. "To try
such a thing at all at this stage is something they
won't even be considering. At least that's what I'm
counting on."

They moved toward the Stork, talking in low
tones. Hoffer drove the Mercedes into the garage,
and Ritter closed the doors again.

The sergeant major whispered, "But that man
isn't Herr Strasser. It's the *Reichsleiter* himself.
What's going on here?"

"I know, Erich, and Berger said they hadn't
met, when it's obvious they know each other very
well indeed."

"So Berger knows who he really is?"

"And who would that be, Erich?" Ritter put a
cigarette in his mouth. "Martin Bormann or
Heinrich Strasser—what's in a name, and if he
prefers one to the other, who are we to argue?"

"Major Ritter," Strasser called. "One moment,
if you don't mind." They crossed to the plane, and
Strasser looked at his watch. "Nine o'clock now.
Captain Berger thinks we should leave around
midnight."

"So I understand," Ritter said. "What about takeoff? I mean, it will be pitch-dark—unless they send bombers over and start a few more fires, that is."

"When we go, we go very fast," Berger said. "I've got a case of parachute flares in the Stork. I'll start the engine, and the moment I'm ready to go, I'd like you to fire the first one. After the first hundred yards, another. We might even need a third, I'm not sure. You'll be able to fire the pistol quite easily through the side window."

"During the actual takeoff period, then, we will be considerably exposed," Strasser said.

"For two or three minutes only. Of course, once we're airborne, the darker the better, but unless you want to end up on top of the Victory Column. . . ." He shrugged.

"Anything but that, Captain," Strasser said. "It should, however, prove an exhilarating few minutes."

Ritter went and sat on a packing case near the door. He put a cigarette in his mouth and felt for a match. Strasser walked across and produced a lighter.

"Thank you," Ritter said.

"Is there anything you would like me to explain?"

"I don't think so," Ritter said. "The *Reichsleiter*'s orders were quite explicit."

"Good, then I think I'll get a little rest. Something tells me I'm going to need my strength before the night is out."

He moved away, and Hoffer, who had been hovering nearby, came and squatted beside Ritter, his back against the wall. "Well, what did he have to say?"

"What did you expect?" Ritter asked.

"Didn't he offer you some sort of explanation?"

"He asked me if there was anything I'd like him to explain. I said there wasn't. Is that what you meant?"

"Yes, Major." Hoffer's voice sounded totally resigned now. "That was exactly what I meant."

■

At eleven-thirty the Russian bombardment started again, spasmodically at first, but within fifteen minutes it was in full voice.

Berger stood by the doors, checking his watch in the glow of his flashlight. At five minutes to midnight precisely, he said, "All right, let's have those doors open and take her out."

The night sky was very dark, occasionally illuminated by brilliant flashes as shells exploded, although they seemed to be concentrating on the area farther to the east. The four men took the Stork out, two on each wing, and turned her around in the side street. There was just enough room, the wall on either side only inches away from the wing tips.

The sounds of battle increased in the middle distance, and Berger, who pushed beside Ritter, said, "Just think, hundreds of thousands of people trapped in this holocaust tonight face certain death, and yet, if the engine starts and the propeller turns, we, by some special dispensation, will live."

"Perhaps—perhaps not."

"You've no faith, my friend."

"Ask me again when we're passing over the Victory Column."

They turned the Stork into the East–West Avenue, the wheels crunching over broken glass.

"What about your wind direction, Berger?" Strasser asked. "These things should always be pointing the right way, am I right?"

"As far as I can judge, there's a crosswind," Berger said. "North to south, not that it makes much difference. We don't, after all, have a great deal of choice."

The avenue was very dark and quiet, the Russian artillery devoting itself exclusively to the district around Potsdamerplatz. Berger said, "Right. Everybody in, except Major Ritter."

Ritter said, "What do you want me to do?"

Berger handed him a flare gun and cartridge. "Walk up the avenue about fifty yards and wait. The moment you hear the engine start, fire the pistol, then turn and run back as fast as you can."

"All right," Ritter said. "I think I can handle that."

Hoffer pulled at his sleeve. "Let me, Major."

"Don't be stupid," Ritter said coldly.

He walked away into the darkness, suddenly angry—with himself as well as Hoffer. The sergeant major meant well, he knew that, but there were times. . . . Perhaps they'd been together for too long.

He was counting out the paces under his breath as he walked, and now he paused and rammed the cartridge home. It was quiet, except for the dull rumble of the guns, and when the engine of the

Fieseler Storch roared into life, the noise was shattering. Ritter raised the pistol and fired a couple of seconds later. The flare started to descend on its parachute, bathing the avenue in a cold, white glare for a few moments only.

There were two Russian tanks and half a company of infantry sixty or seventy yards up the street. Ritter saw the white faces, heard the voices raised excitedly, and turned and ran like hell toward the Stork.

They picked him up on the move—Strasser holding the door open while Hoffer reached out to grab him by the scruff of the neck—and already the Russians were firing.

Ritter fell into the cabin on his hands and knees, and Berger yelled excitedly, "More light. I'm going to need more light."

Ritter fumbled in the box for another flare. The Stork was roaring down the avenue now, its tail lifting, but already one of the tanks had started to move. Berger had to swerve violently at the last moment, his starboard wing tip just missing the tank's turret, and for a moment seemed to lose control.

But a second later he was back on course again. Ritter put his hand out of the window and discharged the flare. In its sudden glare, the Victory Column seemed terrifyingly close, but Berger held on grimly. She yawed to starboard in the crosswind, and he applied a little rudder correction.

And then, quite suddenly, they were airborne, lifting off the avenue in a hail of rifle bullets, the Victory Column rushing to meet them.

"We'll hit! We'll hit!" Hoffer cried, but Berger

held on grimly, refusing to sacrifice power for height, and only at the very last moment did he pull the stick back into his stomach, taking the Stork clear of the top of the Victory Column by fifteen or twenty feet.

"Dear God, we made it. How truly amazing," Strasser said.

"Surely you never doubted me, *Reichsleiter?*" Berger laughed—unaware in the excitement of the moment of his slip of the tongue—stamped on the right rudder, and turned away across what was left of the rooftops of Berlin.

▪

It was at roughly the same moment that the SS guard on duty at the exit of the bunker leading onto Hermann-Göringstrasse heard a vehicle approach. A field car turned into the entrance of the ramp and braked to a halt. The driver, a shadowy figure in the gloom, got out and came forward.

"Identify yourself!" the sentry demanded.

Martin Bormann moved into the circle of lamplight. The sentry drew himself together. "I'm sorry, *Reichsleiter.* I didn't realize it was you."

"A bad night out there."

"Yes, *Reichsleiter.*"

"But it will get better, my friend, very soon now, for all of us. You must believe that." Bormann patted him on the shoulder and moved down the ramp into the darkness.

Eight

THERE was no immediate easing of tension in the Stork, for as they flew across Berlin, the Russian artillery bombardment seemed to chase them all the way. There were numerous fires in many parts of the city, and the darkness crackled with electricity on the edge of things as one shell after another found its target.

"Something to remember—eh, Major?" Strasser said, looking down at the holocaust. "The Twilight of the Gods."

"All we need is a score by Wagner," Ritter said, "to thoroughly enjoy ourselves. We have been well trained, we Germans, to appreciate the finer things."

"Oh, it could be worse," Strasser pointed out. "We could be down there."

The Stork rocked violently, and something rattled against the fuselage. "Antiaircraft fire," Berger cried. "I'm going down."

He threw the Stork into a sudden, violent corkscrew that seemed to last forever, the whine of the engine rising to fever pitch, but finally—and only when the fires below seemed very close indeed—he pulled back the stick and leveled out.

Hoffer turned his head away and was violently sick. Strasser said, with a slight edge of contempt to his voice, "He has no stomach for it, I think, your sergeant major."

"So what?" Ritter said. "They tell me Grand Admiral Dönitz is sick every time he puts to sea, but he's still Germany's greatest sailor."

Gradually, the flames—the darting points of light on the ground—faded into the night. Berger shouted above the roar of the engine, "I'll tell you something now we're out of it. I never thought we'd make it. Not for a moment."

"You did well," Strasser said. "A brilliant piece of flying."

It was Ritter, suddenly irritated, who said, "We're not out of the woods yet."

"Nonsense," Berger shouted. "A milk run from now on."

■

And he was right, for conditions could not have been more in their favor. They flew on through the night at five hundred feet in darkness and heavy rain, Berger sitting there at the controls, a slight, fixed smile on his mouth, obviously thoroughly enjoying himself.

Hoffer fell asleep. Strasser, who was sitting next to Berger, made notes in his diary in the light from the control panel. Ritter smoked a cigarette and watched him, wondering what was going on behind the eyes in that calm, expressionless face—but that was a pointless exercise. Just as much a waste of time as asking himself what the hell he was doing here.

It was like a chess game. You made a move in answer to one. A totally open-ended situation. No means of knowing what the end would be until it was reached. And in the final analysis, did it really matter? He leaned back in his seat and closed his eyes.

■

He came awake instantly in response to a hand on his shoulder. Strasser said, "We're close to Plauen now. Berger's trying to raise the airstrip."

Ritter glanced at his watch and saw, with a slight shock of surprise, that it was three o'clock. He turned to Hoffer. "How are you?"

"Better, Major, much better, now that there's nothing left to come up. I never could stand flying—any kind of flying. Remember that transport plane which brought us out of Stalingrad?"

Berger was talking, using his throat mike. "Red Fox, this is Valhalla. Do you read me?" There was only the confused crackling of the static. He tried again, adjusting one of the dials. "Red Fox, this is Valhalla." A moment later, a voice broke through the static. "Valhalla, this is Red Fox. I read you strength five."

"I am coming in now for refueling as arranged," Berger said. "What is your situation?"

"Heavy rain, slight ground mist, visibility about a hundred and fifty yards. We'll put the landing lights on for you."

"All the comforts of home," Berger said. "My thanks." A moment later, two parallel lines of light flared in the darkness to starboard. "I can see you now," he called. "I'm coming in."

He turned into the wind and started his descent. Ritter said, "Do we stay here for any length of time?"

"For as long as it takes to fill the tanks," Strasser said. "We've still got a long way to go."

They drifted down through the rain and mist into the light, there was the sudden squeal of the tires biting as Berger applied the brakes, they slowed, the tail going down.

And then Berger gave a cry of dismay, for the trucks that raced out of the darkness on either side, converging on them, had red stars emblazoned on their sides.

"Get out of here!" Strasser cried.

Berger increased engine revs. The soldiers in the trucks were already firing. A bullet shattered one of the side windows. Ritter shoved the barrel of a Schmeisser through and let off a long burst. And then they were really moving again, racing toward the end of the runway, the trucks trying to keep up with them, and losing. Berger pulled back the stick; they climbed up into the darkness.

He leveled off at three thousand feet. Strasser said, "Now what?"

For the first time, his composure seemed to have deserted him, and he actually looked worried. For some reason, Ritter found the spectacle strangely comforting.

"The only thing I'm certain of at the moment is that I've got fuel for forty minutes, and that includes the reserve tank," Berger said. And, in the crisis, it was Ritter he turned to. "Have a look at the *Luftwaffe* area map, the one on top. See what there is close to our line fifty miles south of here."

Ritter spread the map across his knees and switched on his flashlight. "There's a place called Plodin marked with a red ring. Perhaps forty miles. According to the key, that means reserve feeder station. What's that?"

"Part of the backup system for nightfighters. The sort of place they can put down if they run into trouble. A hangar and a single runway, usually grass. Probably a private air club before the war. I'll see if I can raise them."

"You raised somebody last time," Strasser said. "They answered in excellent German, and look what happened."

"What do you want me to do?" Berger demanded. "I can't see what we're getting into unless I go down because you won't get even a touch of gray in the sky before four o'clock. I'll be out of fuel twenty minutes before then by my reckoning. You may have read that in such situations people often jump for it. Unfortunately, we only have one parachute, and I'm sitting on it."

"All right, I get the point," Strasser said. "Do as you think fit."

He sat there, his jaw working, fists tightly clenched. He's thrown, Ritter thought—and badly —because, for once, he isn't in charge. He has no control. He isn't playing the game—the game's playing him.

Berger was using plain language. "This is Fieseler Storch AK40, calling Plodin. I am dangerously short of fuel and urgently require assistance. Come in, please."

There was an immediate response. A voice said urgently, "Suggest you try elsewhere. We've been completely cut off by Russian troops since seven o'clock last night."

"I'm afraid I have no choice in the matter," Berger told him. "My estimated time of arrival is oh-three-forty. Five minutes after that, if I'm still airborne, I'll be gliding."

There was silence, only the static, and then the voice said, "Very well, we'll do what we can."

"Right, gentlemen, here we go again," Berger said, and he started to descend.

Two aircraft were burning at the side of the runway as they went in. "Expensive landing lights," Berger said, "but I'm grateful, nevertheless."

There were a couple of hangars, a small control tower, a complex of huts a hundred yards or so away, some trucks parked beside them. There was no sound of conflict, no shooting, only the two planes burning at the side of the runway as they touched down, an old Dornier-17 and a JU-88S nightfighter.

As Berger taxied toward the control tower, half a dozen ground crew ran forward, two of them carrying wheel blocks, and the door opened and an officer stood there framed in the light.

He was an *Oberleutnant,* his *Luftwaffe Flieger-blüse* open at the neck. He was twenty-three or -four, badly in need of a shave, and looked tired.

Berger held out his hand. "Heini Berger. Not too worried about the blackout, I see?"

"What would be the point," the *Oberleutnant* said, "with those two blazing like the candles on a

Christmas tree? Our water main was fractured in the initial bombardment, so we've no firefighting facilities. My name's Fraenkel, by the way."

"You are in command here?" Strasser asked.

"Yes, the commanding officer, *Hauptsturmführer* Hagen, was killed last night. Russian tanks shelled us at eleven o'clock and raked the buildings with machine-gun fire."

"No infantry attack?" Ritter asked.

Fraenkel took in the uniform, the Knight's Cross with Oak Leaves and Swords, and straightened his shoulders. "No, they stayed out there in the dark, *Sturmbannführer*. Shelled us again approximately an hour ago. That's when the planes got it."

Ritter walked forward into the shadows. There were bodies here and there, and on the far side of the runway another Junkers tilted forward on its nose, tail up, an enormous ragged furrow in the ground indicating where it had belly-landed.

He turned and came back to the others. "How many men have you left?"

"Half a dozen," Fraenkel said. "The aircrews of those planes all got away before we were hit. And then there are some of your people. Arrived last night just before the Russians. They're down at the huts now. You can just see their trucks—four of them."

"My people?" Ritter said. "You mean by this SS, I presume. Which unit?"

"Einsatzgruppen, Sturmbannführer."

Ritter's face was very pale. He reached out and grabbed Fraenkel by the front of his *Fliegerblüse*. "You will not mention scum like that in the same breath with the *Waffen*-SS, you hear me?"

Einsatzgruppen, action groups or special commandos, had been formed by Himmler prior to the invasion of Russia. They were, in effect, extermination squads, recruited from the jails of Germany, officered by SD and Gestapo officers. Occasionally soldiers of the *Waffen-*SS convicted of some criminal offense were transferred to them as punishment. The phrase "scum of the earth" summed them up perfectly.

It was Strasser who moved forward to pull Ritter away. "Easy, Major. Easy does it. What are they doing now, down there?"

"Drinking," Fraenkel said. "And they have some women with them."

"Women?"

"Girls—from the camps. Jewish, I think."

There was a nasty silence. Berger said, nodding toward the blazing wrecks, "Why didn't they fly those out while the going was good?"

"They landed here because they were low on fuel in the first place, and we didn't have any. Used our last a fortnight ago."

"No fuel," Strasser cut in. "But you must have something, surely, and the Stork doesn't need much—isn't that right, Berger?"

"If it were only ten gallons you wanted, I still couldn't oblige," Fraenkel said.

Berger looked toward the Junkers on the far side of the hangar, the one that had crash-landed. "What about that? Nothing in the tanks?"

"We siphoned the fuel out of her a couple of weeks ago." Fraenkel hesitated. "There might be a few gallons left, but not enough to get you anywhere."

There was a sudden burst of laughter and singing from the huts. Ritter said to Berger, "Am I right in assuming that a workhorse like the Fieseler Storch doesn't necessarily need high-octane aviation gasoline to be able to fly?"

"No. She'll function on stuff a lot more crude than that. With reduced performance, of course."

Ritter nodded toward the huts. "Four trucks down there. I should think their tanks between them would hold forty or fifty gallons. Would that do?"

"I don't see why not," Berger said. "Especially if we can siphon a few gallons out of the Junkers to mix with it."

Ritter said to Fraenkel, "All right?"

The *Oberleutnant* nodded. "As far as I'm concerned. But the gentlemen of the *Einsatzgruppen* may have other ideas."

Strasser said, "We are on a special mission of vital importance to the Reich. My orders are signed by the *Führer* himself."

"Sorry, *mein Herr*," Fraenkel said, "but strange things are happening in Germany today. There are actually people around for whom that kind of talk doesn't cut much ice. I suspect that's particularly true of these characters."

"Then we must change their minds for them," Ritter said. "How many are there?"

"Thirty or so."

"Good. Put a couple of your men to the task of siphoning the Junkers. Send the rest to the trucks. I'll deal with these"—here he hesitated—"these gentlemen of the *Einsatzgruppen*." He turned to Strasser. "You agree?"

Strasser smiled slightly. "My dear Ritter, I wouldn't miss it for anything."

■

There was no one at the trucks, no guard at the steps leading up to the door of the mess hall, as Ritter marched briskly across the compound, Strasser a pace behind his left shoulder.

"I must be mad," Strasser said.

"Oh, I don't know. Like we used to say about those chairborne bastards at headquarters, it does a man good to get up off his backside occasionally and go up to the front to see what it's like for the ordinary troops. A little action and passion for you, *Reichsleiter*."

He paused at the bottom of the steps to adjust his gloves. Strasser said, "Why do you call me that, Major?"

"You mean I'm mistaken?"

"To the best of my knowledge, *Reichsleiter* Martin Bormann is at present in his office in the *Führerbunker*, in Berlin. Even in this day and age, it would take a rather large miracle for a man to be in two places at once."

"Simple enough if there were two of him."

"Which would raise the problem of who is real and who is only the image in the mirror," Strasser said. "A neat point, but relevant, I think you'll agree."

"True," Ritter said. "And perhaps, in the final analysis, an academic point only." He smiled ironically. "Shall we go in now?"

He opened the door and stepped into the light. At first he and Strasser went completely unnoticed, which was hardly surprising, for the men who crowded the tables before them were mostly drunk. There were perhaps a dozen girls huddled in a corner at the far end of the room, hair unkempt, clothes tattered, faces grimy with dirt. In fact, the faces were the most interesting feature about them, the eyes dull, totally without hope, with the look of trapped animals waiting for the butcher's knife.

There was a burly *Hauptsturmführer* seated at one end of the longest table. He was a brute of a man, with slanting eyes and high, Slavic cheekbones. He had a small, dark-haired girl on his knee, an arm around her neck, holding her tight, while his other hand was busy under her skirt. She couldn't have been more than sixteen. She saw Ritter first, her eyes widening in amazement, and the *Hauptsturmführer,* becoming aware of her stillness, turned to see what she was looking at.

Ritter stood, hands on hips, legs slightly apart, and it was as if a chill wind had swept into the room, Death himself come to join them. The *Hauptsturmführer* took in that magnificent black uniform, the decorations, the dark eyes under the peak of the service cap, the silver death's-head gleaming.

"You are in charge here, I presume?" Ritter inquired softly.

The captain shoved the girl off his knee and stood up. The room had gone absolutely quiet. "That's right," he said. "Grushetsky."

"Ukrainian?" Ritter said, his distaste plain. "I thought so."

Grushetsky turned red with anger. "And who the hell might you be?"

"Your superior officer," Ritter told him calmly. "You're aware that there are Russians out there in the dark who might have a more than passing interest in getting their hands on you, and yet you don't even post a guard."

"No need," Grushetsky said. "They won't come in before dawn, I know how they work. We'll be driving out of here long before then. In the meantime . . ." He put an arm around the girl and pulled her close.

"Sorry," Ritter said, "but you won't be driving anywhere, I'm afraid. We need your gasoline for our aircraft."

"You what?" Grushetsky cried.

"Show him your orders," Ritter said casually to Strasser. He glanced at the girl again, ignoring Grushetsky, then walked to the end of the room and looked at the others.

Strasser said, "I'll read it to you. From the leader and chancellor of the State. Most secret. You recognize the name at the bottom of the page, I trust. Adolf Hitler."

"Yes, well, he's in Berlin, and this is here," Grushetsky said. "And you'll take the gasoline from those tanks over my dead body."

"That can be arranged." Ritter raised his right arm casually and clicked his fingers. A window was smashed as a Schmeisser poked through, Berger's smiling face behind it. The door crashed open, and Hoffer came in, holding another Schmeisser.

"You see," Ritter said to the girl, whom Grushetsky had released now. "It is still possible

for the best to happen in this worst of all possible worlds. What's your name?"

"Bernstein," she said. "Clara Bernstein."

He recognized her accent instantly. "French?"

"That's what it says on my birth certificate, but to you bastards I'm just another dirty Jew."

In a strange way, it was as if they were alone. "What do you want me to do, say I'm sorry?" Ritter asked her in French. "Would that help?"

"Not in the slightest."

"Positive action then, Clara Bernstein. You and your friends go now. Out there in the darkness beyond the perimeter wire there are Russian soldiers. I suggest you turn toward them, hands high in the air, yelling like hell. I think you will find they will take you in."

"Here, what the hell is going on here?" Grushetsky demanded in his bad German.

Ritter rounded on him. "Shut your mouth, damn you. Feet together when you speak to me, you understand? Attention, all of you."

And they responded, all of them, even those far gone in drink trying to draw themselves together. The girl called to the others in German. They hesitated. She cried, "All right, stay and die here if you want, but I'm getting out."

She ran outside, and the rest of the girls broke instantly and went after her. Their voices could be heard clearly as they ran across the runway to the perimeter wire.

Ritter paced up and down between the tables. "You believe yourselves to be soldiers of the German Reich—a natural assumption in view of the

uniforms you wear—but you are mistaken. Now, let me tell you what you are, in simple terms, so that you can understand."

Grushetsky gave a roar of rage and pulled out his Luger, and Strasser, who'd been waiting for something like this to happen for the past few moments, fired twice through the pocket of his leather coat, shattering the Ukrainian's spine, killing him instantly, driving him across one of the tables.

Several men cried out and reached for weapons, and Berger and Hoffer both fired at the same moment, dropping four men between them.

Ritter said to Hoffer, "All right, collect their weapons and hold them here until we're ready to go."

One of the *Einsatzgruppen* took an involuntary step forward. "But *Sturmbannführer*. Without weapons we shall be totally unable to defend ourselves, and the Russians . . ."

"Can have you," Ritter said, and he walked outside, followed by Strasser.

Fraenkel walked to meet them. "It's worked quite well. We've managed to get about fifteen gallons of aviation fuel out of the Junkers. Mixed with gasoline from the trucks, it means we can give you full tanks."

"How long," Strasser asked, "before we're ready to go?"

"Five or ten minutes."

Ritter offered the young *Luftwaffe* lieutenant a cigarette. "I'm sorry we can't take you with us, you and your men. We leave you in a bad situation."

"The moment you've gone, I'm going to go out there and ask for terms," Fraenkel said. "I can't see much point in any other course of action, not at this stage."

"Perhaps you're right," Ritter said. "And I'd keep those bastards back there in the mess hall under lock and key until the Russians get here if I were you. It might help."

A sergeant hurried toward them and saluted. "The Stork's all ready to go now, *Herr Leutnant*."

There was some movement in the darkness beyond the perimeter, the sound of an engine starting up. Ritter turned and shouted, "Berger! Erich! Let's get out of here. It looks as if the Russians are starting to move in."

He ran back toward the hangar, followed by Strasser. As they scrambled up into the cabin of the Stork, Hoffer and Berger arrived. Berger didn't even bother to strap himself in. He got the door closed and started the engines instantly, so that the Stork was moving down the runway and turning into the wind in a matter of seconds.

The flames from the burning planes had died down, and the field was almost totally dark now. "If you believe in prayer, now's the time," Berger cried, and he pushed up the engine revs and took the Stork forward.

They plunged headlong into darkness, and Ritter leaned back in the seat and closed his eyes, totally unafraid, consumed only by curiosity to know what it would be like. Is this it? he asked himself. Could this possibly be the final moment after all these years? And then the Stork lifted as

Berger pulled back the stick, and they climbed up into the darkness.

Ritter turned to find Strasser examining the bullet holes in his coat. "My thanks, but I hardly expected to see the day when you would lay yourself on the line to defend the rights of Jews."

"What happens to those girls back there is a matter of complete indifference to me," Strasser told him. "You, on the other hand, are an essential part of this operation, which could well fail without you. That was the only reason I shot that Slavic ape back there."

"I should be thankful for small mercies, it would seem."

"No more empty gestures, my dear Ritter, I beg you."

"Empty?"

"A fair description. I should imagine the Russians will rape those girls with an enthusiasm at least equal to that of Grushetsky and his motley crew, or had you really imagined it would be different?"

■

Dawn was a gradual affair from about four-thirty as they flew onward through heavy clouds—at first merely an impression of light, no more than that. Strasser and Hoffer both slept, but Berger seemed as cheerful and relaxed as ever, whistling softly through his teeth.

"You love it," Ritter said. "Flying, I mean."

"More than any woman." Berger grinned. "Which is saying a lot. For a long time I worried about what I would do when it was all over—the war, I mean. No more flying, not for the defeated."

"But now you don't?"

It was a statement as much as a question, and caught Berger off guard. "Plenty of places to go, when you think about it. Places where there's always work for a good pilot. South America, for instance. The *Reichs*—" He pulled himself up quickly. "Herr Strasser already has a pipeline organized that should ensure that some of us will live to fight another day."

"A charming prospect," Ritter said. "I congratulate you."

When he leaned back, he realized that Strasser was awake and watching through half-open eyes. He smiled and leaned forward, a hand on Berger's shoulder.

"He likes to talk, my young friend here. A conversationalist by nature. A good thing he's such a brilliant pilot."

Strasser was smiling genially, but his fingers were hooked into the shoulder so tightly that Berger winced with pain. "I'll take her up now," he shouted. "Try to get above this shit and see what's what. We should be nearly there."

He pulled back the stick and started to climb, but the heavy clouds showed no signs of diminishing. Finally he leveled out. "No good. I'll have to try it the other way. Nothing else for it. Hang on and we'll see what the state of things is downstairs."

He pushed the stick forward, taking the Stork into a shallow dive. The clouds became darker, more menacing, boiling around them, hail rattling against the fuselage, and Berger had to hang onto the stick with all his strength. They were at four thousand and still descending, Berger hanging on grimly, and Hoffer gave an involuntary cry of fear. And then, at three thousand feet, they emerged into the light of day and found themselves, as Berger leveled out, drifting along the course of a wide valley, pine trees very green against the snow, the peaks of the Bavarian Alps rising on either side of them.

"Somebody on board must live right," Berger said. "Now have a look at the *Luftwaffe* area map and see if you can find Arnheim, Major."

■

It was no more than a feeder station, had never been any more than that. There were a single runway, two hangars. No control tower, simply a couple of single-story concrete huts with tin roofs.

Snow was falling gently, but there was no wind to speak of, and the Fieseler Storch came in from the north like a gray ghost, her engine barely a murmur. Her wheels touched, and there were two puffs of white as snow spurted beneath them.

Strasser said, "Straight up to the hangars. I want her under cover."

"All right." Berger nodded.

When they were close enough, Strasser, Ritter, and Hoffer all got out and opened the hangar doors. Berger taxied inside and cut the engine. He laughed out loud as he jumped to the ground.

"So, we made it. The Victory Column to Arnheim in five and a half hours." He helped Ritter pull the doors closed. "Smell that mountain air."

Hoffer had gone through the connecting door into the next hangar, and now he returned. "There's a field car in there, Major," he told Ritter. "A basket in the back."

"Good," Strasser said. "I've been expecting that."

He led the way in, and the others followed. The basket was of the picnic type. There was also a small leather suitcase with it. Strasser placed it on the hood of the car and opened it. Inside, there was a radio transmitter and receiver of a kind Ritter had never seen before.

"Excellent," Strasser said. "The best in the world at the present time. Came to us courtesy of an agent of the British Special Operations Executive." He checked his watch. "Five-thirty—am I right?"

"So it would appear," Ritter said.

"Good." Strasser rubbed his hands briskly. "There's a nip in this mountain air. We'll have something to eat, a hot drink, and then . . ."

"Something to eat?" Berger said.

"But of course. What do you think is in the basket?"

Berger unstrapped it and raised the lid. Inside there were three loaves of black bread, sausages, butter, boiled eggs, two large thermos flasks, and a bottle of schnapps. Berger unscrewed the cap of one of the flasks and removed the cork. He inhaled deeply, an expression of delight appearing on his face.

"Coffee—hot coffee." He poured a little into the cup and tasted it. "And it's real," he announced. "A miracle."

"See how good I am to you?" Strasser said.

"You certainly have a flair for organization," Ritter told him.

"It's been said before." Strasser glanced at his watch.

"And then," Ritter said, "after we've eaten? You were saying?"

Strasser smiled. "I'm expecting another aircraft at seven o'clock. A very reliable man, so he should get here right on time." He opened the small judas gate set in the main door and stepped outside, turning his face up to the snow. "What air. It makes things feel clean again."

Hoffer passed Ritter a cup of coffee and a piece of black bread. "But I don't understand, Major. This other plane he's expecting. Who is it? Why won't he tell us?"

"Probably the *Führer* himself, Erich." Ritter smiled. "After the events of the past couple of days, nothing would surprise me."

■

It was at precisely five minutes to seven when Berger, lounging against the hood of the field car, smoking a cigarette, straightened. "There's a plane coming now—I hear it."

Ritter opened the judas and stepped outside. Snow was still falling softly, the flakes brushing against his face when he looked up. The sound was still some distance away, but real enough.

He went back inside. "He's right."

Strasser had the suitcase open, the microphone in his hand. He adjusted the dials and said, in English, to everyone's surprise, "Valhalla Exchange. Valhalla Exchange. Plain language. Do you receive me?"

An American voice answered with startling clarity. "Valhalla Exchange. Odin here. Am I cleared for landing?"

"All clear. Closing down now."

He stowed away the microphone and closed the case. Ritter said, "Are we permitted to know what that was all about?"

"Later," Strasser said impatiently. "For the moment, let's get these doors open. I want him under cover and out of sight the moment he's landed."

Ritter shrugged and nodded to Hoffer and, with Berger's assistance, they got the doors open. The sound of the plane, whatever it was, was very close now, and they all moved outside and waited.

And then, suddenly, she was there, coming in out of the grayness at the north end of the runway, twin-engined, camouflaged, and entirely familiar to at least one man there—Berger—who cried, "God in heaven, that's an American Dakota."

"So it would appear," Strasser said.

"Is nothing impossible to you, then?" Ritter asked.

"My dear Ritter, if I'd needed it, I could have had a Flying Fortress or an RAF Lancaster."

The Dakota landed, snow rising in a cloud around her as she rolled forward, turning in toward them as Strasser waved his arms, and then she was close enough for them to see the pilot in the cockpit, the American Army Air Corps insignia plain against the green-and-brown camouflage.

The plane taxied into the hangar; for a moment, the din was colossal, and then, suddenly, the engines were cut. "Right. Get these doors closed," Strasser ordered.

As they turned from the task, the hatch was opened and the pilot appeared. He had a dark, saturnine face and appeared to be in his early thirties. He was wearing a sidecap with an SS death's-head badge, and a flying jacket. He removed the jacket and caused something of a sensation.

He wore a beautifully tailored uniform of field gray. Under the eagle on his left sleeve was a Stars and Stripes shield, and the cuff-title on his left wrist carried the legend "George Washington Legion" in Gothic lettering. His decorations included the Iron Cross, Second and First Class, and he wore the Winter War ribbon. When he spoke, his German was excellent, but with a definite American accent.

"So, you made it?" he said to Strasser. "Amazing, but then I should have learned to believe you by now."

"Good to see you." Strasser shook hands, then turned to the others. "Gentlemen, allow me to introduce *Hauptsturmführer* Earl Jackson. This is Heini Berger, who got us out of Berlin in the Stork."

"Captain." Berger shook hands. "It gave me something of a shock when I saw you dropping down out of the sky, I can tell you."

"And *Sturmbannführer* Karl Ritter."

Jackson held out his hand, but Ritter ignored him and turned to Strasser. "And now we talk, I think."

"My dear Ritter," Strasser began.

"Now!" Ritter said sharply, and he opened the connecting door and went into the next hangar.

"All right," Strasser said. "What is it now?"

"This American—Jackson—who is he? I want to know."

"Come now, Ritter, the *Waffen*-SS has recruited men from almost every nation possible, you know that. Everything from Frenchmen to Turks. There's even an English contingent—the *Britisches Freikorps*. There have been, admittedly, only a handful of Americans in the George Washington Legion. Ex-prisoners of war, recruited by prospects of unlimited liquor and women. Jackson is a different specimen, believe me. He flew for the Finns against the Russians in their first war, stayed on in their air force, and got caught up in their second bout with the Russians when they joined our side. When the Finns sued for peace last year, he transferred to us."

"A traitor is a traitor, however you wrap it up."

"A point of view, but not objective enough, my friend. All I see is a superb pilot, a brave and resourceful man with a highly specialized background which makes him peculiarly suitable for my purposes. May I also add that, as his own people would most certainly hang him if ever they succeeded in getting their hands on him, he has no choice other than to serve my cause. It is his only chance to live. Now, have you anything else to say?"

"I think you've made your point," Ritter said.

Strasser opened the door and led the way back into the other hangar. He made no reference to what had happened, simply took a map from his pocket and unfolded it across the hood of the field car. They all crowded around.

"Here is Arnheim. Arlberg is eight or nine miles south of here. Ten miles to the west, there's a farm on the edge of the forest. That's where the Finns are."

"Do we all go?" Ritter asked.

"No, *Hauptsturmführer* Berger can stay with the planes."

"And me?" Jackson said.

"No, you might well be useful in other ways. You come with us." The American didn't look too pleased, but there was obviously nothing he could do about it. Strasser added, "And from now on, as what might be termed the military part of the operation starts, *Sturmbannführer* Ritter will be in sole command."

"You mean I have a totally free hand?" Ritter said.

"Well, a little advice now and then never hurt anyone, did it?" Strasser smiled. "Still, no point in crossing bridges until we come to them, Major. Let's get these Finnish barbarians sorted out first."

Nine

AT the field hospital, Mullholland had had a hard night. Eleven wounded from a skirmish near Innsbruck had been brought in at ten o'clock. He and his team had worked steadily through the night on cases of varying seriousness.

His final patient, a young lieutenant, had two machine-gun bullets in the left lung. Mullholland had used every trick in his now considerable repertoire for more than two hours. The boy had died at seven A.M. after suffering a massive hemorrhage.

When Mullholland went outside, it was snowing gently. He lit a cigarette and stood there, breathing in the clean air, and Sergeant Major Grant approached with a cup of tea.

"A rotten night, sir."

"I could have done without it. The bloody war is as good as over, or so they tell us, and here we are, still up to our armpits in blood and destruction. If I sound depressed, it's because I've just lost a patient. A bad way to start the day." He sipped some of the tea. "How's our German friend?"

"Not too bad, sir. He's been asking for you."

"All right, Sergeant Major," Mullholland said wearily. "Let's see what he wants."

Grant led the way down the line of hospital tents and turned into No. 3. Schenck was in the end bed. He lay there, his heavily bandaged arm on top of the blankets. Mullholland unhooked the chart from the foot of the bed to check on his condition, and Schenck's eyes fluttered open.

"Good morning, *Herr Oberst.*"

"And how are you today?"

"Alive, it would seem, for which I am grateful. I thought that perhaps the arm . . ."

"No, it's fine, or it will be. You speak excellent English."

"I worked for ten years in the City of London—not far from St. Paul's—for an export agency."

"I see."

There was a pause, then Schenck said, "Have you had a chance to consider General Canning's letter?"

Mullholland sat on the edge of the bed, suddenly very tired. "I'm in something of a difficulty here. This isn't a combat unit. We're medical people. I've been thinking that perhaps the best thing I can do is get onto brigade headquarters and see if they can manage anything."

"Are they nearby?"

"Last I heard, about twenty miles west of here, but the situation, of course, is very fluid."

Schenck tried to push himself up. "Forgive me, *Herr Oberst,* but time is of the essence in this matter. I must stress that, to our certain knowledge, orders from Berlin have gone out, authorizing the execution of all *prominenti*. If the SS reach Arlberg first, then General Canning, your own Colonel Birr, and the rest are certain to die. Colonel Hesser wishes to avoid this situation at all costs and is willing to formally surrender his command immediately."

"But the area between here and Arlberg is in a very confused state—no one knows that better than you yourself. It would require a fighting unit to get through. They could run into trouble."

"A small patrol, that's all I ask. A couple of jeeps, perhaps. An officer and a few men. If I go with them to show the best route, we could be there in four hours, with any kind of luck at all. They could return at once with the prisoners. General Canning and the others could be here by this evening."

"And just as much chance that they might run into units of your forces on the way back. They could be taking a hell of a chance, especially the ladies."

"So, what do you suggest, *Herr Oberst?* That they wait for the SS?"

Mullholland sighed wearily. "No, you're right, of course. Give me half an hour. I'll see what I can work out."

He went straight to his command tent and sat behind the desk. "It's a mess, isn't it, but he's right. We've got to do something."

"I've been thinking, sir," Grant said. "What about the three Americans? Captain Howard, the Ranger officer, and his men?"

Mullholland paused in the act of taking a bottle of Scotch from his drawer. "The survivors of that mess on the Salzburg road last week? By God, you might have something there. What shape is Howard in?"

"It took about fifty stitches to sew him up, sir, if you remember. Shrapnel wounds, but he was on his feet when I last saw him yesterday, and his sergeant and the other bloke weren't wounded."

"See if you can dig him up, and bring him to me."

Grant went out. Mullholland looked at the whisky bottle for a long moment, then he sighed, replaced the cork, and put the bottle back into the drawer, closing it firmly. He lit a cigarette and started on some paperwork. A few moments later, Grant entered.

"Captain Howard, sir."

Mullholland looked up. "Fine, Sergeant Major. Show him in, and see if you can rustle up some tea."

Grant went out, and Howard ducked under the flap a moment later. He wasn't wearing a helmet, and a red, angry-looking scar bisected his forehead, stopping short of the left eye, the stitches still clearly visible. His left hand was heavily bandaged. He was very pale, the eyes sunken, an expression of ineffable weariness on his face.

My God, Mullholland thought, this boy's had about all he can take, and no mistake. He smiled. "Come in, Captain, sit down. With any luck, we might get some tea in a few minutes. Cigarette?"

"Thank you, sir."

Mullholland gave him a light. "How are you feeling?"

"Fine."

Which was as fair a lie as Mullholland had heard in many a day, but he carried on. "I've got a problem I thought you might be able to help me with."

Howard showed no emotion at all. "I see, sir."

"We carted a German officer in here yesterday with a couple of bullets in him. The unfortunate thing was that he'd been looking for an Allied unit anyway. Had a letter on him from an American general called Canning. Have you heard of him?"

"Hamilton Canning?"

"That's him. He's being held prisoner, along with four other *prominenti*, as the Germans call them." He pushed the bloodstained letter across the table. "But you'll find all the details there."

Howard picked up the letter, read it with lackluster eyes. Grant came in with two mugs of tea and placed them on the desk. Mullholland motioned him to stay.

After a while, the American looked up. "They seem to be in a mess, these people. What do you want me to do about it?"

"I'd like you to go and get them. Accept this Colonel Hesser's surrender formally, then return with the prisoners as soon as possible. The German officer who brought this letter, Lieutenant Schenck, is willing to return with you to show you the way. He was quite badly wounded, but I think we can fix him up well enough to stand the trip."

"You want me to go?" Howard said.

"And those two men of yours. I've been thinking

about it. We could give you an ambulance. Plenty of room then for the others for the return trip."

"Have you any idea what it's like out there, sir, between here and Arlberg?"

"I can guess," Mullholland said evenly.

"And you want me to go with two men and a crippled German?" Howard's voice was flat, unemotional. "Is this an order?"

"No, I've no authority to order you to do anything, Captain, as I think you know. The blunt truth is that I just haven't got anyone else available. This is a medical unit, and as you've seen for yourself, we're up to our eyes in it."

Howard stared down at the letter for a long moment, then he nodded slowly. "I'll put it to Sergeant Hoover and Private Finebaum if that's all right with you, sir. I think, under the circumstances, they should have some choice in the matter."

"Fine," Mullholland said. "But don't take too long about making your decision, please." And he used the phrase Schenck had used to him. "Time really is of the essence in this one."

Howard went out, and Mullholland looked up at Grant. "What do you think?"

"I don't know, sir. He looks as if he's had it to me."

"Haven't we all, Sergeant Major?" Mullholland said wearily.

■

Finebaum and Hoover shared a pup tent at the end of the rows on the other side of the vehicle area. Hoover was busily writing a letter, while Finebaum crouched in the entrance, heating beans in a mess tin on a portable stove.

"Beans and yet more beans. Don't these Limeys eat anything else?"

"Maybe you'd prefer K-rations," Hoover said.

"Oh, I've got plans for that stuff, Harry," Finebaum said. "After the war, I'm going to buy a whole load of that crap—war surplus, you understand? Then I'm going to take it around to my old grannie, who runs a strictly kosher house. So kosher that even the cat's got religion."

"You mean you're going to feed K-rations to the cat?"

"That's it."

"And break that old woman's heart? I mean, what did she ever do to you?"

"I'll tell you what she did. The day after the Japs bombed Pearl Harbor, she called me in and said, 'Mannie, you know what you've got to do.' Then she opened the front door, pointed me in the general direction of the recruiting office, and shoved."

He spooned beans onto a tin plate and handed it to Hoover. The sergeant said, "You talk too much, but I know how you feel. I'm bored to hell with this place, too."

"When are we going to get out of here?" Finebaum demanded. "I mean, I respect and love our noble captain—nobody more so—but how much longer do we stand around and wait for him to find his goddamned soul?"

"You cut that out," Hoover said. "He's had about all he can take."

"In this game there's only two ways to be—alive or dead. Now I've seen a lot of good men go under in the year I've served with you and him. But they're dead, and I'm not. I don't rejoice in it, but it's a fact of life, and I ain't going to sit and cry over them, either."

Hoover put down his plate. "Why, you son of a bitch, I've just made a discovery. You're not doing it because you're here or a patriot or something. You're doing it because you like it. Because it gives you kicks like you've never had before."

"Screw you!"

"What are you after—another battle star? You want to be right up there in the line with those other heroes?"

"What do you want me to do, go back to sewing on flybuttons in an East Side cellar for thirty bucks a week when I can't get work blowing clarinet? No, thank you. Before I got back to that, I'd rather pull the pin on one of my own grenades. I'll tell you something, Harry." His voice was low, urgent. "I live more in a single day than I did in a year before the war. When my time comes, I hope I take it right between the eyes about one minute before they sign the peace treaty, and if you and the noble captain don't like it, baby, then you can do the other thing."

He got up and, turning, found Howard listening. They stood there, neither Hoover nor Finebaum knowing what the hell to say. It was Howard who spoke first. "Tell me, Finebaum—Garland, Anderson, O'Grady, all those other guys in the outfit, all the way across Europe since D-Day—don't you ever think about them at all? Doesn't the fact of their death have any meaning for you?"

"Those guys are dead—so they're dead. Right, Captain? I mean, maybe some part of my brain is missing or something, but I don't see it any other way."

"And you don't think they accomplished anything?"

"You mean the nobility of war, sir? The strength of our purpose and all that crap? I'm afraid I don't buy that, either. The way I figure it, every day for the past ten thousand years, someone somewhere in the world has been beating hell out of someone else. I think it's in the nature of the species."

"You know something, Finebaum? I'm beginning to think you might have read a book or two."

"Could be, Captain. That just could be."

"All right," Howard said. "You want a little action—I've got a pretty large helping for you. Ever heard of General Hamilton Canning?"

He quickly outlined the situation. When he was finished, Finebaum said, "That's the craziest thing I ever heard of. That's Indian territory out there."

"Forty or fifty miles of it between here and Arlberg."

"And they want *us* to go? Three guys in an ambulance with some Kraut stretcher case?" He started to laugh. "You know? I like it, Captain. Yes, I definitely like it."

"Okay. So you go and tell Sergeant Major Grant we're going. Tell him I'll go along in five minutes to speak to this German lieutenant, Schenck. And move it. If we're going, we've got to go now."

Finebaum went off on the double, and Howard squatted down and helped himself to coffee from the stove. Hoover said, "You sure you're doing the right thing? You don't look too good."

"You want to know something, Harry?" Howard said. "I'm tired right through to my backbone. More tired than I've ever been in my life, and yet I can't sleep. I can't feel. I don't seem to be able to react." He shrugged. "Maybe I need to smell a little gunpowder. Maybe I've gotten like Finebaum and need it." He stuck a cigarette between his lips. "I know one thing. Right now, I'd rather be out there taking my chances than squatting on my backside here, waiting for the war to finish."

■

The Finns were encamped on a farm just off the main road, about ten miles west of Arnheim. There were thirty-eight of them under the command of a *Hauptsturmführer* named Erik Sorsa.

The Fifth SS Panzer Division Wiking was the first, and without a doubt the best, foreign division of the *Waffen*-SS, composed mainly of Dutch, Flemings, Danes, and Norwegians. The Finns had joined in 1941, providing the ski-troop expertise so essential in the Russian campaign.

The losses on the Eastern Front by January 1945 had been so colossal that it was decided to raise a new regiment, a joint German-Finnish affair. The project had foundered when the few dozen Finnish survivors, with Sorsa as their senior officer, had made it clear that they would not renew their contracts with the German government after May 1. So, from divisional headquarters in Klagenfurt had come the order which had sent them to the farm at Oberfeld to await further instructions, which was what they had been doing for precisely three weeks now.

Sorsa was a handsome, fair-haired young man of twenty-seven. His mountain cap was identical in cut to that of the army, the edelweiss on the left-hand side, the usual SS death's-head at the front. His cuff-title read *"Finnisches Freiwilligen Bataillon der Waffen-*SS" in two lines, and his armshield was black with a white lion. He wore two Iron Crosses, the wound badge in silver, and the Winter War ribbon.

He stood at the door of the farm, smoking a cigarette, watching half a dozen of his men skiing down through the trees on the hillside above, led by the unit's senior sergeant major, Matti Gestrin. Gestrin soared over the wall by the barn, jumping superbly, and they followed him, one by one, with rhythmic precision—tough, competent-looking men in reversible winter uniforms, white on one side, autumn-pattern camouflage on the other.

"Did you see anything?" Sorsa inquired.

"Were we supposed to?" Gestrin grinned. "I thought we were just out for the exercise. Still no word from headquarters?"

"No, I think they've forgotten about us."

Gestrin, in the act of lighting a cigarette, stopped smiling, looking over Sorsa's shoulder. "From the looks of things, I'd say they've just found us again."

■

The field car came down the track through the snow, Hoffer at the wheel, Ritter beside him wearing a camouflaged parka with the hood up over his cap. Strasser and Jackson were in the back seat. Hoffer drove into the farmyard and braked to a halt. Sorsa and Gestrin stayed where they were by the front door, but the rest of the Finns moved forward perceptibly, one or two un-slinging their Mauser infantry rifles. Sorsa said something quietly to them in Finnish.

"What did he say?" Strasser asked Jackson.

"He said, 'Easy, children. Nothing I can't handle.' "

Another dozen or fifteen Finns came out of the barn, mostly in shirtsleeves and all carrying weapons of one sort or another. There was total silence as everyone waited, just the snow falling perfectly straight, and then, with a sudden whispering rush, another white-clad skier lifted over the wall to land perfectly, skidding to a halt a yard or two from Sorsa. Another, and yet another, followed.

It was poetry in motion, total perfection, and there was a slight fixed smile on Sorsa's face that seemed to say: That's what we are. What about you?

Jackson murmured, "The greatest skiers in the world, these boys. They knocked hell out of the Russians in the first Winter War. And they're great throat-cutters—maybe I should have warned you."

"Wait here," Ritter said tonelessly. "All of you."

He got out of the field car and walked across the yard to Sorsa. For a moment, he confronted the tall Finn, who could see only the death's-head on his cap, then said, "Not bad, not bad at all."

"You think so?" Sorsa said.

"A fair jump, certainly."

"You could do better?"

"Perhaps."

There were several pairs of skis leaning against the wall. Ritter helped himself, kneeling to adjust the bindings to fit his heavy panzer boots.

Hoffer appeared at his side and knelt down. "Allow me, *Sturmbannführer*."

Sorsa took in the sergeant major's black panzer uniform, the Knight's Cross. There was a sudden change of expression in his eyes, and he turned and glanced briefly at Gestrin.

Ritter stamped his feet and took the sticks Hoffer offered him. He smiled. "A long time, Erich, eh?"

He pushed forward, past the field car, out of the gate, and started up the steep slope through the pine trees. Nobody said a word. Everyone waited. He felt curiously calm and peaceful as he followed the zigzag of the farm trail, totally absorbed, thoroughly enjoying the whole thing.

When he turned, he was perhaps a hundred feet above the yard, the trail the Finns had made clear before him. Every face was turned, looking up, and he suddenly felt immensely happy, laughter bubbling up inside him.

He threw back his head, howled like a wolf— the old Harz woodcutters' signal—and launched himself forward, away from the track of the Finns, taking the steepest slope down, zigzagging through the pine trees in a series of stem turns that were breathtaking in their audacity. And then he lifted, soaring effortlessly over the wall, the field car, drifting broadside for a second only, then turning on his left stick, landing in a spray of snow at a dead halt in a perfectly executed stem christiania, no more than a yard from Sorsa.

There was a shout of approval from the Finns. Ritter stood there, Hoffer kneeling to unfasten his bindings for him, then he threw back his hood, unbuttoned the parka, and took it off.

"He should have been on the stage, that one," Strasser whispered to Jackson.

Ritter tightened his gloves and spoke without looking at Sorsa. "My name is Ritter, *Sturmbann-führer*, Five Hundred and Second SS Heavy Tank Battalion, and I am here to assume command of this unit, under special orders from the *Führer* himself in Berlin."

Sorsa looked him over, the Winter War ribbon, the Iron Cross, First and Second Class, the silver badge which meant at least three wounds, the Knight's Cross with Oak Leaves and Swords, the dark eyes, the pale Devil's face.

"Death himself come among us," Matti Gestrin said.

"You will speak German, please, in my presence," Ritter said calmly. "I take it your men are capable of that, *Hauptsturmführer*, considering that they have been in the service of the Reich for some four years now?"

Sorsa said, "Most of them, but never mind that now. What's this nonsense about orders from Berlin? I know nothing of this."

"Herr Strasser?" Ritter called. "You will please show this gentleman our orders?"

"With pleasure, Major."

Strasser came forward, taking them from his

pocket, and Ritter walked a few paces away, ignoring the Finns' stares, took out a silver case and selected a cigarette with care. Hoffer jumped to his side to offer him a light.

"Thank you, *Sturmscharführer*."

It was a nicely calculated piece of theater, a scene they had played many times before, usually with maximum effect.

Sorsa was examining the order Strasser had passed to him. From the leader and chancellor of the State. Most secret. And he was there himself, mentioned by name, everything exactly as Ritter had said. Most explicit. And, most amazing thing of all, the signature at the foot of the paper. *Adolf Hitler.*

He handed the paper back, and Strasser replaced it in his wallet. "Well?" Ritter said, without looking around. "You are satisfied?"

"There is a situation here," Sorsa said awkwardly. "My comrades and I are contract soldiers."

"Mercenaries," Ritter said. "I'm well aware of the fact. So?"

"My men have voted to go home to Helsinki. We have not renewed our contract."

"Why should you," Ritter said loud enough for all to hear, "when your original one is still in force until nine o'clock tomorrow morning—or would you deny that fact?"

"No, what you say is true."

"Then it would appear that you and your men are still soldiers of the *Waffen*-SS, and under the *Führer* directive just shown to you by Herr Strasser here, I now assume command of this unit."

There was a long, long moment while everyone waited for Sorsa's answer. "Yes, *Sturmbann-führer*." There was a further pause, and he raised his voice a little. "Until nine o'clock tomorrow morning, we are still soldiers of the *Waffen*-SS. We have taken the blood money, sworn the oath, and we Finns do not go back on our word."

"Good." Ritter turned to Gestrin. "You will please bring the company to attention, Sergeant Major. I wish to address them."

There was a flurry of movement as Gestrin barked orders, and finally the Finns were drawn up in two lines—thirty-five of them, Ritter noted. They stood there, waiting in the falling snow as he paced up and down. Finally, he stopped and faced them, hands on his hips.

"I know you men. You were at Leningrad, Kurland, Stalingrad. So was I. You fought in the Ardennes. So did I. We've a lot in common, so I'll speak plainly. Captain Sorsa here says that you're *Waffen*-SS only until tomorrow morning. That you want to go home to Helsinki. Well, I've news for you. The Russians are in Berlin, they're with the American Army on the Elbe, cutting Germany in half. You're not going anywhere because there's nowhere to go, and if the Ivans get their hands on you, all you'll get is a bullet—and that's if you're lucky."

The wind increased in force, driving snow down through the trees in a miniature blizzard.

"And I'm in the same boat because the Russians overran my parents' place a month ago. So all we've got is each other and the regiment, but even if it's only till nine o'clock tomorrow morning, you're still soldiers of the *Waffen*-SS, the toughest, most efficient fighting men the world has ever seen, and from now on, you'll start acting that way again. If I ask you a question, you answer *'Jawohl, Sturmbannführer.'* If I give you an order, you get those heels together and shout *'Zu Befehl, Sturmbannführer.'* Do you understand me?" There was silence. He raised his voice. "Do you understand me?"

"*Jawohl, Sturmbannführer,*" they chorused.

"Good." He turned to Sorsa. "Let's go inside, and I'll explain the situation to you."

The door opened directly into a large, stone-flagged kitchen. There were a wooden table, a few chairs, a wood fire burning on the hearth, and a profusion of military equipment of various kinds, including several *Panzerfausts*—one-man antitank weapons which had been produced in quantity during the last few months of the war.

They all gathered around the table—Sorsa, Strasser, Jackson, Hoffer. Ritter unfolded a map of the area. "How many vehicles do you have?"

"One field car, three troop-carrying half-tracks."

"And weapons?"

"A heavy machine gun in each half-track, otherwise only light infantry weapons and grenades. Oh, and a few *Panzerfausts,* as you can see."

Strasser said, "Aren't you overreacting just a little, Major? After all, if things go as smoothly as they should, this could simply be a matter of driving into the Schloss and driving out again half an hour later."

"I stopped believing in miracles some considerable time ago." Ritter tapped his finger on the map and said to Sorsa, "Schloss Arlberg. That's our objective. Herr Strasser here will now tell you what it's all about, and you can then brief the men. We leave in half an hour."

Ten

IT was just after ten o'clock, and Colonel Hesser was working at his desk when there was a knock at the door and Schneider entered.

Hesser glanced up eagerly. "Any news of Schenck?"

"I'm afraid not, sir."

Hesser threw down his pen. "He should have been back by now. It doesn't look good."

"I know, sir."

"Anyway, what did you want?"

"Herr Meyer is here, sir, from the village. There's been some sort of accident. His son, I believe. He wants to know if Herr Gaillard can go down to the village with him. He's the only doctor for miles around at the moment."

"Show him in."

Johann Meyer was mayor of Arlberg and owner of the village inn, the Golden Eagle. He was a tall, robust-looking man with iron-gray hair and beard, a well-known guide in the Bavarian Alps. Just now he was considerably agitated.

"What's the trouble, Meyer?" Colonel Hesser asked.

"It's my boy, Arnie, *Herr Oberst*," Meyer said. "Trying the quick way down the mountain again—tried jumping a tree and ended up taking a bad fall. I think he may have broken his leg. I was wondering whether the *Herr Doktor . . .*"

"Yes, of course." Hesser nodded to Schneider. "Find Gaillard fast as you can and take him and Herr Meyer back to the village in a field car."

"Shall I stay with him, *Herr Oberst?*"

"No, I need you here. Take one of the men with you and leave him there. Anyone will do. Oh, and tell Gaillard that I naturally assume that under the circumstances he gives his word not to try to escape."

Gaillard was, in fact, at that very moment engaged in an animated discussion about their situation with Canning and Birr.

"We can't go on like this, it's crazy," Canning said. "Schenck should have been back last night. Something's gone wrong."

"Probably lying dead in a ditch somewhere," Birr said. "I did tell you, remember?"

"Okay, so what do we do?"

"Well," Gaillard said. "The garrison of this establishment is composed mainly of old men or cripples, as no one knows better than I. I've been treating them all for months now. On the other hand, they still outnumber the three of us by about seven to one, and they are armed to the teeth."

"But we can't just sit here and wait for it to happen," Canning said.

Claire, sitting by the fire with Madame Chevalier, said, "Has it ever occurred to you, Hamilton, that you just might be making a mountain out of a molehill here? An American or British unit could roll up to that gate at any time, and all our troubles would be over."

"And pigs might also fly."

"You know what your trouble is?" she told him. "You want it this way. Drama, intrigue—up to your ears in the most dangerous game of all again."

"Now you listen to me," he began, thoroughly angry, and then the door opened and Schneider entered.

He clicked his heels. "Excuse me, Herr General, but Dr. Gaillard is wanted urgently in the village. Herr Meyer's son has had a skiing accident."

"I'll come at once," Gaillard said. "Just give me a moment to get my bag."

He hurried out, followed by Schneider. Birr said, "Always work for the healers, eh? Nice to think there are people like Gaillard around to put us together again when we fall down."

"Philosophy now?" Canning said. "May God preserve me."

"Oh, he will, Hamilton. He will," Birr said. "I've got a feeling the Almighty has something very special lined up for you."

As Claire and Madame Chevalier started to laugh, Canning said, "I wonder whether you'll still be smiling when the SS drive into that courtyard down there," and he stalked angrily from the room.

■

Arnie Meyer was only twelve years old, and small

for his age. Just now his face was twisted in agony, the sweat springing to his forehead, trickling down from the fair hair. He had no mother, and his father stood anxiously at one side of the bed and watched as Gaillard cut the trouser leg open with a pair of scissors.

He ran his fingers around the angry swelling below the right knee, and in spite of his gentleness the boy cried out sharply.

"Is it broken, *Herr Doktor?*" Meyer asked.

"Without a doubt. You have splints, of course, with your mountain rescue equipment?"

"Yes, I'll get them."

"In the meantime, I'll give him a morphine injection. I'll have to set the leg, and that would be too painful for him to bear. Oh, and that private Schneider left—Voss, I think his name is. Send him in here. He can assist me."

The mayor went out, and Gaillard broke open a morphine ampul. "Were you coming down the north track again?"

"Yes, *Herr Doktor.*"

"How many times have I warned you? Out of the sun among the trees when it's below freezing, conditions are too fast for you. Your father says you tried to jump a tree, but that isn't true, is it?" Here, he gave the boy the injection.

Arnie winced. "No, *Herr Doktor,*" he said faintly. "I came out of the track onto the slope and tried to do a stem christie like I've seen you do, only everything went wrong."

"As well it might, you idiot," Gaillard told him. "Frozen ground—hardly any snow. What were you trying to do, commit suicide?"

There was a knock at the door, and Private Voss came in, a small, middle-aged man with steel spectacles. He was a clerk from Hamburg whose bad eyes had kept him out of the war until the previous July.

"You wanted me, *Herr Doktor?*"

"I'll need your asistance in a short while to set the boy's leg. Have you ever done anything like this before?"

"No." Voss looked faintly alarmed.

"Don't worry. You'll soon learn."

Meyer came back a moment later with mountain rescue splints and several rolls of bandage.

"If I had hospital facilities, I'd put this leg in a pot," Gaillard said. "It is absolutely essential that, once it's set, it remain immobile, especially so in the case of a boy of this age. It will be your responsibility to see that he behaves himself."

"He will, I promise you, *Herr Doktor.*"

"Good. Now let's see how brave you can be, Arnie."

But Arnie, in spite of the morphine, fainted dead away at the first touch. Which was all to the good, of course, for Gaillard was really able to get to work then, setting the bone with an audible crack that turned Voss's face pale. The little private hauled on the foot as instructed and held a splint on the other side from Meyer as Gaillard skillfully wound the bandages.

When he was finished, the Frenchman stepped back and smiled at Meyer. "And now, my friend, you can serve me a very large brandy. Nothing less than Armagnac will be accepted."

"Do we return to the castle now, *Herr Doktor?*" Voss asked.

"No, my friend. We adjourn to the bar with the mayor here, who will no doubt consider your efforts no less worthy of his hospitality. We will wait there until my patient recovers consciousness, however long it takes—possibly all day—so be prepared."

They started downstairs and at the same moment heard a motor vehicle draw up outside. Meyer went to the window on the landing halfway down, then turned. "There's a military ambulance outside, *Herr Doktor,* and it isn't German, from the looks of it."

Gaillard joined him at the window in time to see Jack Howard jump down from the passenger seat and stand looking up at the Golden Eagle, a Thompson gun under one arm.

Gaillard got the window open. "In here," he called in English. "A pleasure to see you." Howard looked up, hesitated, then advanced to the door. Gaillard turned to Voss. "A great day, my friend, perhaps the most important in your life, because from this moment, for you, the war is over."

The journey in the ambulance from the field hospital had been a total anticlimax. They had driven through a countryside covered with snow, from which the population seemed to have vanished—a strange, lost land of deserted villages and shuttered farms. Most important of all, except for a few abandoned vehicles at various places, they had seen no sign of the enemy.

"But where the hell is everybody?" Hoover demanded at one point.

"With their heads under the bed, waiting for the ax to fall," Finebaum told him.

"The Alpine Fortress," Hoover said. "What a load of crap. One good armored column could go from one end of this country to the other in a day, as far as I can see, and nobody to stop them." He turned to Howard. "What do you think, sir?"

"I think it's all very mysterious," Howard said, "and that's good because if my map reading is correct, we're coming down into Arlberg now."

They came around the corner, saw the village at the bottom of the hill, the spires of the castle peeping above the wooded crest on the other side of the valley.

"And there she is," Finebaum said. "Schloss Arlberg. Sounds like a tailor I used to know in New York."

They drove down the deserted street, turned into the cobbled square, and halted in front of the Golden Eagle.

"Even here," Hoover said, "not a soul in sight. It gives me the creeps."

Howard reached for his Thompson gun and got out of the ambulance's cab. He stood there looking up at the building, and then a window was thrown open and a voice called excitedly in English with a French accent, "In here!"

■

Gaillard embraced the American enthusiastically. "My friend, I don't think I've ever been more pleased to see anyone in my life. My name is Paul Gaillard. I am a prisoner with several others here at Schloss Arlberg."

"I know," Howard said. "That's why we're here. I'm Jack Howard, by the way."

"Ah, then Schenck got through?"

"Yes, but he stopped a couple of bullets on the way. He's outside now in the ambulance."

"Then I'd better take a look at him. I was once a doctor by profession. My training has been useful of late."

Just then, Voss appeared hesitantly at the bottom of the stairs. Finebaum called a warning from the doorway. "Watch it, Captain."

As he raised his M1, Gaillard hastily got in the way. "No need for that. Although poor Voss here is technically supposed to be guarding me, he has, to my certain knowledge, never fired a shot in anger in his life." Finebaum lowered his rifle, and Gaillard said to Howard, "There will be no need for shooting by anyone, believe me. Colonel Hesser has already said that he will surrender to the first Allied troops who appear. Didn't Schenck make this clear?"

"It's been a long, hard war, Doctor," Finebaum said. "We only got this far by never taking a Kraut on trust."

"Like perspective, I suppose it's all a question of your point of view," Gaillard said. "It has been my experience that they are as good, bad, or indifferent as the rest of us. Still, I'd better have a look at Schenck now. Voss, please bring my bag."

At the door he paused, looking at the ambulance, then glanced along the street. "There are no others? No one else is coming?"

"You were lucky to get us," Howard told him.

He opened the rear door of the ambulance, and

Gaillard climbed inside. Schenck lay there, the heavily bandaged arm outside the blankets, the eyes closed. He opened them slowly and, on finding Gaillard, managed a smile.

"So, *Herr Doktor,* here we are again."

"You did well." Gaillard felt his pulse. "What about Schmidt?"

"Dead."

"He was a good man. I'm sorry. You have a slight fever. Is there much pain?"

"For the past hour it has been hell."

"I'll give you something for that, then you can sleep."

He opened the bag which Voss had brought, found a morphine ampul, and gave Schenck an injection. Then he climbed out of the ambulance again.

"Will he be okay?" Howard asked.

"I think so."

They went back into the inn and found Hoover and Finebaum at one end of the bar, Voss at the other, looking worried. Meyer had the Armagnac out and several glasses.

"Excellent," Gaillard said. "Herr Meyer, here, who is mayor of Arlberg as well as a most excellent innkeeper, was about to treat me to a shot—as I believe you Americans call it—of his best brandy. Perhaps you gentlemen will join me."

Meyer filled the glasses hurriedly. Finebaum grabbed for his, and Hoover said, "Not yet, you dummy. This is a special occasion. It calls for a toast."

Howard turned to Gaillard. "I'd say it was your prerogative, Doctor."

"Very well," Gaillard said. "I could drink to you, my friends, but I think the circumstances demand something more appropriate. Something for all of us. For you and me, but also for Schenck and Voss and Meyer here, all those who have suffered the disabilities of this terrible war. I give you love and life and happiness, commodities which have been in short supply for some considerable time now."

"I'll drink to that," Finebaum said and emptied the glass at a swallow.

"We'd better get on up to the castle now," Howard said.

"Where you will find them awaiting your arrival with a considerable degree of impatience—General Canning in particular," Gaillard told him. "I'll hang on here for the moment. I have a patient upstairs."

"Okay, Doctor," Howard said. "But I'd better warn you. My orders are to pick you people up, turn straight around, and get the hell out. I'd say you've got an hour—that's all."

They moved outside. Finebaum said, "What about the Kraut? We take him along?"

"Voss stays with me," Gaillard said firmly. "I'll very probably need him."

"Anything you say, Doctor." Howard shoved Finebaum up into the cab of the ambulance. "Finebaum's survived on the idea the only good one is a dead one for so long, it's become a way of life."

"So what does that make me, some kind of animal? It means I'm alive, doesn't it?" Finebaum leaned down to Gaillard as Hoover started the engine. "You look like a philosopher, Doc. Here's some philosophy for you. A funny thing about war. It gets easier as you go along."

The ambulance drove away across the square. Meyer, who was standing on the porch, said in German, "What did he say—the small one—*Herr Doktor?*"

"He said a terrible thing, my friend." Gaillard smiled sadly. "But true, unfortunately. And now, I think, we'll take another look at that boy of yours."

■

Hesser was seated at his desk, writing a letter to his wife, when the door was flung open unceremoniously and Schneider rushed in. He had the Alsatian with him, and his excitement had even infected the dog, which circled him, whining, so that the leash got entangled in his legs.

"What is it, man?" Hesser demanded. "What's wrong with you?"

"They're coming, *Herr Oberst*. A British vehicle has just started up the hill."

"Only one? You are certain?"

"They've just phoned through from the guardhouse, *Herr Oberst*. An ambulance, apparently."

"Strange," Hesser said. "However, we must prepare to receive them with all speed. Turn out the garrison and notify General Canning and the others. I'll be down myself, directly."

Schneider went out, and Hesser sat there, hands flat on the table, a slight frown on his face. Now that the moment had come he felt curiously deflated, but then that was only to be expected. The end of something, after all, and what did he have to show

for it? One arm, one eye. But there was still Gerda
—and the children—and it was over now. Soon he
could go home. When he got up and reached for his
cap and belt, he was actually smiling.

■

As the ambulance came out of the last bend and
Schloss Arlberg loomed above them, Finebaum
leaned out of the cab and looked up at the pointed
roofs of the towers in awe.

"Hey, I seen this place before. The moat, the
drawbridge—everything. *The Prisoner of Zenda*.
Ronald Colman swam across, and some dame
helped him in through the window."

"That was Hollywood—this is for real, man,"
Hoover said. "This place was built to stand a siege.
Those walls must be ten feet thick."

"They're hospitable enough, that's for sure,"
Howard said. "They've left the gate open for us.
Straight in, Harry, nice and slow, and let's see what
we've got here."

Hoover dropped into bottom gear, and they trun-
dled across the drawbridge. The iron-bound gates
stood open, and they moved on through the darkness of the entrance tunnel and emerged into the
great inner courtyard.

The garrison was drawn up in a single line, all
eighteen of them, Colonel Hesser at the front. General Canning, Colonel Birr, Claire, and Madame
Chevalier stood together at the top of the steps leading up to the main entrance.

The ambulance rolled to a halt, and Howard got
out. Hesser called his men to attention and saluted
politely. "My name is Hesser—*Oberstleutnant,*

Forty-second Panzer Grenadiers, at present in command of this establishment. And you, sir?"

"Captain John H. Howard, Second Ranger Battalion, United States Army."

Hesser turned and called, "General Canning? Colonel Birr? Will you join me, please?"

They came down the steps and crossed the yard. It was snowing quite hard now. Howard saluted, and Canning held out his hand. "We're certainly pleased to see you, son, believe me."

"Our pleasure, General."

Hesser said, "Then, in the presence of these officers as witnesses, I formally surrender this establishment, Captain Howard." He saluted, turned, and said to Schneider, "Have the men lay down their arms."

There was a flurry of movement. Within a matter of seconds, the men were back in line, their rifles standing in three triangular stacks before them.

Hesser saluted again. "Very well, Captain," he said. "What are your orders?"

■

Sorsa headed the German column in one of the armored half-tracks, Ritter and Hoffer, Strasser and Jackson next in line in their field car, the rest of the Finns trailing behind.

Just after noon they emerged from a side road to join the road from Innsbruck to Arlberg, along which the ambulance had passed a short time before. As they reached the crest of the hill above the village, Sorsa signaled a halt. Ritter, Strasser, and Jackson got out of the field car and went to join him.

"What is it?" Ritter demanded.

"Something's passed along this road very recently. Heavy vehicle. See the tire marks? It stopped here before starting down to the village."

There was fresh oil on the snow. Ritter looked down the hill. "So this is Arlberg."

"Quiet little place, isn't it?" Jackson said. "They're certainly staying out of the way down there."

Ritter held out his hand for Sorsa's field glasses and trained them on the turrets of Schloss Arlberg peeping above the crest of the far ridge. He handed them back to Strasser. "Nothing worth seeing. The vehicle which has preceded us could be anything, but under the circumstances, I think we should press on."

"I agree," Strasser said and for the first time seemed less calm than usual, filled with a kind of nervous excitement. "Let's get there as fast as possible and get things sewn up. We've come too far for anything to be allowed to go wrong now."

They got back into the vehicles, Sorsa waved the column on, and they started down the hill.

■

It was Meyer who saw them first, when they were halfway down—sheer luck that he'd gone to the landing window to close it. He took one look, then hurried to the bedroom where Gaillard was checking on the boy, who was still unconscious.

"There's an SS column coming down the hill," Meyer said. "Three half-tracks, two field cars. About forty men in all."

Voss's face turned deathly pale. Gaillard said, "You're certain?"

Meyer opened a cupboard and took out an old brass telescope. "See for yourself."

They all went out onto the landing, and Meyer leveled the telescope on the lead half-track. Immediately the divisional signs on the vehicle leaped into view—the SS runes, the death's-head painted in white. He moved on to the field car, picking out Ritter first, then Strasser.

He frowned, and Meyer said, "What is it, *Herr Doktor?*"

"Nothing," Gaillard said. "There's a civilian with them I thought I knew for a moment, but I must be wrong. They're mountain troops—judging by their uniforms and the skis they carry in the half-tracks."

He closed the telescope and handed it to Meyer. Voss plucked at his sleeve. "What are we going to do, *Herr Doktor?* Those devils are capable of anything."

"No need to panic," Gaillard said. "Keep calm, above all things." He turned to Meyer. "They'll be here within the next two or three minutes. Go out and meet them."

"And what about the Americans? Look, the tracks of the ambulance are plain in the snow. What if they ask me who made them?"

"Play it by ear. Whatever happens, don't tell them Voss and I are here. We'll keep out of sight for the time being. We can always clear off the back way if we have to, but I want to see how the situation develops here first, and besides, Arnie is going to need me when he wakes up."

"As you say." Meyer took a deep breath and started downstairs as the first vehicle braked to a halt outside. Gaillard and Voss, peering around the edge of the curtain, saw Ritter, Strasser, and Jackson get out of the field car.

"Strange," Gaillard said. "One of the SS officers has a Stars and Stripes shield sewn on his left sleeve below the eagle. What on earth does that mean?"

"I don't know, *Herr Doktor*," Voss whispered. "Where the SS are concerned, I've always kept well out of the way. Who's the one in the leather coat speaking to Meyer now? Gestapo, perhaps?"

"I don't know," Gaillard said. "I still have that irritating feeling we've met somewhere before." He eased the window open in time to hear Sorsa shout an order to Matti Gestrin in the rear half-track. "My God," Gaillard whispered, "they're Finns."

He peered down at them, suddenly fearful. Hard, tough, competent-looking men, armed to the teeth, and there was only one road up to the castle, one road down. He turned and grabbed Voss by the shirt front.

"Right, my friend. Your chance to be a hero for the first time in your miserable life. Out the back door, through the trees, take the woodcutters' trail up to the castle, and run til your heart bursts. Tell Hesser the SS are coming. Now get moving!" And he shoved Voss violently along the landing toward the back stairs.

As he turned to the window again, Ritter was saying to Meyer, "From these tracks a vehicle would seem to have passed this way during the past half hour. A heavy vehicle. What was it?"

A direct question—and in the circumstances, there was only one answer Meyer could give. "It was an ambulance, *Sturmbannführer*."

"A German ambulance?" Strasser asked.

"No, *mein Herr*. A British Army ambulance. There were three American soldiers in the cab. One was an officer—a captain, I think."

"And they took that street there out of the square?" Ritter nodded. "Which leads to . . ."

"Schloss Arlberg."

"And is there any other way up or down?"

"Only on foot."

"One more question. How many men in the garrison at Schloss Arlberg now?"

Meyer hesitated, but he was a simple man with his son to consider, and Ritter's pale face, the dark eyes under the silver death's-head were too much.

"Eighteen, *Sturmbannführer*. Nineteen, with the commandant."

Ritter turned to the others. "What you might call a damn close thing."

"No problem, surely," Strasser said.

"Let's go and see, shall we?" Ritter replied calmly, and he turned back to the field car.

Meyer waited on the step until the last half-track in the column had disappeared up the narrow street before going back inside. Gaillard was at the bottom of the stairs.

"Well?" the Frenchman demanded.

"What could I do? I had to tell them." Meyer shivered. "But now what, *Herr Doktor*? I mean, what can they do up there in the castle? Colonel Hesser has no option but to turn your friends over to the SS now."

But before Gaillard could reply, Arnie called out

feverishly from the bedroom, and Gaillard turned and hurried upstairs.

■

In the courtyard, the *prominenti* were making ready to leave. Schenck had been left on board the ambulance, and three German soldiers were loading the prisoners' personal belongings. Claire and Madame Chevalier waited on the porch while Hesser, Birr, and Canning stood at the bottom of the steps smoking cigarettes. Beyond the ambulance, the rest of the tiny garrison still stood in line before their stacked rifles.

It was Magda, Schneider's Alsatian, who first showed signs of agitation, whining and straining at her leash and then breaking into furious barking.

Canning frowned. "What is it, old girl? What's wrong with you?"

There was the hollow booming of feet thundering across the drawbridge, and Voss staggered out of the tunnel.

"Herr Oberst!" he called weakly, lurching from side to side like a drunken man. "The SS are coming! The SS are coming!"

Hesser reached out his one good arm to steady him as Voss almost fell down, chest heaving, sweat pouring down his face.

"What are you telling me, man?"

"SS, *Herr Oberst.* On their way up from the village. It's true. Finnish mountain troops in charge of a *Sturmbannführer* in panzer uniform."

Canning caught him by the arm and pulled him around. "How many?"

"Forty or so altogether. Three half-tracks and two field cars."

"What kind of armaments did they carry?"

"There was a heavy machine gun with each vehicle, *Herr General,* I noticed that. The rest was just the usual hand stuff. Schmeissers, rifles, and so on."

Finebaum said to Hoover, "They keep telling me the war's over, but here we are, the three of us, with nineteen Kraut prisoners on our hands and forty of those SS bastards coming around the bend fast."

Howard turned to Canning. "It's an impossible situation, sir, and even if we tried to make a run for it, we'd just run slap into them. There's only one road in and out of here."

Canning turned to face Hesser, trying to think of the right words, but strangely enough it was Madame Chevalier who played a hand now.

"Well, Max," she called. "What's it to be? Checkmate? Or have you still got enough juice left in you to act like a man?" She moved forward, leaning on Claire's shoulder. "Not for us, Max, not even for yourself. For Gerda, for your children."

Max Hesser stared up at her wildly for a moment, then he turned to the garrison. "Grab your rifles, quick as you can. Schneider—take two men, get to the guardroom on the double, and shut the gates."

There was a sudden flurry of activity. He turned to Canning, drew himself up, and saluted formally. "General Canning, as you are the senior Allied officer here, I place myself and my men at your command. What are your orders, sir?"

Canning's nostrils flared, his eyes sparkled, tension erupting from deep inside him in a harsh laugh. "By God, that's more like it. All right, for the time being, deploy your men on the walls above the guardroom, and let's see what these bastards want." He clapped his hands together and shouted furiously, "Come on, come on, come on! Let's get this show on the road."

Eleven

THE column, Sorsa still leading the way in the front half-track, was no more than fifty yards from the castle entrance when the gates clanged shut. Sorsa immediately signaled a halt.

Ritter stood up in the field car and called, "Line of assault. Quickly, now."

The Finns moved into action instantly. The other two half-tracks took up position on either side of Sorsa; the machine-gun crews made themselves ready for action; the rest of the men jumped to the ground and fanned out.

There was silence for a moment after the engines were cut. Ritter raised his field glasses and looked to where there was movement on the wall.

"What is it? What's happening?" Strasser demanded.

"Interesting," Ritter said softly. "I see American helmets up there, together with German ones. Perhaps the Third World War has started?"

On the wall, Canning, Birr, Hesser, and Howard

grouped together in the shelter of the west guard-room turret and peered out.

"Now what?" Birr said. He carried a Schmeisser in one hand, and Canning a Walther pistol.

"We'll stir things up a bit, just to show them we mean business." Canning moved to where Schneider crouched beside the machine-gun crew, who had positioned their weapons to point out through an embrasure beside one of the castle's eighteenth-century cannon. "I want you to fire a long burst into the ground about ten yards in front of the lead half-track," he said in German.

Schneider turned in alarm and looked to Hesser. *"Herr Oberst,* what do I do?"

"As General Canning commands," Hesser said. "We are under his orders now."

Schneider patted the lead gunner on the shoulder. He was another reservist, a man named Strang, who, like most of them, had never in his life fired a shot in anger. He hesitated, sweat on his face, and Fine-baum unslung his M1, pushed him out of the way, and grabbed for the handles.

"Maybe you got qualms, uncle, but not me."

He squeezed off a long burst, swinging the bar-rel so that snow and gravel spurted in a darting line right across the front of the half-tracks.

Ritter turned, arms flung wide. "No return fire. It's a warning only."

Hoover whispered to Howard, "Did you see that? Those guys didn't even move."

Finebaum got up and turned. "They're hot stuff, Harry, believe me. I tell you, this thing could get very interesting."

Ritter jumped down from the field car, and Sorsa moved to meet him. "Do we go in?"

"No, first we talk. They'll want to talk, I think." He turned to Strasser. "You agree?"

"Yes, I think so. Hesser will already be beginning to have second thoughts. Let's give him a chance to change his mind."

"Good," Ritter said and called to Hoffer. "Over here, Erich. We'll go for a little walk, you and I."

"Zu Befehl, Sturmbannführer," Hoffer replied crisply.

"I, too, could do with some exercise, I think," Strasser said. "If you've no objection, Major Ritter?"

"As you like."

Strasser turned to Jackson. "You stay back out of the way. Borrow a parka and get the hood up. I don't want them to see you, you understand?"

Jackson frowned, but did as he was told, moving back to one of the half-tracks.

Sorsa said, "What if they open fire?"

"Then you'll have to take command, won't you?" Ritter said and started forward.

Their feet crunched in the snow. Ritter took out his case, selected a cigarette, and offered one to Strasser.

"No, thank you. I never use them. You are surprised, I think, that I felt the need for exercise?"

"Perhaps. On the other hand, I could say that it shows confidence in my judgment."

"Or a belief in my own destiny—have you considered that?"

"A point of view, I suppose. If it's of any comfort, good luck to you."

On the wall, Canning said, "By God, he's a cool one, the devil in black out there. Obviously in need of conversation."

"What do we do, General?" Hesser asked.

"Why, accommodate him, of course. You, me, and Captain Howard here. Not you, Justin. You stay up here in command, just in case some trigger-happy jerk in one of the half-tracks decides to open up." He smiled savagely, giving every appearance of thoroughly enjoying himself. "All right, gentlemen. Let's see what they have to say."

■

Ritter, Strasser, and Hoffer paused at their side of the drawbridge and waited. After a while, the small judas door in the main gate opened, and Canning stepped out, followed by Hesser and Howard. As they came forward, Ritter and his party moved also, and they met in the middle of the drawbridge.

Ritter saluted and said in excellent English, *"Sturmbannführer* Karl Ritter, Five Hundred and Second SS Heavy Tank Battalion, at present in command of this unit, and this is Herr Strasser."

"Of the Prisoner-of-War Administration in Berlin," Strasser put in.

"And I am Brigadier General Hamilton Canning of the Army of the United States, Captain Howard here, Second Rangers. *Oberstleutnant* Hesser, you may know."

It was all very polite, very formal, except for Jack Howard, whose face had turned deathly pale and who clutched the Thompson gun in his hands till the knuckles turned white. There was life in his eyes again for the first time in days, for he had recognized Ritter instantly.

"What can we do for you?" Canning said.

"*Oberstleutnant* Hesser." Strasser produced the Hitler directive and unfolded it. "I have here an order from my department in Berlin, signed, as you will see, by the *Führer* himself, ordering you to place the five prisoners remaining at Schloss Arlberg in my care."

He held out the letter. Max Hesser waved it away. "Too late, gentlemen. I surrendered my command to Captain Howard on his arrival not more than thirty minutes ago. General Canning is in command here now."

There was silence for a while. The snow falling harder than ever, a sudden, small wind churning it into a miniature blizzard that danced around them.

Strasser said, "This is a totally illegal act, Colonel Hesser. To my certain knowledge there has been no general surrender, no discussion of peace terms— cannot be while the *Führer* still lives to direct the struggle of the German people from his headquarters in Berlin."

"There has been a surrender here," Hesser said, "according to the rules of war. I have done nothing dishonorable."

"A surrender to three members of the American Army?" Strasser said. "You tell me there is nothing dishonorable in this?"

"You will speak to me, if you please," Canning said. "As this gentleman has made plain, I command here now as senior Allied officer present."

"No, General, I think not," Ritter said calmly. "Our business is with the officer in command of Schloss Arlberg, and to us he must still be *Oberstleutnant* Max Hesser, until relieved of that duty by the High Command of the German Army." He turned to Hesser. "You took an oath, Colonel Hesser, as did we all, I think. An oath as a German soldier to your *Führer* and the State."

"To a madman," Hesser said, "who has brought Germany to her knees."

"But also to the State, to your country," Ritter said. "You and I are soldiers, Hesser, like General Canning here and Captain Howard. No difference. We play the game on our side, they on theirs. We can't hope to change the rules in the middle, to suit our personal convenience. Not any of us. Is that not so, General?"

It was Howard who answered him. "Is that how you see it? A game? Nothing more?"

"Perhaps," Ritter said. "The greatest game of all, where the stakes are a country and its people, and if a man can't stand by his own, he is less than nothing."

He turned back to Hesser, waiting. Hesser said, "It is my information that a direct order has gone to the SS from the *Führer* himself, authorizing the execution of all prominent prisoners. I consider this order monstrous. A direct violation of the Geneva Convention and a crime against humanity. I will not be a party to it, and neither will the men of this garrison."

Strasser said, "This is, of course, total nonsense. A tissue of lies. As the representative for this area of the Prisoner-of-War Administration, I can give you my word on this absolutely."

"Then why do you want us?" Canning asked. "Tell me that."

"All prominent prisoners are being brought together in one center, for their own protection."

"As hostages against the evil day?"

"A sensible precaution only, *Herr General*, I assure you."

"Who for—you or us?"

There was another brief silence. The snow danced around them. Hesser said slowly, "I stand by what I have done. General Canning is in command here now."

"Which just about wraps it up," Canning said. "I can't see that we have anything further to discuss. If you'll take the advice of an old hand, Major, I'd say you and your men had better get the hell out of here while you still can. Let's go, gentlemen."

He turned and walked briskly back toward the gate, Hesser at his side. Howard stayed there, holding the Thompson gun across his chest. Hoffer never took his eyes off him, his hand close to the butt of the holstered Walther at his belt. Ritter ignored him as he lit a cigarette calmly and examined the gate, the walls above.

"It would seem they mean business," Strasser said.

Ritter nodded. "So it would appear." He turned on his heel.

Howard said, "Major Karl Ritter, of the Five Hundred and Second SS Heavy Tank Battalion, you said?"

Ritter turned slowly. "That is correct."

"We've met before."

"Have we?"

"Last Wednesday morning. That little affair on the way to Innsbruck, when you took out an entire

British armored column. I was one of the survivors, along with my two friends up there on the wall."

"Congratulations," Ritter said calmly. "Your luck is good."

"You can tell your man there to take his hand off the butt of that Walther. I'm not going to kill you —yet. I mean, that wouldn't be playing this game of yours according to the rules—now would it?"

"Your choice, my friend."

"You'll be coming in?" Howard said. "Or you'll try to?"

"Yes, I think so."

"I'll be looking for you."

Canning called from the gate, "Captain Howard." Howard turned and ran back through the snow.

"He means it, that one," Strasser said. "For the past five minutes I've had a finger on the trigger, imagining I might have to put another hole through the pocket of my coat. I wonder if he knew."

"Oh, yes," Ritter said, "he knew." And he turned and led the way back to the half-tracks.

■

"What in hell kept you?" Canning demanded as Howard slipped inside and the gate closed. "Go on —up on the wall—and tell Colonel Birr I'll join you in a couple of minutes."

Howard mounted the stone steps, and Canning turned to Hesser. "As I recall, you raised the draw-bridge six or seven months back?"

"That's right, *Herr General*. To see if it was work-ing."

"Then let's see if the damn thing still does."

Hesser nodded to Schneider, who immediately opened the door at the foot of the tower on the left-hand side of the gate and led the way in. He switched on the light, disclosing a massive steel drum ten feet across, chains wrapped around it, lifting up into the gloom. There were great spoked wheels on either side.

"Let's get it done." Canning moved to one of the wheels, Schneider ran to the other, and together they started to turn.

■

Howard crouched beside the cannon, peering out through the embrasure, watching Ritter and his two companions walk back toward the Finns. Hoover and Finebaum dropped down beside him.

"What was going on out there, Captain?" the sergeant asked. "Between you and the Kraut officer?"

"It was him," Howard said. "The guy who took the column out Wednesday. His name's Ritter— Karl Ritter."

"The guy in the Tiger who flattened the jeep?" Finebaum demanded. "Are you saying that's him out there?" He raised the M1 and leaned across the cannon. "Jesus, maybe I can still get him."

Howard pulled him down. "Not now," he said. "And anyway, he's mine."

■

"Attack now!" Strasser said. "The only way. Use the front half-track as a battering ram. Straight in while they're still wondering what our next move will be."

"There are twenty armed men on that wall. At least one heavy machine gun mounted beside the old cannon between the turrets. I had a good look at that while I was lighting my cigarette. Rate of fire not far short of a thousand rounds a minute. You served in the First World War, did you not, Herr Strasser? I should have thought you might have remembered what happens to those who attempt frontal attacks on heavy machine guns skillfully positioned."

"And in any case, the argument now becomes a wholly academic one." Sorsa pointed, and Strasser and Ritter turned in time to see the end of the drawbridge lift above the moat.

They watched as it continued its steady progress and finally came to a halt. Strasser said, "So, a situation which can only be described as medieval. Impossible for us to get in . . ."

"And equally impossible for them to get out," Ritter said. "Which is, after all, the important thing. There is one thing which worries me, however."

"What's that?" Strasser asked.

"The question of radio communication with the outside world. A distress call at random might well be picked up by some Allied unit or other in the vicinity."

"No danger of that," Strasser said. "They've had problems in the communications room at Schloss Arlberg for several days now. Believe me, Major, there is no way in which they can communicate with the outside world."

"Another example of your flair for organization, I presume," Ritter said. "Anyway, that problem being solved, we will now leave, I think."

"You mean that literally, or do you have a plan?"

"The fact of our going may comfort the general and his friends, however temporarily. The question of planning must wait until I've handled the immediate situation." He nodded to Sorsa. "Move out and stop the column around the first bend out of sight of the castle."

"Zu Befehl, Sturmbannführer."

■

From the walls, Canning and the others watched them go. "What do you think, Hamilton?" Birr asked.

"I'm not sure," Canning said. "Strasser, the guy who said he was from the Prisoner-of-War Administration, intrigues me. I'm sure I've seen the bastard before somewhere."

"And the other one—Ritter?"

"The kind who never lets go. Did you see his medals, for Christ's sake?"

"He has quite a reputation, this man," Hesser said. "Something of a legend. A great tank destroyer on the Eastern Front. They made much of him in the magazines last year."

"And Strasser—you've never seen him before?"

"No, never."

Canning nodded. "Right. This is what we do. I want two lookouts in the top of the north tower, linked to here by field telephone. From up there they should be able to see outside the walls for the entire circuit. Any kind of movement must be reported instantly. I want the rest of the garrison split into three fire parties of six or seven each, ready to rush to any point on the wall as directed by the lookouts." He turned to Howard. "You take charge of that operation with Hoover. Finebaum can accompany me as my runner."

"I'm with you, General," Finebaum said. "We'll make a hell of a team, believe me—no disrespect intended, General."

"Which remains to be seen." Canning turned to Hesser. "And now I want to see the armory. Everything you've got here."

■

Beyond the first bend in the road, the column had halted. Ritter said to Sorsa, "I'm returning to the village now. I'll take Sergeant Major Gestrin and four men with me. They can use the other field car. You stay here with the half-tracks. I want fifteen or twenty men on skis circling those walls without pause. Keep to the woods, but make sure they can be seen. Field-telephone communication at all times."

"And then what?" Sorsa asked.

"I'll let you know," Ritter said.

■

Paul Gaillard and Meyer were at the landing window as the two field cars drove into the square and pulled up outside the Golden Eagle. Gestrin and his men carried their skis in their car and had a field radio.

Gaillard said, "Better go down and find out what they want. I'll hide in the closet in the dressing room if I hear anyone coming."

Meyer went downstairs as the front door opened, and Ritter led the way into the bar. Strasser and Jackson followed, then Hoffer carrying Strasser's suitcase containing the radio.

Strasser said to Meyer, "You have a room I can use privately?"

Meyer, with little choice in the matter, said, "Through here, *mein Herr*. My office."

"Excellent." Strasser turned to Jackson. "Tell me. The American pilot's uniform—they managed to procure one for you?"

"It's in the Dakota," Jackson told him.

"Good. I want you to run up there now in one of the field cars and get it. Take a couple of Gestrin's men with you. And I want you back here as soon as possible." Jackson hesitated, a look of puzzlement on his face, and Strasser said, "No questions—just do it."

Jackson turned and went out. Strasser picked up his case. "And now," he said to Ritter, "if you will excuse me, I have a little communicating to do," and he nodded to Meyer and followed him out.

Hoffer went behind the bar. "A drink, *Sturmbannführer?*"

"Why not?" Ritter said. "Brandy, I think," and then he gave a small exclamation and crossed the room quickly.

On the opposite wall hung a large, framed, eighteenth-century print of Schloss Arlberg, a perfect plan of the entire castle—every walk, every strongpoint, all clearly defined.

∎

The armory contained few surprises. Perhaps a dozen extra Schmeissers, twenty spare rifles, a couple of boxes of grenades, some plastic explosive. No heavy stuff at all.

"Plenty of ammunition, that's one good thing," Canning said. He hefted a couple of Walther service pistols and said to the others, "All right, let's go and see the ladies."

They found Madame Chevalier warming herself in front of the log fire in the upper dining hall in the north tower. Canning said, "Where's Claire?"

"She went to her room. She was feeling the cold very badly. We stood outside too long."

Canning held up the Walther. "You know how to use one of those things?"

"I play a different instrument, as you well know."

"You'd better learn this one fast, believe me." He turned to Finebaum. "See if you can get the finer points across to Madame Chevalier in a fast five minutes, soldier."

"Anything you say, General."

Madame Chevalier looked him over, horror on her face, and Finebaum tried his most ingratiating smile. "They tell me you play piano, lady. You know 'GI Jive'?"

Madame Chevalier closed her eyes momentarily, then opened them again. "If you could show me how the pistol works now," she said.

∎

When Canning tried the handle on Claire's door, it was locked. He knocked and called her name. It was two or three minutes before the bolt was drawn back and she peered out at him. Her eyes seemed very large, the face pale.

"I'm sorry, Hamilton. Come in," she said.

He walked past her into the bedroom. "You don't look too good."

"As a matter of fact, I've just been thoroughly sick. I panicked down there when I heard that the SS had arrived."

Canning remembered how her husband had died.

"It made you think of Etienne and what happened to him?"

When she looked up at him, her face was very pale. "No, it made me think of myself, Hamilton. You see, I'm a total physical coward and the very thought of those devils . . ."

He placed a finger on her lips and took the Walther from his pocket. "I've brought you a life preserver. You know how to use it, I believe."

She took it from him, holding it in both hands. "On myself," she said. "Before I allow them to take me from this place."

"Hush." Canning kissed her gently. "Nobody's taking you anywhere, believe me. Now come down and join the others."

■

Ritter had taken the print down from the wall and was examining it closely when Strasser entered.

"A useful find," Ritter told him. "A plan of Schloss Arlberg."

"Never mind that now," Strasser said. "I've made an even more interesting discovery. Hoffer, bring friend Meyer in here."

"What is it?" Ritter inquired.

"It appears that a certain Dr. Paul Gaillard is actually on the premises. Meyer's boy broke a leg this morning."

"You're sure of this?"

"Oh, yes, my informant is completely reliable."

Ritter frowned. "You've been on the radio. Where to? The castle? You mean you've actually got an agent planted up there? I really must congratulate you, *Reichsleiter*. My apologies—Herr Strasser.

That really is taking organization to the outer limits."

"I do like efficiency, you see, Major. A fatal flaw, if you like, all my life."

The door opened, and Hoffer ushered Meyer into the room. Strasser turned to him and smiled. "So, Herr Meyer, it would appear you have not been strictly honest with us."

■

A few moments later, Paul Gaillard, bending over the still-unconscious boy, heard footsteps on the stairs. They approached the door confidently. He hesitated, then withdrew into the dressing room and stepped into the closet.

There was a long period of silence—or so it seemed—a slight creaking, and then, quite unexpectedly, the closet door opened and light flooded in.

Ritter was standing there. He didn't bother to draw his pistol. Simply smiled and said, "Dr. Gaillard, I believe? Your patient seems to be reviving."

Gaillard hesitated, then brushed past him and went into the other room, where he found Strasser and Meyer bending over the boy, who was moaning feverishly.

Meyer turned in appeal to Ritter, his concern wholly for his son now. "When you first arrived, *Sturmbannführer*, we didn't know what to think, the doctor and I. And there was the boy to consider."

"Yes, I can see that," Ritter said. "How bad is he?"

"Not good," Gaillard said. "A badly broken leg, high fever. He needs constant attention, that's why I stayed. But I can't have you in here. You'll have to go."

Ritter glanced at Strasser, who nodded slightly. Gaillard was ignoring them, sponging the boy's forehead. "So you didn't manage to get into the castle, it would seem."

"We will, Doctor, we will," Ritter said. "I'll have to put a sentry in here, of course, but we'll leave you for now."

He nodded to Meyer, who went out. Gaillard said, "All right, if you must, I suppose." He glanced up, saw Strasser for the first time. His mouth opened wide; there was a look of astonishment on his face. "Good God, I know you."

"I don't think so," Strasser said. "My name is Strasser, of the Prisoner-of-War Administration in Berlin, as the major here will confirm."

Gaillard turned to Ritter, who smiled. "We'll leave you to your patient, Doctor." And he ushered Strasser outside and closed the door.

"Bormann," Gaillard whispered. "When was it we were introduced? Munich, 1935? *Reichsleiter* Martin Bormann. I'd stake my life on it."

•

And at the same moment, in the bunker in Berlin, Martin Bormann and General Wilhelm Burgdorf, Hitler's army adjutant, waited in the central passage outside the *Führer*'s personal suite. Since he was the man who had delivered the poison with which Field Marshal Erwin Rommel had been obliged to kill himself after the July 20 plot, it might be thought that Burgdorf was used to such situations, but just now he looked terrified and was sweating profusely.

At three-thirty there was a pistol shot. Martin Bormann rushed into the *Führer*'s suite, followed by Hitler's valet, Heinz Linge, and Colonel Otto

Günsche, his SS adjutant. The room reeked of the cyanide which Eva Hitler had used to take her life. The *Führer* sprawled beside her, his face shattered.

Dr. Stumpfegger, the *Führer*'s personal doctor, and Linge, the valet, carried his body up to the Chancellery garden, wrapped in a gray blanket. Martin Bormann came next, carrying Eva Hitler.

A curious incident then took place, for the *Führer*'s chauffeur, Erich Kempka, was reminded of the fact that, in life, Bormann had been Eva Hitler's greatest enemy. He stepped forward and took her body from the *Reichsleiter*, for it did not seem right to him to leave her in his charge.

The bodies were placed in a shallow pit, and fifty gallons of gasoline were poured over them and set on fire. As the flames cascaded into the sky, those present stood at attention, arms extended in a final party salute.

The Russians, at that point in time, were perhaps a hundred and fifty yards away from the bunker.

Twelve

RITTER sat at the desk in Meyer's office, going over the print of the ground plan of Schloss Arlberg yet again. Hoffer stood by the door, waiting quietly. Ritter put down his pencil and sat back.

Hoffer said, "Can it be done?"

"I don't see why not," Ritter said. "All it requires is good discipline and a little nerve, and I think our Finns aren't noticeably lacking in either."

The door opened, and Strasser entered. "Jackson is back."

"Ah, yes," Ritter said. "You sent him to Arnheim. May one ask why?"

"First tell me of your plan of attack."

"Very well." Ritter looked down at the print of the castle again. "I will wait until dark. In fact, well after. Say, midnight, when the defenders will already have been on the alert for a considerable period of time, which means they will be tired. No use moving in with the half-tracks because we alert them the instant we start the engines."

"So?"

"A force of, say, twenty men will approach the edge of the moat under cover of darkness. Two of them will cross the moat, climb the drawbridge, and set a couple of demolition charges. Very easy to make up from what we've got, and it won't need a particularly powerful charge to blow these chains. Another charge against the gate will be timed to explode at the same instant."

"I see," Strasser said. "The drawbridge falls, the gate opens, and your shock troops rush across to take possession."

"Backed up by the half-tracks, which start moving the instant they hear the explosion. What do you think?"

"Very good," Strasser said.

"Any weak points?"

"Only one. As it happens, there's an outside floodlight at the entrance. They turned it on about fifteen minutes ago. I'm sure Sorsa will confirm that if you raise him on the field telephone."

Ritter leaned back. "You have an excellent and very immediate source of information."

"So it would appear," Strasser said, but made no effort to enlighten him. "Of course, you could have a sniper shoot out this floodlight."

"And immediately alert them to the fact that we were up to something."

"An excellent plan, however, and it could still work."

"How?"

"If we had someone able to do exactly the same thing from the inside." Strasser walked to the door and opened it. "All right," he said.

Earl Jackson entered the room, wearing a flying

jacket with a sheepskin collar over the uniform of a captain in the United States Army Air Corps.

■

As Colonel Hesser and Schneider mounted the steps to the east wall, the wind dashed frozen sleet in their faces. It was bitterly cold, and the sergeant major adjusted his grip on Magda's leash.

"A bitch of a night," Hesser said. "Takes me back to 1942 and the Winter War. The kind of cold that eats into the brain."

He shuddered, remembering, and Schneider said, "I wouldn't think they'd bother us on a night like this."

"Isn't that what we used to say about the Russians?" Hesser said. "Until we learned better? And so, I presume, did Ritter. He's spent enough time on the Eastern Front, God knows."

The sentries were spread woefully thin—not that he could do much about that. There was one at the east watchtower. Hesser had a word with him, then leaned out of an embrasure in the wall and looked back toward the pool of light at the gate.

"I wonder how long it will be before one of them can't resist shooting that out? I almost wish they would. An end to this damned uncertainty."

"You think they'll come, then, *Herr Oberst?*" Schneider asked.

"You saw Ritter yourself, didn't you? Did he look like the kind of man to just run away? And what about those ski patrols circling through the forest right up until dark. No, he's there, all right. And when he's ready, you'll know about it. Anyway, let's check the water gate."

They went down the watchtower steps. There was

a small, damp tunnel blocked by a heavy iron grille. A corporal called Wagner stood guard there, a veteran of the Eastern Front, his left arm partially wasted away from bad shrapnel wounds. Just now, he was leaning against the gate, looking out, his Schmeisser ready in his right hand.

"Everything is in order here?" Hesser demanded.

"I'm not sure, *Herr Oberst*. I thought I heard something."

They stood, listening. Snow drifted through the grille, and Hesser said, "Only the wind."

And then Magda whined, straining forward on the leash. "No, *Herr Oberst*," Schneider said. "He's right. Something moves."

He and Hesser drew their pistols. There was a distinct slithering sound on the other side of the moat, snow falling into the water, and then a hoarse whisper in English. "Is there anyone there? Don't shoot. I'm an American officer."

Someone entered the water. Hesser said to Schneider, "Switch on your flashlight, a second only, then down on the ground."

There was a pause, then Schneider's flashlight picked Earl Jackson out of the darkness instantly. He was in the middle of the moat, swimming strongly, only his head and the sheepskin collar of his flying jacket showing above the water.

"Kamerad!" he called, gasping for breath. "American officer. I'm looking for General Hamilton Canning."

■

It was Finebaum, crouched in the shadow of the wall above the main gate, who spotted the momentary spot of light on his left. Below him, Howard and

Hoover crouched against the wall, smoking cigarettes.

"Hey, Captain, there was a light down there, below the east watchtower, in the moat."

They were on their feet instantly. "You're certain?" Howard leaned out of the embrasure. "I can't see a thing."

"There was a light. Just for a minute."

"Okay, let's move it," Howard said and started along the wall.

■

When they entered the water gate tunnel, Jackson was on the other side from Hesser and his men, clutching the grille, knee-deep in water. "Let me in, for Christ's sake. I've got to see General Canning."

"What is it?" Howard demanded. "What's going on?"

Hesser switched on the flashlight without a word. Jackson blinked in the sudden light. He was soaked to the skin, water dripping from his uniform, teeth chattering. He tried to peer into the darkness at Howard.

"You an American, buddy? For Christ's sake, make these crazy bastards let me in. Another five minutes of this, and I'll die of exposure."

"Hey, he's right, Captain," Finebaum said. "He don't look too good."

"Who are you?" Howard demanded.

"Harry Bannerman's the name. Crash-landed this morning about ten miles from here in a P-47. Got picked up by an SS unit. They had me down in the village here until an hour ago. In an inn called the Golden Eagle."

"How did you get away?"

"The landlord helped me—a guy called Meyer. There was another prisoner there. He put him up to it. A Frenchman named Gaillard. He told me to get up here fast and see General Canning. I've got information about when the Krauts intend to hit this place." He rattled the grille ineffectually, his voice breaking. "Let me in, for Christ's sake—if you don't want to die, that is."

"Okay," Howard said to Hesser. "Open the gate and drag him in—but fast. And you, Finebaum, I make personally responsible for blowing his backbone in half if he makes a wrong move."

In the darkness among the trees on the far side of the moat, Strasser, Ritter, and Hoffer listened to the clang of the grille shutting.

"So he's in," Ritter said. "Let's hope they buy his story."

"I don't see why not," Strasser said. "Jackson's strength, as I said before, lies in the fact that he's a genuine American, not the ersatz variety that let Skorzeny down so badly in the Ardennes."

"So now we wait," Ritter said.

"Until it's time for my part in this rather interesting drama." Strasser smiled through the darkness. "You know, I'm really rather looking forward to it."

General Canning, Birr, Madame Chevalier, and Claire were having a late supper of sandwiches and coffee when Hesser and Howard entered, followed by Jackson, an army blanket draped around his shoulders. Finebaum was right behind him, the muzzle of his M1 no more than an inch away from Jackson's backbone.

"What have we here?" Canning demanded, rising to his feet.

"Swam across the moat to the water gate, General," Howard said. "Claims to be an Army Air Corps officer. No papers, no identification on him whatsoever. Not even his dog tags."

"They took them off me," Jackson said. "Those damned SS stripped me of everything. I mean, how many times do I have to tell you?"

"What outfit?" Canning demanded.

"Five Hundred and Tenth Squadron, Four Hundred and Fifth Group, sir. Operating out of what was a *Luftwaffe* base at Hellenbach until we took it four days ago."

"What's your story?"

"My squadron was ordered to hit a panzer column on the other side of Salzburg from here. This morning it was, General. We dropped our bombs dead on target—no problem, there being no *Luftwaffe* to speak of in this area anymore. Then, on the way back, my battery went dead and I had to crash-land."

"What was your aircraft?"

"P-47 Thunderbolt, sir. I made it down in one piece in a clearing in the forest, then struck out for the main road. It's a pretty fluid situation in this area, General. There are plenty of our people around. It's just a question of knowing where."

"And you say you were picked up by an SS unit?"

"That's right, sir. Mostly Finns, but there was a German officer in charge. A man called Ritter."

"And they've been holding you all day?"

"That's right, sir, at an inn called the Golden Eagle in Arlberg." There was a slight pause. He gazed around him wildly. "Say, what goes on here? What do you people think I am—a Kraut or something?"

"Well, I'll tell you, Captain," Finebaum put in, "because it's really funny you should say that. When we were in the Ardennes in 'forty-four—and it was snowing then, too, I might add—there was guys popping up all over the place, just like you, GI uniform, everything. Saying they'd lost their units, asking the way to Malmédy. Stuff like that. An interesting thing—they was all Krautheads."

"Any chance of you shutting this man up?" Canning inquired coldly.

Howard said, "Button it, Finebaum."

Canning said to Jackson, "We're in a hell of a position in here, Bannerman. We can't afford to take anything on trust—you understand?"

"He says he's met Dr. Gaillard, sir," Howard put in.

"Sure I've seen him."

"How is he?"

"He's looking after a sick kid down there at the inn. Son of the landlord, a guy named Meyer."

"And the SS have him?" Canning asked.

"Oh, yes. Major Ritter, the officer in command, lets him see to the kid regularly, but they had us locked up together for quite a while. Meyer brought our food, and Gaillard saw him quite a lot each time he went to see to the kid. He's in a pretty bad way."

"All right, how did you escape?"

"Well, it was mostly Meyer who made that possible. He overheard Ritter and some guy called

Strasser—a civilian he had with him—discussing their plans for an attack just before dawn. They're going to put some guys across the moat with explosives to blow down your drawbridge. When Gaillard heard that, he told me I'd have to get away somehow and come and warn you people."

"Which you seem to have managed without too much trouble," Birr said.

"That was Meyer again. He tipped me off he'd leave the back door near the kitchen unlocked. I asked to go to the john, gave the Finn who was escorting me a shove at the right moment, got the door open, and ran like hell."

There was a long and heavy silence now, in which everyone seemed to be looking at him. Jackson said, "General, I'm Captain Harry Bannerman of the United States Army Air Corps and when that drawbridge of yours is blown to hell and gone just before dawn tomorrow, you'll know I was telling the truth. Just now, I'd settle for a cup of coffee, dry clothes, and somewhere to lay my head."

Canning smiled suddenly and held out his hand. "I'll tell you something, son. All of a sudden I've decided to believe you." He turned to Hesser. "Can you find him some dry clothes?"

"Certainly," Hesser said, "if the captain doesn't mind a German uniform. This way, if you please."

Jackson started to follow him, paused, and turned. "Hey, there's just one thing, General. Something kind of funny. It doesn't mean a damn thing to me. Maybe it does to you."

"What's that?" Canning asked him.

225

"This guy Strasser—the civilian I told you about?"

"Well?"

"It's just that he seems to swing a lot of weight. I mean, a couple of times there he acted as if he was in charge, and I heard Ritter call him *'Reichsleiter.'* That ring any bells with you?"

Hesser turned pale. "Bormann?" he whispered.

"That's it," Canning said excitedly. "I knew I'd seen that ugly face somewhere before. Martin Bormann, secretary to Hitler himself. I saw him just once on the stand at the Berlin Olympic Games in 'thirty-six." He turned on Hesser. "You didn't recognize him?"

"I've never laid eyes on Bormann in my life," Hesser said. "He's a man of the shadows—always has been."

"Now we know why they wanted us so urgently," Canning said. "Hostages to bargain with in the hope he might save his rotten neck." He rubbed his hands together excitedly. "Good work, Bannerman. You've really earned your keep with that one. Take him away now, Max, and get some dry clothes on him."

Hesser and Jackson went out. Madame Chevalier said, "What does this mean, General? I've heard of this man Bormann. A member of the inner circle, isn't that so?"

"Not a thing to worry about, I assure you," Canning said. "Now have some more coffee, sit down and take it easy, and I'll be back in a moment."

He went out with Howard and Finebaum, closed the door behind him, and paused in the shadows at the head of the stairs.

"What do you think, sir?" Howard asked.

Canning looked down at Finebaum. "Is he any good?"

"A sackful of medals. You see, he seems to have a talent for killing people, General."

"Okay, soldier," Canning said. "You watch Bannerman like a hawk. Not too close, but be around just in case."

"I'm your man, General." Finebaum went down the stairs into the shadows.

"You don't believe Bannerman, sir?" Howard asked.

"I had a Scottish grandmother, Captain, from the Isle of Skye, who used to say she had an instinct for things. No proof because there was no need. She just knew. I sometimes think some of it rubbed off on me. Now get back to that gate. I'll join you there as soon as I can."

He opened the door and went back into the dining hall.

■

When Howard climbed up to the ramparts above the gate, it was snowing hard—large flakes drifting down through the yellow glare of the spotlight spiraling in the slight wind. Hoover was up there with three Germans. Like them, the American was wearing a *Wehrmacht* winter-issue parka.

"Decided to change sides, I see," Howard said. "Kind of late in the war, isn't it?"

"The romantic in me," Hoover said. "My great-grandfather was in the Army of the Confederacy. We Hoovers just take to losing naturally, I guess. What about Bannerman?"

"He tells a convincing story. Says the opposition

are going to hit us just before dawn. Slip a couple of guys across the moat with explosives and come running."

He explained the rest of it, and when he was finished Hoover said, "That last part doesn't make too much sense to me. I never even heard of this guy Bormann. Did you?"

"Somewhere or other," Howard said. "But I never thought he was particularly important. I mean not like Ribbentrop or Goebbels or one of those guys. Sending someone like him sure lays it on the line how much they want to get their hands on these people as hostages."

"Where's Finebaum?"

"Somewhere back there in the north tower, keeping an eye on Bannerman. General Canning's orders."

One of the sentries said quickly in German, "Something moves—out there."

He grabbed Howard's arm and pointed. A moment later, Ritter, Hoffer, and Strasser moved out of the darkness into the circle of light.

"Hello, the wall," Ritter called. "Is General Canning there?"

Howard stayed back in the shadows. "What do you want?"

"Herr Strasser would like a word with General Canning. He has a proposition to put to him."

"Tell me," Howard called.

Ritter shrugged. "If that is your attitude, then I can see we are wasting your time. Thank you and good night."

They turned to go, and Hoover whispered, "Sir, this could be important."

"Okay, Harry, okay." Howard leaned forward into the light. "Hold it. I'll see what he says."

A moment later, he was speaking to Canning on the field telephone. "It could be a trap, sir."

"I don't think so," Canning said. "They must know they'd be cut down in half a second at the first sign of trouble, and I don't think they'd make that kind of sacrifice—not if Strasser is who Jackson says he is. No, drop the drawbridge and let them in. Send Strasser up here to me. Keep Ritter with you."

A few moments later, the drawbridge started to descend with a rattle of chains. Ritter said softly, "So, the fish bite. Are you always so correct in your prophecies?"

"Only where matters of importance are concerned," Strasser said, and as the drawbridge thudded down into place, they walked across together, Hoffer following.

The judas door opened, and Howard peered through briefly. He stepped back, and they moved inside. As he closed the gate and barred it, Howard said to Hoover, "Take Herr Strasser up to the north tower. General Canning is waiting. You, Major," he continued to Ritter, "will have to put up with my company until he gets back, I'm afraid."

Strasser moved off without a word, following Hoover. Hoffer stood, back to the gate, stony-faced. Ritter took out his case, selected a cigarette, then offered one to Howard.

"I must warn you they're Russian—an acquired taste."

Howard took one and leaned back against the

wall, the butt of his Thompson braced against his hip. "So here we are again," he said.

■

When Hoover knocked on the door and led the way into the upper dining hall, only Canning and Justin Birr stood by the fire. Strasser paused nonchalantly in the center of the room, hands in the pockets of his leather coat, slouch hat slanted over one ear.

"Good evening, gentlemen."

Canning nodded to Hoover. "You can wait outside, Sergeant. I'll call you if I need you."

The door closed. Strasser crossed to the fireplace and spread his hands to the blaze. "Nothing like a log fire to take the chill off. It's cold out there tonight. The kind that eats into your bones like acid."

Canning glanced at Birr and nodded. Birr crossed to the sideboard, poured a generous measure of brandy into a glass, and returned.

"Just to show how humanitarian we are. Now what the hell do you want, Bormann?"

Strasser paused in the act of drinking some of the brandy. "Strasser, General. The name is Strasser."

"Strange," Canning said. "You look exactly like the man I saw in Berlin in 1936 standing on the rostrum behind Adolf Hitler at the Olympic Games. *Reichsleiter* Martin Bormann."

"You flatter me, General. I am, I assure you, a relatively unimportant official of the Department of Prisoner-of-War Administration."

"I have difficulty in imagining you as relatively unimportant. But go on."

"Let us consider your situation here. There are twenty-four of you in this garrison, twenty-six if we count the ladies. Most of your men are reservists who have never fought, or cripples who can barely lift a rifle."

"So?"

"We, on the other hand, have almost forty battle-hardened shock troops to call upon. Men of the *Waffen*-SS, and whatever you may think, General, however much you disapprove, that means the best in the world."

"Get on with it," Justin Birr said. "Just what are you trying to prove?"

"That if we decide to move against you, the consequences will be disastrous—for you."

"A matter of opinion," Canning said. "But accepting that what you say is true, what do you suggest we do about it. I mean, that is why you're here, isn't it? To offer us some kind of alternative solution? I mean, before you try slipping a couple of men across the moat just before dawn to blow the drawbridge chains?"

"My goodness, somebody has been busy," Strasser said. "All right, General, it's simple. We have Dr. Gaillard, whom we found at the Golden Eagle in Arlberg attending to the landlord's sick son. Sad, how good deeds can so often prove our undoing. However, if you and Colonel Birr will hand yourselves over, we'll be content with that and let the ladies go free."

"Not a chance," Canning said.

Strasser turned to Birr. "You agree?"

"I'm afraid so, old boy. You see, we don't really trust you—that's the truth of it. Terribly sorry, but there it is."

"And the ladies?" Strasser said. "They have no say in this?"

Canning hesitated, then went and opened the door. He spoke briefly to Hoover, then returned. "They'll be here directly."

He and Birr lit cigarettes. Strasser turned to survey the room and immediately saw the great silver bowl of scarlet winter roses on the piano.

"Ah, my favorite flowers." He was genuinely delighted and crossed the room to admire them. "Winter roses. Like life in the midst of death—they fill the heart with gladness."

The door opened, and as he turned, Claire de Beauville, Madame Chevalier, and Earl Jackson entered the room. Strasser smiled at the American. "We missed you at supper."

"Sorry I couldn't stay."

Strasser turned to Canning. "An explanation of one or two things which were puzzling me. I was beginning to think you were a wonder-worker. It's nice to know you're just a man like the rest of us."

"Okay," Canning said. "I've had just about enough for one night. You wanted a word with the ladies. Well, they're here, so make the most of it."

"I can't imagine what you could possibly have to say to me that I would be interested in hearing, *monsieur*," Madame Chevalier said. "Thankfully, I can use the time to some advantage."

She sat down at the piano and started to play a Debussy nocturne. Strasser, not in the least put out, said, "I have offered you ladies your freedom— guaranteed it—on condition that the general and Colonel Birr come quietly and with no fuss."

Madame Chevalier ignored him, and Claire

simply walked across to the bowl of roses and buried her face in them.

Strasser said, "I should have known. Above all flowers, they need delicate hands and infinite patience in their rearing. Your work, *madame?*"

"Yes," she said. "So, as you can see, I am fully occupied and cannot leave at the present time."

Canning moved in. "You heard the lady."

Strasser selected one of the blooms, snapped the stem, and placed it in his buttonhole. "Ah, well, it was worth the trip. You like winter roses, General?"

"I like whatever Madame de Beauville cultivates."

"Good," Strasser said. "I'll remember that at your funeral. One gets so bored with lilies. A single scarlet winter rose should look very good. And now, I think, I will bid you good night. There is obviously nothing more for me here."

He walked to the door. Hoover glanced at Canning, who nodded. The sergeant led the way out.

There was a heavy silence, and Madame Chevalier stopped playing. "I must be getting old. Suddenly I feel cold—very, very cold."

■

Strasser stepped through the judas door, followed by Hoffer. As Ritter moved out, Howard said softly, "I'll be seeing you."

"When?" Ritter said. "Under the elms at dawn? Six paces each way, turn and fire? You take it all too seriously, Captain."

He followed the others across. As they stepped onto the bank, the drawbridge lifted behind them.

"Are you satisfied?" Ritter asked Strasser softly.

"Oh, yes, I think so. Jackson should be well enough entrenched now. The rest is up to him."

He started to whistle cheerfully.

■

It was just after midnight, and in Berlin, at his office in the bunker, Bormann worked steadily, the scratching of his pen the only sound, the noise of the Russian shelling muted, faraway. There was a light tap on the door. It opened, and Goebbels entered. He looked pale and haggard, the skin drawn tightly over his face. A dead man walking.

Bormann put down his pen. "How goes it?"

Goebbels passed a flimsy across the desk. "That's the radiogram I've just dispatched to Plön."

> GRAND ADMIRAL DONITZ *(Personal and Secret)*
> *To be handled only by an officer.*
> *Führer died yesterday, 1530 hours. In his will, dated April 29, he appoints you as president of the Reich, Goebbels as Reich chancellor, Bormann as party minister. . . .*

There was more, but Bormann didn't bother to read it. "Paper, Joseph. Just so much paper."

"Perhaps," Goebbels said, "but we must preserve the formalities, even at this desperate stage."

"Why?"

"For posterity, if nothing else. For those who will come after us."

"Nobody comes after us. Not here—not in Germany for many years to come. Our destiny lies elsewhere, for the time being."

"For you, perhaps, but not for me," Goebbels said, his voice flat, toneless.

"I see," Bormann said. "You intend to emulate the *Führer*?"

"No shame in ending a life which will have no further value to me if I cannot stand at his side. I have no intention of spending the rest of my life running around the world like some eternal refugee. Preparations are already in hand. The children will be given cyanide capsules."

"What, all six of them?" Bormann actually smiled. "Thorough and painstaking to the end, I see. And you and Magda?"

"I have already detailed an SS orderly to shoot us when the moment comes."

Bormann shrugged. "Then I can only wish you better luck in the hereafter than you've had here."

"And you?" Goebbels said.

"Oh, I'll try my luck in the outside world, I think. We should be all right here for the rest of today. I'll make a run for it tonight with Axmann, Stumpfegger, and one or two more. We intend to try the underground railway tunnel. That should get us to Friedrichstrasse Station all right. Mohnke is still holding out there with a battle group of three thousand. SS, sailors, *Volkssturm,* and a whole batch of Hitler Youth. They seem to be holding their own."

"And then?"

"With their help we'll try to cross the Weiden-dammer Bridge over the Spree. Once on the other side, we should stand an excellent chance. Not many Russians in the northwestern suburbs yet."

"I can only wish you luck." Suddenly Goebbels sounded very tired indeed. He turned to the door, started to open it, and paused. "What comes afterward—if you get away?"

"Oh, I'll make out."

"Come to think of it, you always did, didn't you?"

Goebbels went out, closing the door. Bormann sat there, thinking about what he had said. *I have no intention of spending my life running around the world like some eternal refugee.* He shrugged, picked up his pen, and resumed his writing.

■

Jackson lay on the bed, waiting in the dark in the room they'd given him. He glanced at the luminous dial of his watch. It was twenty past midnight—ten minutes to go. He lit a cigarette and drew on it nervously. Not that he was afraid—simply keyed up. A brilliant suggestion of Strasser's, to tell them he was the *Reichsleiter*. Coupled with Strasser's personal appearance, it had effectively clouded the entire issue. He was certain they'd accepted him completely now.

He checked his watch again. Time to go. He got up and padded to the door, and when he opened it, the passageway was deserted, a place of shadows partially illuminated by a single small bulb at the far end. He caught a brief glimpse of himself in a full-length gilt mirror. He was wearing Hesser's best uniform, and it fitted rather well. He moved on, past one oil painting after another—blank, eighteenth-century faces staring down at him. He turned the stairs at the end, paused by the white door on the small landing, and knocked.

The door opened slightly and instantly, as if the

occupant had been waiting. "Valhalla Exchange," Jackson whispered.

"Good—everything's ready for you," Claire de Beauville said.

Jackson stepped into the room. On the washstand were plastic explosive, detonators, and a Schmeisser. He put the explosive in one pocket, the detonators in the other, and picked up the machine pistol.

"Anything else?" she said. Her face was pale, unnaturally calm.

"Yes. Some sort of handgun. Can you manage that?"

"I think so."

She opened the drawer of the bedside table and produced a Walther. Jackson checked that it was loaded, then pushed it down into his waistband at the small of his back under the tunic.

"I like an ace-in-the-hole, just in case things go wrong. Amazing how often even an expert search misses that particular spot. Have you spoken to him on the radio again since he was here?"

"Twenty minutes ago. Everything is arranged, exactly as planned. They wait on you. You'll need a greatcoat and a cap to get you across the square unnoticed. There are men working out there. The small staircase at the end of the passage takes you to the main entrance hall, you'll find a cloakroom at the bottom, and the room that houses the drawbridge mechanism is the first door on the left in the gate tunnel."

"You've done well." Jackson grinned. "Well, mustn't stand here gossiping. Once more into the breach, dear friends . . ." And he picked up the Schmeisser and slipped out.

■

In the dining hall, Canning was standing alone in front of the fire when Hesser entered. "Cold," the German said. "Too cold. Schneider said you wanted a word."

"Yes. Let's say that the drawbridge falls and the gate blows, what happens then?"

"They'll come in at full speed in those half-tracks, I should imagine."

"Exactly. Armored troop carriers, and we don't even have anything capable of blowing off a track unless someone gets lucky and close enough with one of your stick grenades."

"True, but you have some sort of solution, I think, or you would not be raising the matter."

"We've been together too long, Max." Canning smiled. "Okay—that cannon in the center of the square. Big Bertha."

Hesser said, "She hasn't been fired since the Franco-Prussian War."

"I know, but she could still have one good belt left in her. Get Schneider on the job. You can soon make up some sort of charge. Prise open a few cartridges to make touch powder. Stoke up the barrel with old metal, chains, anything you can find, then have the men haul her down to the tunnel. Say, twenty or thirty yards from the entrance. It could knock hell out of the first vehicle to come out of there."

"Or simply explode in the face of whoever puts a light to the touch hole."

"Well, that's me," Canning told him. "I thought of it, so I'll stick with it."

Hesser sighed, "Very well, *Herr General,* you command here, not I," and he went out.

Thirteen

JACKSON went down the rear staircase quickly and paused at the bottom, staying well back in the shadows; but his caution was unnecessary, for the hall was quite deserted. He opened the door on his left, slipped inside, and switched on the light.

As Claire de Beauville had indicated, it was a cloakroom, and there was an assortment of coats and caps hanging on the pegs—even a couple of helmets. He hesitated, debating, then selected a field cap and heavy officer's greatcoat. He and Hesser were, after all, of the same build, and it was a reasonable assumption that in the darkness he would be mistaken for the colonel by anyone who saw him.

When he opened the front door, snow filtered through. He moved out quickly and paused at the top of the steps to get his bearings. Most of the courtyard was in darkness, but in the center a group of German soldiers supervised by Howard and Sergeant Hoover worked in the light of a storm lantern on Big Bertha.

Jackson went down the steps to the left and moved into the protecting dark, following the line of the wall toward the main gate. He paused at the end of the tunnel. It was very quiet, except for an occasional murmur of voices from the men in the middle of the courtyard, and a sudden, small wind dashed snow in his face.

It was as if he were listening for something— waiting, he wasn't sure what for—and he felt a shiver of loneliness. Suddenly, in one of those instant flashes of recall, he was once again the fifteen-year-old minister's son standing in a Michigan snowstorm at one o'clock in the morning, despair in his heart. Home late, and the door locked against him for the last time.

And from that to Arlberg—so much in between, and yet in some ways so little. He smiled wryly, moved into the tunnel. First door on the left, Claire de Beauville had said. He held the Schmeisser ready and tried the handle of the iron-bound door. It opened gently; he pushed it wide and stepped inside.

The place was lit by a single bulb. Gunther Voss, Gaillard's erstwhile guard, sat in helmet and greatcoat on a stool by a small woodstove, his back to the door, reading a magazine.

"Is that you, Hans?" he demanded without turning around. "About time."

Jackson pushed the door shut with a very definite click. Voss glanced over his shoulder; his mouth gaped in astonishment.

"Just do as you're told," Jackson said, "and everything will be fine."

He stepped lightly across the room, picked up Voss's Mauser rifle, and tossed it on top of one of the bunks, out of the way.

"What are you going to do?" Voss asked hoarsely. He was absolutely terrified, sweat on his face.

"You've got it wrong, my friend. It's what you're going to do that counts."

A cold breeze touched him in the back of the neck; there was the faintest of creakings from the door. Finebaum said, "That's it, hotshot—you're all through."

Jackson turned in the same moment, the Schmeisser coming up, and Finebaum shot him through the right arm just above the elbow. Jackson was knocked back against the table, dropping the Schmeisser. He forced himself up, clutching his arm, blood spurting between his fingers.

"What are you bucking for—a coffin?" Finebaum demanded, and he nodded to Voss. "Search him."

Voss went through Jackson's pockets and found the plastic explosive and the detonators. He held them up without a word, and the door was flung open and Howard and Hoover rushed in.

"What's going on here?" Howard demanded.

Finebaum took one of the packets of plastic explosive from Voss and threw it across to him. "Just like I said, Captain. The Ardennes all over again."

Claire de Beauville, waiting in the darkness of her

room, heard the shot. Her window looked out over the water garden, not the courtyard, so she couldn't see anything, yet the shot was trouble, whatever the cause. It meant that Jackson had failed. She lit a cigarette and sat on the bed in the dark, smoking nervously, but that wasn't any good. She had to know what had happened, there was no avoiding that fact. She opened the wash-stand door, took out another Walther automatic pistol, slipped it into her jacket pocket, and went out.

When she went into the dining hall, Madame Chevalier was already there with Canning, Birr, and Hesser.

"What's happened?" Claire said. "I heard a shot."

"Nothing to be alarmed about." Canning put an arm about her shoulders. "Everything's under control. I've just had Howard on the field telephone from the gate. It seems friend Jackson wasn't all he pretended to be. They're bringing him up now."

She turned away and moved to join Madame Chevalier by the fire. The door opened and Howard entered, followed by Jackson and Finebaum. Jackson was no longer wearing the greatcoat. A scarf was tied about his right arm, blood soaking through.

"Okay, what happened?" Canning demanded.

Howard held up the packets of plastic explosive. "He was going to blow up the drawbridge winding gear with this. Lucky for all of us, Finebaum was on the ball."

Canning turned to Jackson. "All right, Bannerman, or whatever your name is. Who are you? What are you?"

"Sorry, General," Jackson said. "I've been trying to work that one out for myself for the past thirty years, with a total lack of success."

Before Canning could reply, the door opened and Hoover looked in. "General, sir?"

"What is it?"

"The German sentry who was on duty in the winding-gear room, Private Voss, is out here asking to see you or Colonel Hesser. He says he has information about this man."

"Let's have him in, then."

Hoover snapped his fingers, and Voss stepped into the room. His army greatcoat and the helmet were too big for him, and he looked faintly ridiculous.

"He doesn't speak English," Hesser said. "I'll deal with this. You've got something to say, Voss?" he asked in German.

It poured out of Voss like a dam bursting, the words seeming to spill over themselves, and several times he gestured toward Jackson. He finally stopped, and Hesser turned, a frown on his face.

"What is it?" Canning demanded. "Good news or bad?"

Hesser looked at Jackson gravely. "He says he's seen this man before—yesterday at Arlberg, sitting in a field car with Strasser and Ritter when they first drove into the square."

"He was at that time wearing the uniform of a *Hauptsturmführer* in the SS."

"Now that," Canning said, "really is interesting. Where did you learn your English, Bannerman? I must congratulate you. They did a first-class job."

"I think you'll find he was raised to it," Hesser said. "You see, Voss noticed that the armshield on this—this gentleman's uniform was a Stars and Stripes."

There was a heavy silence. Canning glanced at Jackson, then turned back to Hesser incredulously. "Are you saying this man is a genuine American?"

"In the *Waffen*-SS, *Herr General*, there are what are known as the foreign legions. Units of volunteers raised from every country in Europe. There is even a *Britisches Freikorps* raised from English soldiers recruited from prisoner-of-war camps."

"And you're trying to tell me there are Americans who would sell out their country like that?"

"Not many," Hesser said gently. "A handful only. They are called the George Washington Legion."

Canning turned, his arm swinging, and struck Jackson backhanded across the face. "You dirty yellow bastard," he shouted.

Jackson staggered back, cannoning into Madame Chevalier. In a second he had an arm around her throat and produced the Walther from the waistband at his back.

"Okay, just stand clear—all of you."

Claire de Beauville remained where she was on his left, apparently frozen, hands thrust deep into the pockets of her jacket.

Jackson said, "It's a funny world, General. Not too long ago I was one of the gallant American boys flying for the Finns against the Russians. Remember that one? Then, all of a sudden, the Finns are allies of the Nazis and back fighting the Russians again. Now that kind of thing can be just a little confusing."

"You should have got out," Canning said hoarsely.

"Maybe you're right. All I know is I was flying with the same guys against the same enemy. Hurricanes, by the way, with swastikas on them. Can you beat that?"

"Just let her go," Canning said. "She's an old woman."

"I'm sorry, General. I can't do that. She's going to walk me right out of that front gate—aren't you, *Liebling?*"

Claire stepped in close; her right hand came out of her pocket, clutching the Walther. She rammed the muzzle into his side and pulled the trigger.

The sound seemed very loud, sending shock waves around the room. Jackson bucked, crying out in agony, and staggered back. She swung the Walther up, clutching it in both hands now, and pulled the trigger again and again until the gun was empty, driving him back against the wall beside the fireplace.

As his body slumped to the floor, she threw the Walther away from her and turned to Canning, her face contorted.

"Hamilton?"

He opened his arms, and she ran into them.

■

She lay on her bed in the dark, as Jackson had lain no more than an hour ago, waiting, afraid to move in case they came back. And then, finally, when all seemed quiet, she got up, went to the door, and shot the bolt.

She lifted the washbasin out of its mahogany stand and took out the small compact radio which was secreted inside. An S-phone, they had told her. A British invention, far in advance of any German counterpart, obtained when an OSS agent in France had been picked up by the Gestapo.

She pressed the electronic buzzer that processed the call sign automatically, and waited. Strasser's voice sounded in her ear almost instantly, clear and distinct.

"Valhalla here."

"Exchange. It didn't work. He was caught in the act."

"Dead?"

She hesitated, but only for a moment. "Yes."

"Very well. You'll have to do it yourself. You have sufficient materials left?"

"Yes." She hesitated again. "I'm not sure that I can."

"No choice. You know the consequences if you fail. You should stand a good chance. The Jackson affair will have taken the edge off things. They won't be expecting a similar move from inside. Why should they?" He paused, then said, "I repeat—you know the consequences if you fail."

"All right." Her voice was barely a whisper, a dying fall.

"Good. Valhalla out."

She sat there for a long, long moment, then got

up slowly and took the S-phone back to the wash-stand. Then she got down on her knees, removed the bottom drawer, and took out the two packets of plastic explosive and detonators that remained from what she had stolen from the armory earlier.

■

Strasser, seated at the desk in Meyer's office, closed the lid of the case containing the radio and locked it. He sat there thinking for a moment, his face grave, then stood up and went out.

Ritter was seated by the fire in the bar, enjoying a late supper. Cheese, black bread, and beer. Hoffer lurked in the background as usual, in case of need.

As Ritter looked up, Strasser said, "Total failure, I'm afraid. He's dead."

Ritter said calmly, "What now?"

"The plan still stands. My agent will make another attempt."

Ritter selected a cigarette from his case and lit it with a twig from the fire. "One thing puzzles me. Why didn't this contact of yours make the attempt in the first place? Why the elaborate charade with Jackson?"

"It's really very simple," Strasser said. "You see, she's a woman."

■

Meyer went up the stairs from the kitchen, carrying a tray containing sandwiches, a pot of coffee, and a cup. The big Finn at the door regarded him impassively—one of the few who didn't speak a word of German, as Meyer well knew. In fact, communication had proved impossible. Meyer spoke fair English, but that had provoked no response, nor had the few phrases of French that he knew. He raised the tray and gestured at the door. The Finn slung his Schmeisser, unlocked the door, and stood back.

Gaillard was sitting beside the bed, wiping Arnie's damp forehead. The boy, obviously still feverish, moaned, tossing and turning, clutching at the blankets.

"Ah, there you are, Johann," Gaillard said in German. "I'm about ready for that."

"How is he, *Herr Doktor?*"

"A little better, though you might not think it to look at him."

Meyer put the tray on the bedside table and started to pour the coffee. "I was in the passageway that leads from the bar to the kitchen just now," he said in a low voice. "Don't worry about this one. He can't understand me."

"So?"

"I heard Herr Strasser and Major Ritter talking. Something about the castle. Strasser said he had a contact in there. A woman."

Gaillard looked up at him in astonishment.

"Impossible. There are only two women in the place, Madame Chevalier and Claire de Beauville. Frenchwomen to the core, both of them. What are you saying, man?"

"Only what I heard, *Herr Doktor.* I think they're waiting for something to happen."

The Finn said something unintelligible, strode into the room, and grabbed Meyer by the shoulder. He shoved him outside quickly and closed the door.

Gaillard sat there, staring into space. Impossible to believe. Meyer must have got it wrong. Must have. The boy cried out, and Gaillard turned quickly, squeezed out his cloth in the bowl of water, and wiped the forehead gently.

■

Claire de Beauville paused in the shadows at the bottom of the back stairs, listening. All was still. She opened the door on her left gently and stepped into the cloakroom. When she slipped out a few seconds later, she was wearing a military great-coat and a steel helmet, both far too large for her, but that didn't matter. In the darkness it was only the general impression that was important.

It was snowing lightly when she went outside, and the entire courtyard was shrouded in dark-ness, no one working on Big Bertha this time. She took a deep breath to steady her nerves, went down the steps, and started across to the gate.

There was a murmur of conversation up on the wall where the sentries talked in subdued voices. In the tunnel itself, silence. She hesitated at the door of the winding-gear room, then tried the han-dle gently. The door opened with a slight creak. It was dark in there. With a tremendous surge of relief, she stepped inside. Her groping hand found the switch, and she turned on the light.

Canning was standing there with Hesser and Birr, Howard and Finebaum against the wall. She stood there, very pale, looking suddenly like some little girl in a macabre game of dressing up that had gone wrong, lost in that ridiculous greatcoat and steel helmet.

"How did you know?" she said tonelessly.

"Well, I'll tell you, miss, you'll have to blame

me for that." Finebaum slung his M1, crossed to her side, and searched her pockets, finding the explosive and detonators instantly. "You see, the general here, being highly suspicious of our old pal Bannerman, put me on his trail. I was watching his door when he came out and went to your room. The rest, as they say in the movies, you know. I didn't get a chance to tell the general about it right away because everything happened pretty fast after that."

"That'll do, Finebaum," Canning said.

"Anything you say, sir."

Finebaum moved away. She stood there, defenseless. Canning glared at her, eyes burning, agony on his face.

It was Hesser who said, strangely gentle, "Strasser is Bormann, then?"

"I don't know. I've never met him. Remember the Gestapo security check on the castle two months ago, when we were all interviewed privately? I received my instructions then from that SS colonel, Rattenhuber. He said he was acting for Bormann. A special radio was secreted in my room. I was given times when I could expect messages."

"The damage to our own radio spares," Hesser said. "That was you?"

"Yes."

"Why, for God's sake?" Canning cried harshly.

"It's really quite simple," she said. "Remember my husband, Etienne?"

"Of course. Shot dead while trying to escape from SD headquarters in Paris."

"So I believed," she said, "until Rattenhuber

was able to prove to me that wasn't true. Etienne is alive, Hamilton. Has been all along. An inmate of Mauthausen concentration camp."

"I see," Justin Birr said. "And the price of his continued existence was your cooperation."

"It wasn't enough," Canning cried. "You hear me? Not to excuse what you have done."

The rage, the anguish in him was personal, and obvious to everyone there. His hand came up, clutching his Walther.

"Shoot me, then, Hamilton, if you must," she said in the same flat voice. "It doesn't matter. Nothing matters any longer. Etienne is as good as dead now."

It was Finebaum who moved first, getting in front of her and facing Canning, his M1 still slung from his shoulder.

"General, I respect you—I respect you like hell—but this isn't the way, sir, and I can't just stand by and let you do it."

Canning gazed at him wildly, the Walther shaking in his hand, and then something seemed to die inside him, the light faded, he lowered the pistol.

"Captain Howard."

"Sir."

"Lower the drawbridge, then open the gate."

"I beg your pardon, sir?"

"You heard me." Canning's voice was flat. "I don't want her here, you hear me? Let her go. She can't harm us now."

He brushed past her and went outside.

■

It was Sorsa, in the observation post the Finns had set up in the trees above the first bend, who noticed the drawbridge descending. Ritter had only just arrived from the village and was still in the field car on the road below.

Sorsa called softly, "Something going on up there at the gate. They're lowering the drawbridge."

Ritter scrambled up the bank to join him, and as he did so, the judas door opened and Claire de Beauville stepped into the light. She started across without hesitation, and the moment she reached the opposite side, the drawbridge lifted again behind her. She came on.

"You know who it is?" Sorsa demanded.

"Madame de Beauville, one of the *prominenti*." Ritter lowered his night glasses. "Now I wonder what friend Strasser will have to say about this rather singular turn of events?"

■

As the drawbridge started to rise again, Canning went back into the winding-gear room. Finebaum and Hoover were turning the massive wheels by hand, Howard watching them. Hesser and Birr talked together in low voices.

Canning's face was white with fury. "Okay, that's it. I've had enough of hanging around and nothing happening. I'm going out there to see what the situation is."

"Good God, Hamilton, how on earth are you going to do that?" Birr demanded.

"Leave by the water gate. There's an old skiff in the tunnel there. We can cross the moat in that. They'll be heavily occupied with the woman at the moment. They won't expect any move like this."

Birr shrugged. "All right, Hamilton. If that's how you want it, I'm your man."

"No, not you. You're needed here."

Howard said, "If you're looking for volunteers, sir . . ."

"Captain, in my entire career, I never asked anyone under my command to volunteer for anything. If I need a man, I tell him." He nodded at Hoover and Finebaum. "I'll take these two. You stay here to back up Colonel Birr. Any questions?"

Birr shrugged helplessly. "You give the orders, Hamilton. You're in command."

■

It was damp in the tunnel, and cold. They waited while Schneider got the water gate unlocked, and then the sergeant major and a couple of his men got the skiff into the water.

Hesser said, "It's in pretty rotten condition, *Herr General*. Careful your boot doesn't go through the bottom."

Howard handed Canning his Thompson. "Better take this, sir. You might need it."

"Thanks," Canning said. "We'll hit those trees as fast as we can, then work our way through and see if we can make out what's happening around that first bend in the road. In and out again, nice and fast. I'd say we should be back here in thirty minutes."

"We'll be looking for you," Birr called softly.

Hoover and Finebaum were already in the skiff. Canning joined them, sitting on the stern rail, and Howard gave them a strong push. The skiff glided across the moat, its prow bit into the snow of the other bank, and Finebaum was ashore in an instant. He knelt there, covering Hoover and Canning while they pulled the skiff up out of the water a little.

"Okay," Canning whispered, "let's go."

"Excuse me, General, but I figure we've got something to settle first."

"What in hell are you talking about, soldier?"

"You did say this was a reconnaissance mission, General?"

"Yes."

"Well, that's good because that's what Harry and me and the captain have been kind of specializing in for the past eighteen months—only I always take point, sir. I mean, I lead the way on account of I seem to have a nose for it and we all live longer. Okay, General?"

"Okay," Canning said. "Just so long as we get moving."

"Right. Just keep your mouth shut and follow my ass."

He was away in an instant, moving very fast, and Canning went after him, Hoover following. They reached the tree line, and Finebaum paused to get his bearings. In spite of the darkness, there was a faint luminosity because of the snow.

Finebaum dropped to one knee, his face close to the ground, then he stood up. "Ski tracks, so those mothers are still around."

He set off again, going straight up the slope through the trees at a speed which had Canning struggling for breath. From the top of the slope, the ground inclined to the east more gently, through pine trees whose branches were covered with snow. Finebaum was some yards ahead by now, and suddenly signaling them to halt, he went forward. He waved them on.

Finebaum was crouched beside a snow-covered bush in a small hollow on the ridge above the road. The Finns were encamped below, beside the three half-tracks and the field car. The scene was illuminated by a couple of storm lanterns, and in their light it was possible to see Sorsa, Ritter, and Claire de Beauville standing by the field car. The Finns squatted around portable field stoves in small groups.

"Hey, this could be a real turkey shoot," Finebaum said. "There must be thirty or thirty-five guys down there. We open up now, we could take half of them out, no trouble." He caressed the barrel of his M1. "On the other hand, that would probably mean the lady getting it, and you wouldn't like that, would you, General?"

"No, I wouldn't like it at all," Canning said.

Strange how different it seemed, now that they were apart. Standing down there in the lamplight, she might have been a stranger. No anger in him at all now.

"But when she moves out, General?" Finebaum said. "That would be different."

"Very different." Canning eased the Thompson forward.

Finebaum leaned across to Hoover. "You move ten yards that way, on the other side of the bank, Harry. Give us a better field of fire. I'll look after the general."

"And who'll look after you!" Hoover asked and wriggled away through the snow.

Finebaum took out a couple of German stick grenades and laid them ready in the snow. They were still talking down there by the field car.

Canning said, "What are you going to do when you get home, Finebaum?"

"Hell, that's easy, General. I'm going to buy something big—like maybe my own hotel in New York someplace. Fill it with high-class women."

"And make a fortune out of them? Or maybe plunge in yourself?"

"That's where I can't make my mind up." They didn't look at each other, but continued to watch the group below. "It's a funny war."

"Is it?"

"If you don't know, who does, General?"

Claire got into the field car. Ritter climbed in beside her and nodded to Hoffer, who started the engine. "Beautiful." Finebaum breathed. "Just too beautiful. Get ready, General."

The field car moved into the night, the engine noise starting to dwindle. And then, as Canning and Finebaum eased forward in the snow to take aim at the men below, there was a sudden whisper in the night, like wings beating.

They both turned as a Finn in white winter uniform, the hood of his parka drawn up over his field cap, erupted from the trees and did a perfect stem turn, coming to a dead halt. Finebaum fired from the hip three times very fast, knocking him back among the bushes.

"Watch it you two!" Hoover yelled. "Three o'clock high!"

Canning swiveled in the right direction and found another Finn coming down the slope through the trees like a rocket. He started to fire the Thompson, snow dancing in fountains across the face of the slope, and the Finn swerved to one side and disappeared. There was uproar down below as Sorsa shouted commands, ordering his men forward in skirmish order. Someone started to fire from the trees above them, and then, below on the road, a big Finnish *Rottenführer* jumped into one of the half-tracks, swung the heavy machine gun, and let off a burst that cut branches from the tree above Canning's head.

"You wanted action, General—you got it," Finebaum said and called to Hoover, "Hey, Harry, get ready to move out, old buddy. One, two, three—the old routine. Understand?"

There was no reply. He emptied his rifle into the men and the road below, and shoved in another clip. "Okay, General, let's move it," he said and crawled through the bushes toward Hoover.

The sergeant was lying on his back, eyes open wide, as if surprised that this could happen to him after all this time. There was a large and very ragged hole in his throat where two machine-gun bullets had hit together.

Finebaum turned and started to crawl back to their original position. The Finns were halfway up the slope at the side of the road now. He picked up the first stick grenade and tossed it over. There was a deafening explosion and cries of anguish. He ducked as the *Rottenführer* in the half-track swung the machine gun in his direction, kicking a wall of snow six feet in the air.

"Good-bye, old buddy," Finebaum shouted and tossed the second grenade.

It seemed to drift through the night in a kind of slow motion. The *Rottenführer* ducked; it dropped into the half-track beside him. A second later, it exploded, lifting him bodily into the air.

Finebaum yelled, "Okay, General, let's get the hell out of here," and he got to his feet and ran up the slope, head down.

Canning lost contact with him almost instantly, but kept on running, clutching the Thompson gun across his chest with both hands, aware of the spotlight over the castle gate in the distance.

There was a whisper of skis somewhere up above him on his right among the trees, and he swung the Thompson and fired. There were two rifle shots in reply, and he kept on running, head down.

As he came out of the trees on the final ridge, there was a sudden swish of skis. He was aware of movement on his right, turned too late as the Finn ran straight into him. They went over the edge together, rolling over and over through deep snow, the man's skis tearing free.

Canning didn't relinquish his hold on the Thompson—not for a second—flailing wildly at the Finn as the man tried to get up, feeling the side of the skull disintegrate under the impact of the steel butt.

He could hardly breathe now, staggering like a drunken man across the final section of open ground, aware of the deadly swish of skis closing behind, but as he fell down the bank of the moat,

Finebaum was there, giving them one burst after another.

"Come on, you mothers! Is that the best you can do?"

Canning lurched into the water, thrashing out wildly, the Thompson still in his right hand. He went under once, and then someone had him by the collar.

"Easy, General. Easy does it," Jack Howard was saying.

Canning crouched against the wall, totally exhausted, in real physical pain. Hesser and Birr leaned over him. The German forced the neck of a flask between his teeth. It was brandy. Canning didn't think anything had ever tasted quite so good in his life before.

He realized that he was still clutching the Thompson and held it up to Howard. "I lost your sergeant."

"Hoover?" Howard said. "You mean he's dead?"

"As a mackerel. Took two heavy-chopper rounds straight in the throat," Finebaum said as he squatted beside Canning. "Anyone got a cigarette? Mine are all wet."

Hesser gave him one and a light. Howard exploded, "Goddammit, Finebaum, is that all you can say? That's Harry out there."

"What the hell do you expect me to do, recite the prayers for the dead or something?"

Howard walked away along the tunnel. Canning said, "You saved my skin out there, Finebaum, I won't forget that."

"You did okay, General. You did as you was told. That's lesson number one in this game."

"Game?" Canning said. "Is that how you see it?"

Finebaum inhaled deeply and took his time replying. "I don't know about that, General, but I'll tell you one thing. Sometimes at night I wake up frightened—scared half to death—and you know why?"

"No."

"Because I'm afraid it'll soon be over."

For the first time since Canning had known him, he didn't sound as if he were trying to make a joke.

Fourteen

RITTER and Claire de Beauville did not exchange a single word during the drive down to the
village. When Hoffer finally braked to a halt in
front of the Golden Eagle, she made no attempt to
get out, simply sat there mute, staring into space,
snowflakes clinging to her eyelashes.

"We will go in now, *madame*," Ritter said
gently as Hoffer opened the door for them.

He took her hand to help her down, and she
started to shake. He put an arm about her shoulder. "Quickly, Erich—inside."

Hoffer ran ahead to get the door open. Ritter
took her up the steps and into the bar. Meyer was
tending the fire. A look of astonishment appeared
on his face when he saw Claire. "Madame de
Beauville—are you all right?"

She was shaking uncontrollably now. Ritter
said, "Where is Herr Strasser?"

"In my office, *Sturmbannführer*."

"I'll take her there now. You get Dr. Gaillard. I

think she's going to need him. Go with him, Erich."

They both went out quickly. Claire leaned heavily against Ritter, and he held her close, afraid that she might fall. He walked her across to the fire and eased her into the large armchair beside it. Then he went to the bar, poured brandy into a glass, and returned.

"Come on, just a little. You'll feel better, I promise you."

She moaned softly, but drank, and then she seemed to choke a little, her fingers tightening on his shoulder as she stared past him.

Strasser said, "What happened? What went wrong?"

Ritter turned to look at him. "She is not well, as you can see."

"This is not your department, so kindly keep out of it," Strasser told him coldly.

Ritter hesitated, then got to his feet and moved a few paces away. Strasser said, "You were discovered?"

"Yes."

"Then how do you come to be here?"

"General Canning threw me out."

Strasser stood there, confronting her, hands clasped behind his back, a slight frown on his face. He nodded slowly. "Exactly the sort of stupidity he would indulge in."

"What happens now?"

"To you? A matter of supreme indifference to me, *madame*."

He started to turn away, and she caught at his sleeve, shaking again now, tears in her eyes.

"Please, Herr Bormann. Etienne—my husband. You promised."

"Strasser," he said. "The name is Strasser, *madame*. And in regard to your husband, I promised nothing. I said I would do what I could."

"But Colonel Rattenhuber . . ."

". . . is dead," Strasser said, "and I can't be responsible for the empty promises of a dead man."

There was horror and incredulity on her face now. "But I did everything I was asked to do. Betrayed my friends—my country. Don't you understand?"

From the doorway Gaillard said, in shocked tones, "For God's sake, Claire, what are you saying?"

She turned on him feverishly. "Oh, yes, it's true. I was the puppet—he pulled the strings. Meet my master, Paul. *Reichsleiter* Martin Bormann."

"I really am growing rather weary of this," Strasser said.

"Would you like to know why I did it, Paul? Shall I tell you? Etienne wasn't killed escaping from SD headquarters in Paris, as we thought. He's alive. A prisoner at Mauthausen concentration camp."

There was agony in Paul Gaillard's face, and an overwhelming pity. He took her hands in his. "I know, Claire, that Etienne wasn't shot trying to escape from Avenue Foch. I've known for a long time. I also know they took him to Mauthausen."

"You know?" she whispered. "But I don't understand."

"Mauthausen is an extermination camp. You

only go in, you never come out. Etienne died there in the stone quarry two years ago, along with forty-seven American, British, and French fliers. There seemed no point in causing you needless distress when you already believed him dead."

"How did they die?"

Gaillard hesitated.

"Please, Paul, I must know."

"Very well. At one point in the quarry there is a flight of steps, a hundred and twenty-seven of them. Etienne and the others were made to climb them, carrying heavy stones. Seventy, eighty, ninety—even a hundred pounds in weight. If they fell down, they were clubbed and kicked until they got up again. By the evening of the first day, half of them were dead. The rest died the following morning."

■

Canning and Justin Birr had a plan of the castle open across the top of the piano. Claudine Chevalier sat opposite them, playing softly. The door opened, and Hesser and Howard entered, the German brushing snowflakes from the fur collar of his great coat.

Canning said, "I've called you together for a final briefing on what the plan must be in case of an all-out assault."

"You think that's still possible, sir?" Howard asked.

"I've no reason to believe otherwise. One thing is absolutely certain. If it comes at all, it must come soon. I'd say no later than dawn because the one thing Strasser or Bormann or whoever he is doesn't have, is time. An Allied column could cross this place at any moment. However"—he pulled the plan forward—"let's say they do attack and force the drawbridge. How long can you hold them before they blast that gate, Howard?"

"Not long enough, General. All we have are rifles, Schmeissers, and grenades—and one machine gun up there. They still have two half-tracks with heavy machine guns, and a lot more manpower."

"Okay—so they force the gates and you have to fall back. What about Big Bertha, Max?"

"She is in position thirty yards from the mouth of the tunnel and overflowing with scrap metal. However, I can't guarantee that she won't blow up in the face of whoever puts a light to her."

"That's my department," Canning told him. "I said it, I meant it. If it works, we dispose of the first half-track out of the tunnel and probably every man in it. That should even things up a little."

"Then what?" Howard demanded.

"We retreat into the north tower, get the door shut, and stand them off for as long as we can."

Justin Birr said mildly, "I hate to mention it, Hamilton, but that door isn't really much of a barrier."

"Then we retreat up the stairs," Canning said. "Fight them floor by floor—or has anybody got a better suggestion?" There was only silence. "All right, gentlemen, let's get moving. I'll see you on the wall in five minutes."

They went out. He stood there looking at the plan for a while, then picked up a German-issue parka and pulled it over his head.

"A long wait until dawn, Hamilton," Claudine Chevalier said. "You really think they'll come?"

"I'm afraid so."

"And Paul and Claire? I wonder what will happen to them."

"I don't know."

"Or care?"

"About Gaillard—yes." Canning buckled on his holstered pistol.

"How strange," she said, still playing, "that love can turn to hate so quickly—or can it? Perhaps we only delude ourselves."

Canning walked out, slamming the door.

■

When Sorsa went into the bar at the Golden Eagle, he found Ritter sitting by the fire, a glass in one hand. Sorsa beat the snow from his parka. Ritter didn't say a word, simply stared into the fire. The door from the kitchen opened, and Hoffer entered with coffee on a tray. He put it down on the side table without a word. Ritter ignored him, also.

Sorsa glanced at the sergeant major, then coughed. Ritter's head turned very slowly. He glanced up, a brooding expression in his eyes.

"Yes, what is it?"

"You sent for me, *Sturmbannführer*."

Ritter stared up at him for a moment longer, then said, "How many did you lose up there?"

"Four dead, two seriously wounded. Three others scratched a bit. We brought the wounded back here for the doctor to deal with. One of the half-tracks is a complete write-off. What happens now?"

"We attack at dawn. Seven o'clock, precisely.

You and your men are still mine until nine, remember?"

"Yes, *Sturmbannführer.*"

"I'll take command personally. Full assault. We'll use *Panzerfausts* on the drawbridge. Hoffer, here, was the best gunner in the battalion. He'll blow those chains for us—won't you, Erich?"

It was delivered as an order, and Hoffer reacted accordingly, springing to attention, heels clicking together. *"Zu Befehl, Sturmbannführer."*

Ritter looked up at Sorsa. "Any questions?"

"Would it make any difference if I had?" Sorsa asked.

"Not really. The same roads lead to hell in the end for all of us."

"A saying we have in Finland, also."

Ritter nodded. "Better leave Sergeant Major Gestrin and four of your best men down here to hold the fort while we're away. You get back to your camp now. I'll be up in a little while."

"And Herr Strasser?"

"I shouldn't imagine so, not for a moment. Herr Strasser is too important to be risked. You understand me?"

"I think so, *Sturmbannführer.*"

"Good, because I'm damned if *I* do." Ritter got to his feet, walked to the bar, and reached for the schnapps. "I've known a lot of good men during the past five or six years who are no longer with us, and for the first time I'm beginning to wonder why." There was a kind of desperation on his face. "Why did they die, Sorsa? What for? Can you tell me?"

"I'm afraid not," Sorsa said gently. "You see, I

fight for wages. We belong to a different club, you and I. Was there anything else?" Ritter shook his head. "Then I'll get back to my boys."

The big Finn gave him a military salute and went out. Ritter moved to the fireplace and stared into the flames. "Why, Erich?" he whispered. "What for?"

"What's this, Major Ritter?" Strasser said from the doorway. "A little late in the day for philosophy, I should think."

Ritter turned, the dark eyes blazing in the pale face. "No more games, *Reichsleiter*. We've gone too far for that now, you and I."

"Have we, indeed?" Strasser went behind the bar and poured himself a brandy.

"Is it Bormann in Berlin and Strasser here—or the other way about?" Ritter said. "On the other hand, does it really matter?"

"Speeches now?"

"I'd say I've earned the right, if only because I had to stand by and watch that sickening spectacle with the Beauville woman. You left her more degraded than a San Pauli whore. You left her nothing."

"I did what had to be done."

"For God, the *Führer,* and the Reich—or have I got that in the wrong order?" Ritter ignored the horror on Hoffer's face. "Hundreds of thousands of young Germans have died, the cream of our nation, who believed. Who had faith and idealism. Who thought they were taking our country out of the degradation and squalor of the twenties into a new age. I now realize they died for nothing. What they believed in never existed in the first place. You and your kind allowed, for your own ends, a madman to lead the German people down the road to hell, and we followed you with joy in our hearts."

Strasser said, "Listen to me, Ritter. This is sentimental nonsense of the worst kind—and from you, a man who has served the Reich as few others have done. Do you think we are finished? If so, you are badly mistaken. We go on—only now the *Kameradenwerk* begins, and there is a place for you in this. A place of honor."

Ritter turned to Hoffer. "We're leaving now, Erich."

Hoffer went out. Strasser said, "What do you intend?"

"I'm attacking at seven o'clock. Full assault. We'll use *Panzerfausts* to blow the drawbridge chains. It might work, but I can't guarantee it. I'm leaving Sergeant Major Gestrin and four men to look after things here."

Hoffer returned and handed him his parka and field cap. Strasser said, "Let me get my coat. I'll come with you."

"No!" Ritter said flatly. "I command, and I say you stay here."

As Ritter buttoned his parka, Strasser said, "As you so obviously feel as you do, why are you doing this?"

"Most of my friends are dead now," Ritter told him. "Why should I get away with it?" And he walked out.

■

Arnie was sleeping peacefully, and the only evidences of the ordeal he had passed through were the dark smudges like purple bruising under each eye. Gaillard placed a hand on the boy's forehead. It was quite cool, and the pulse was normal for the first time in twenty-four hours.

He lit a cigarette, went to the window and opened it. It was quite dark, except for light spilling out from the kitchen window across the courtyard below. It was snowing, and he breathed deeply of the cold bracing air.

There was a knock at the door, and Meyer entered with coffee on a tray. The Finnish guard stayed outside. Gaillard could see him sitting on a chair on the other side of the corridor, smoking a cigarette.

"How is he, *Herr Doktor?*" Meyer asked as he poured coffee.

"Temperature down, pulse normal, fever gone, and sleeping peacefully, as you can see." Gaillard drank some of the coffee gratefully. "And now I must check on Madame de Beauville."

Meyer said softly, "They mount a general assault on Schloss Arlberg at seven."

Gaillard said, "Are you certain?"

"I overheard Major Ritter and Herr Strasser discussing it in the bar a short time ago. Major Ritter has already left for the castle."

"And Strasser?"

"There was trouble between them. Strasser wanted to go, but Ritter wouldn't have it. He stays here with five Finns to guard him."

Gaillard turned and leaned on the windowsill, considerably agitated. "If a general assault is mounted up there, they won't stand a chance. We must do something."

"What can we do, *Herr Doktor?* It's a hopeless situation."

"Not if someone could get out with news of what's happening here." There was new hope on Gaillard's face. "There must be many Allied units in the vicinity of Arlberg now. You could go, Johann." He reached out a hand and gripped Meyer's coat. "You could slip away."

"I am sorry, *Herr Doktor,* I owe you a great deal —possibly even my son's life—but if I went, it would be like leaving the boy to take his chances." Meyer shook his head. "In any case, it would be impossible to steal the field car with those Finns out in front, and how far could anyone hope to get on foot?"

"You're right, of course." Gaillard turned back to the window dejectedly and saw something in the courtyard below that filled him with a sudden fierce hope. A set of skis propped against the wall beside the kitchen window.

He controlled himself with considerable difficulty. "Pour me another coffee before that sentry decides you've been here long enough, and listen. The skis down there—they are yours?"

"Yes, *Herr Doktor.*"

"You are right, my friend, you do owe me something, and now is your chance to repay. You will take those skis, an anorak, mittens, and boots and leave them in the woodshed at the top of the yard. That is all I ask. Getting out of here is my problem."

Meyer still hesitated. "I'm not sure, *Herr Doktor.* If they ever found out . . ."

"Not for me or my friends, Johann," Gaillard said. "For Arnie. You owe him that much, I think."

The Finn moved into the room, said something in his own language, and gestured to Meyer, motioning him outside. Meyer picked up the tray.

"I'm counting on you, Johann."

"I'll try, *Herr Doktor*." Meyer looked distinctly unhappy. "I'll do my best, but I can't promise more than that."

He went out, and the guard made to close the door, but Gaillard shook his head. He picked up his doctor's bag, brushed past him, and went down the corridor to the next room. Claire de Beauville was lying down, and when the Finn tried to follow him in, Gaillard shut the door in his face.

She started to get up, and Gaillard sat on the edge of the bed. "No, stay where you are. How do you feel now?"

"A little better."

"Not if someone comes in, you don't. You feel very ill indeed."

"The sentry?"

"No, he's been rather more amenable since standing by and watching while I patched up two of his comrades in a room along the corridor. Casualties of some fracas up at the castle." He opened his bag and took out a stethoscope. "I haven't got long, so listen carefully. This man Strasser, or whoever he is —do you still wish to serve him?"

She shuddered. "What do you think?"

He glanced at his watch. "In less than an hour, they mount a general assault on Schloss Arlberg. Everything they've got. No holds barred."

Her eyes widened. "Claudine, Hamilton, and the others—they won't stand a chance."

"Exactly, so someone must go for help."

"But how?"

"Meyer is hiding skiing equipment for me in the woodshed behind the inn. Getting out is my own affair. Will you help?"

"Of course." Her hand tightened on his, and she smiled sadly. "If you want the help of someone like me."

"My poor Claire. We are all casualties of war to a greater or lesser degree. Who am I to judge you?" There were voices outside. She lay back hurriedly. The door opened, and Strasser entered.

"How is she?"

"Not very well," Gaillard said. "I'm afraid a total breakdown is quite possible. She has, after all, gone through a lengthy period of intense stress. Add to this the trauma of more recent events. The news of her husband's death."

"Yes, all very sad," Strasser said impatiently. "However, I want to talk to you."

"It will have to wait. Madame de Beauville needs my full attention at the moment, and I would remind you that I have two badly wounded Finns along the corridor."

"Ten minutes," Strasser said. "That's all you can have. Then I want you downstairs in the bar." His voice was cold, incisive. "You understand me?"

"Of course, *Reichsleiter*," Gaillard told him calmly.

Strasser left, leaving the door open, the Finnish guard standing outside. "That's bad," Gaillard said. "It doesn't give us much time."

"If you don't go now, you won't go at all, isn't that how it stands?" she said.

"Very probably."

"Well, then, it's now or never."

She sat up and swung her legs down, somehow managing to knock his bag to the floor. She reached to pick it up, clumsily disgorging most of the contents—instruments, pill bottles, and so on—onto the carpet.

"Now look what I've done."

The Finnish guard moved into the room and stood watching. She stared to kneel, and Gaillard said, "It doesn't matter. I'll get them."

Claire turned to the Finn, trying to look as confused and helpless as possible, and he responded as she had hoped. He grinned, unslung his rifle, and put it on the bed, then dropped to one knee beside Gaillard.

She didn't hesitate. There was a cut-glass decanter half full of water beside her bed. She seized it by the neck and struck with all her strength at the base of the guard's skull. Glass fragmented, bone splintered, the Finn slumped on his face without a sound.

She froze for a few moments, listening, but all was quiet. She said, "Go now, Paul."

"And you?" he asked, standing up.

"Don't worry about me."

He put his hands on her shoulders, kissed her briefly, and hurried out. Claire stood there looking down at the Finn, surprisingly calm, drained of all emotion, and very, very tired. A drink, she thought, that's what I need. And she went out, closing the door behind her.

Gaillard went down the back stairs. As he reached the stone-flagged passage, the door to the courtyard opened and Meyer entered, stamping snow from his boots. He drew back in astonishment at the sight of Gaillard, who grabbed his arm.

"Have you done as I asked?"

"Yes, *Herr Doktor*," Meyer stammered. "I've just come back."

"Good man," Gaillard said. "If Strasser descends on you when I'm gone, just play dumb."

He opened the door, stepped out, and closed it. The first pale luminous light of dawn was filtering through the trees. There was a slight ground mist, and it was snowing a little. Meyer's tracks were plain, and Gaillard followed them quickly across the yard to the woodshed. He got the door open and went inside.

He was excited now, more so than he had been for years, and his hands shook as he took off his shoes and pulled on the woolen socks and heavy ski boots Meyer had provided. The anorak was an old red one which had been patched many times, but the hood was fur-lined, as were the mittens. He pulled them on quickly, picked up the skis and sticks, and went back outside.

It was snowing harder now, cold, early-morning mountain snow, strangely exhilarating, and when he paused on the other side of the wall to put on the skis, he was conscious of the old familiar thrill again. The years fell away and he was in the Vosges, practicing for Chamonix—1924—the first Winter Olympic Games. The greatest moment of his life when he had won that gold medal. Everything afterward had always savored a little of anticlimax.

He smiled wryly to himself and knelt to adjust the bindings to his satisfaction. He pressed on the safety catch, locking his boot in position, then repeated the performance with the other ski. So, he was ready. He pulled on his mittens and reached for the sticks.

■

It was perhaps five minutes later that Strasser, sitting waiting for Gaillard in the bar, heard a cry from outside in the square. He went to the door. Gestrin and the four Finnish soldiers Ritter had left were standing by the field car. One of them was pointing up above the houses to the wooded slope of the mountain behind.

"What is it?" Strasser demanded.

Gestrin lowered his field glasses. "The Frenchman."

"Gaillard?" Strasser said incredulously. "Impossible."

"See for yourself. Up there on the trail."

He handed him the field glasses. Strasser hastily adjusted the lenses. He found the woodcutters' trail that zigzagged up through the trees, and came upon the skier in the red anorak almost instantly. Gaillard glanced back over his shoulder, giving a good view of his face.

Two of the Finns were already taking aim with their Mauser rifles. Gestrin said, "Shall we fire?"

"No, you fool. I want him back," Strasser said. "You understand me?"

"Nothing simpler. In this kind of country, on skis, these lads are the best in the business."

He turned away, giving orders in Finnish. They all moved quickly to the field car and started to unload their skis.

"You go with them," Strasser told Gestrin. "No

excuses, no arguments. Just have him back here within the hour."

"As you say," Gestrin answered calmly.

They had their skis on within a few minutes and moved away in single file, rifles slung over their backs, Gestrin in the lead. Strasser looked up the mountain to the last bend in the trail which could be seen from the square. There was a flash of red among the green, then nothing.

He hurried into the inn, drawing the Walther from his pocket. He went up the stairs two at a time and moved along the corridor. Arnie's door stood open. The boy slept peacefully. Strasser hesitated, then turned to Claire de Beauville's room. The Finnish guard lay where he had fallen, his face turned to one side. The back of the skull was soft, matted with blood. There was a trickle of red from the corner of his mouth. He was quite dead, and Strasser went out quickly.

"Meyer, where are you, damn you?" he called as he went downstairs.

Meyer emerged from the kitchen and stood there, fear in his eyes. In the same moment, Strasser saw that Claire de Beauville was behind the bar, opening a champagne bottle.

"Ah, there you are, *Reichsleiter*. Just in time to join me. Krug. An excellent year, too. Not as chilled as I would normally expect, but one can't have everything in this life."

Strasser ignored her and menaced Meyer with his pistol, beside himself with rage. "You helped him, didn't you? Where else would he obtain skis and winter clothing?"

"Please, Herr Strasser. Don't shoot." Meyer broke

down completely. "I had nothing to do with this business. You are mistaken if you think otherwise."

Claire poured herself a glass of champagne, perched on one of the high stools, and sipped it appreciatively. "Excellent. Really excellent. And he's quite right, by the way. I was the one who helped Paul. I had the greatest of pleasure in crowning that SS man of yours."

Strasser glared at her. "You?" he said. "He's dead, the man you assaulted, did you know that?"

The smile left her face, but she replied instantly. "And so is Etienne."

"You bitch. Do you realize what you've done?"

"Ruined everything for you, I hope. There must be British and American troops all over the area by now. I'm sure Paul will run across one of their columns quite quickly."

"No chance," he said. "Gestrin and four of those Finns of his have just taken off after him. Probably five of the finest skiers in the German Army. You think it will take them long to run down a sixty-year-old man?"

"Who won an Olympic gold medal in 1924. The greatest skier in the world in his day. I would have thought that would still count for something, wouldn't you?" She raised her glass. "*A votre santé, Reichsleiter*—and may you rot in hell."

He fired several times as the black rage erupted inside him. His first bullet caught her in the right shoulder, knocking her off the stool and turning her around. His second and third shattered her spine, driving her headlong into the wall, the woolen material of her jacket smoldering, then bursting into flame. He moved forward, firing again and again until the gun was empty.

He stood looking down at her, and Meyer, his face contorted with horror, backed away quietly, then turned and rushed upstairs. When he reached Arnie's room, the boy was still asleep. He closed the door, bolted it, then dragged a heavy chest of drawers across it as an additional barrier.

He went into the dressing room, lifted the carpet in the corner, and removed a loose floorboard. Inside, wrapped in a piece of blanket, was his old sawed-off shotgun from the poaching days of his youth, and a box of cartridges, both hidden since before the war. He loaded both barrels and went back into the bedroom. He placed a chair in the center of the room facing the door, sat down with the gun across his knees, and waited.

■

It had been a long time, but some things you never forgot. Gaillard moved out of the trees and started onto a flat plateau perhaps two hundred yards across, more trees on the other side. He was using the sliding, forward stride much favored by Scandinavians, a technique he had picked up in his youth and which ate up the miles at a surprising rate.

If you were fit, of course—always that—though at the moment he felt better than he had for years. Free, yes, but more than that—the knowledge that they'd come to the end of something. That freedom was just around the corner for everyone.

But this was no time for such considerations. He needed a destination and didn't have one. On the other hand, it seemed reasonable to assume that the help he was seeking was more than likely to be found on the main roads, which meant climbing higher, traversing the eastern shoulder of the mountain, and then descending.

Something made him glance back, some sixth sense. The Finns were halfway across the plateau, moving in single file, Gestrin leading. He was not afraid, but filled with a fierce delight, and started into the trees moving at a fast, loping rate. He was already a hundred feet up the side of the mountain when the Finns reached the edge of the trees and Gestrin called them to a halt.

"All right," he said. "The party's over. He's good, this one. Too good to play with. From now on, it's every man for himself, and remember—we want him alive."

He started up the slope, and they moved after him.

■

Ritter and Sorsa stood beside one of the two remaining half-tracks, drinking coffee and examining the ground plan of Schloss Arlberg which the German had brought from the inn.

"Once we're in, they'll fall back to the north tower," Ritter said. "Nowhere else to go."

"And what's that going to be like?"

"According to Strasser, a heavy oak door opening in two sections. That shouldn't take long. Inside, a hall, then a broad stairway that diminishes in size, becoming a spiral at the higher levels. The dining hall, then a maze of passages and rooms right on up to the top."

"If they take it room by room, it could be nasty."

"Not if we keep after them, right from the word *go*. No hesitation, no letup."

The Finns were ready and waiting in the half-tracks, half a dozen with the *Panzerfausts*. Ritter moved closer to examine the ugly-looking antitank projectiles. "Are they good with these things?"

"We've had our successes. On target, one of these can open a T-Thirty-four like a can of meat."

"How many have we got?"

"Ten."

"Then we can't afford to take chances. I'm putting Hoffer in charge. Make that clear to your men. He's the finest gunner I know."

At that moment, Hoffer called from the field car, "Herr Strasser on the radio for you, *Sturmbannführer*."

Ritter leaned into the car. There was no static, and Strasser's voice sounded clear and distinct. "You've not started the assault?"

"Any minute now. Why?"

Strasser told him. When he was finished, Ritter said, "So we don't have too much time, that's what you're trying to say? You needn't have bothered, *Reichsleiter*. We've been a little short on that commodity from the beginning. Over and out."

He replaced the handmike and turned to Sorsa. "Trouble?" the Finn asked.

"Gaillard's managed to escape. He's taken to the mountain on skis. Strasser's sent Gestrin and his boys after him."

"No problem," Sorsa said. "They're the best in the business. They'll lay him by the heels soon enough."

"I wouldn't count on it. He was an Olympic gold

medalist at Chamonix in 1924. If he runs across a British or American column before Gestrin and his men get to him . . ."

Sorsa looked grave. "I see what you mean. So, what do we do?"

"Get this little affair over with as quickly as possible. We move out now."

He started toward one of the half-tracks, and Sorsa caught his arm. "A moment, *Sturmbann-führer*. The first half-track through that tunnel is likely to have a hard time. I'd like to be in it."

"I command here," Ritter said. "I thought I'd made that clear."

"But these are my boys," Sorsa persisted. "We've been together a long time."

Ritter stared at him, a slight frown on his face, and then nodded. "I get the point. Very well, for this occasion only, you lead and I follow. Now let's get moving."

He turned and scrambled up into the second half-track.

Fifteen

CLAUDINE Chevalier was sitting at the piano in the dining hall, playing "The Girl with the Flaxen Hair," by Debussy. It was one of her favorite pieces, mainly because the composer himself had taught her how to play it when she was twelve years of age.

There was a knock at the door, and Finebaum entered. His M1 was slung from his left shoulder, a Schmeisser from his right, and there were three stick grenades in his belt.

She kept on playing. "Trouble, Mr. Finebaum?"

"Well, I'll tell you, ma'am. General Canning, he thought it would be a good idea to have someone look out for you personally. You know what I mean?"

"You?" she said.

"I'm afraid so, ma'am. Mind if I smoke?"

"Not at all—and I couldn't be in better hands. What do we do?"

"I'll take you up to the top of the tower when the time comes—out of the way of things."

"But not now?"

"No need. They haven't even knocked at the gate yet. Say, my old lady used to play piano. Nothing like that, though. I learned the clarinet when she got one cheap from my Uncle Paul. He was a pawn-broker in Brooklyn."

"Did you enjoy it?"

"Well, I ain't Benny Goodman, but I made front row with Glenn Miller."

"But that's wonderful. Do you like this piece that I'm playing now?"

"No, ma'am. It makes my stomach feel cold. It worries me—I don't know why—and that ain't good because I've got enough to worry about."

"Ah, I see. Perhaps you would prefer something like this?"

She started to play "Night and Day." Finebaum moved around the piano to look down at the keys. "Hey, that's great. That's really something. I mean, where did you ever learn to play like that?"

"Oh, one gets around, Mr. Finebaum. Isn't that the phrase?"

"I guess so."

A roar of engines shattered the early-morning stillness. "Oh, my God," she whispered and stopped playing.

As Finebaum ran to the window, there was a sudden booming explosion and the rattle of machine-gun fire.

■

Gaillard, high in the woods now, on the upper slopes of the mountain, heard the echoes of that first out-break of firing and paused to listen. His lungs were aching as he struggled for breath, leaning heavily on his sticks, and his legs were trembling slightly.

He was too old, of course. Too many years under his belt, and the truth was, he simply wasn't fit enough. When it came right down to it, the only thing he really had going for him was technique and the skill born of his natural genius and years of experience.

The Finns, on the other hand, were young men, battle-hardened to endure anything, and at the peak of their physical fitness. He really didn't stand a chance—had not from the beginning.

He langlaufed across the small plateau that tilted gently upward, and paused on the ridge. On the other side, the snow slope was almost vertical, dropping into gray mist, no means of knowing what was down there at all.

He turned and saw the first of the Finns appear from the trees on the other side of the plateau, no more than thirty yards away. Gestrin was number three, and the big Finn waved his hand to bring the patrol to a halt.

He pushed up his goggles. "All right, Doctor. You've put up a wonderful show, and we admire you for it, but enough of this foolishness. Now we go home."

There were two more violent explosions somewhere in the mist below. The rattle of small-arms fire persisted. Gaillard thought of his friends—of Claudine Chevalier and of Claire de Beauville and what had happened to her.

He was filled with a fierce, sudden anger and shouted down at the Finns, "All right, you bastards. Let's see what you're made of."

He went straight over the edge of the near-vertical drop, crouching, skis nailed together, and plunged into the mist. The Finns, as they reached the edge, followed, one after the other, without hesitation.

■

Canning, Birr, and Hesser were in the tunnel, Howard on the wall, when the engine's roar first shattered the morning calm. A few moments later, the half-tracks emerged into view and took up position. The Finns spilled out and started to deploy. Hoffer and the men under his personal command took up position to the left.

Howard trained his glasses on them, trying to make out what they were doing. In the moment of realization, there came a tongue of orange flame and, a second later, a violent explosion as the first *Panzerfaust* projectile struck the wall beside the drawbridge.

Everyone crouched. "What the hell was that?" Birr demanded.

"Panzerfaust," Hesser replied. "It's an antitank weapon rather like your bazooka."

"So I see," Canning said grimly, ducking as another violent explosion rocked the drawbridge—a direct hit, this time.

"Obviously it's the chains they're after," Birr said. "I wonder how long it will take?"

Heavy machine-gun fire raked the top of the wall, bullets ricocheting into space. "Give them everything we've got," Canning cried. "Really pour it on."

Schneider opened up with the MG34, and the rest of the Germans backed him with their Mauser rifles, sniping from the embrasures in the wall. The Finns took refuge behind the half-tracks, one of which moved position slightly to cover the *Panzerfaust* group.

The fourth projectile, fired by Hoffer personally, scored a direct hit on the drawbridge just below the chain mounting on the left-hand side. The woodwork disintegrated, the chain coupling tore free, the drawbridge sagged.

"Strike one," Howard said. "Not long now."

Two more projectiles homed in, a third landing just below the top of the wall above the gate, its shrapnel killing Schneider and the other two men in the machine-gun crew instantly, hurling the MG34 on its side, battered and useless.

Canning crawled across to Howard, blood on his face. "Not long now." He turned to Birr and Hesser. "Justin, you and Howard stay up here as long as you can, with half a dozen men. Max, you drop back on the tower."

"And what about you?" Birr demanded.

"Big Bertha and I have business together. You make things as hot for those bastards as you can on the way in, then get off the wall and join Max in the tower."

Birr started to argue, but in the same moment there was another frightful explosion just below them. The remaining chain disintegrated; the drawbridge fell down across the moat with a resounding crash.

◼

There was a general cheer from the Finns, and Ritter jumped from the half-track to join Hoffer.

"How many have you left?"

"Two, *Sturmbannführer*."

"Make them count, Erich. The gate this time." He ran to the other half-track, and Sorsa leaned down. "Hoffer is going to blast the gate," Ritter said. "You make your move as soon as you like. Smash straight in, and we'll cover you. Good luck."

Sorsa smiled, waved a gloved hand, and pulled down his panzer goggles. He shouted an order in Finnish, and a dozen men scrambled over the side and joined him in the half-track. He clapped his driver on the shoulder and, as they started to move forward, took over the machine gun himself.

■

The first of Hoffer's last two projectiles punched a hole through a massive gate and exploded at the end of the tunnel. The blast knocked Canning, standing beside Big Bertha, clean off his feet, showering him with dirt and tiny fragments of shrapnel.

There was more blood on his face, his own this time, and as he started to get up, Hoffer fired the remaining *Panzerfaust*. The left-hand side of the gate sagged and fell in.

The lead half-track was halfway there, Sorsa firing the machine gun furiously, his men backing him up, and Ritter followed in the second half-track, spraying the top of the wall with such a volume of fire that it was virtually impossible for the handful of defenders to reply.

Howard tossed a couple of stick grenades over at random as the lead half-track got close and Birr grabbed his arm. "Let's get out of here!"

Of the German soldiers who had stayed on the wall with them, only three were left on their feet. Howard beckoned to them now, and they all went down the steps on the run and started across the courtyard to where Hesser and seven of his men waited on the steps of the tower entrance.

Canning leaned heavily on the cannon, blood running into his eyes, and Howard swerved toward him. The general sagged to one knee, groping for the length of smoldering fuse he had dropped, as Howard joined him.

"Get the hell out of here!" Canning ordered.

But by then it was too late, for as Howard handed him the fuse, the lead half-track smashed what was left of the gate from its hinges. The half-track emerged from the tunnel, Sorsa firing the machine gun, and Canning touched the end of his fuse to the powder charge.

Big Bertha belched fire and smoke in a thunderous roar, rocking back on her solid wheels, disgorging her improvised charge of assorted metal fragments and chain at point-blank range, killing Sorsa and every man in the half-track instantly, hurling the vehicle over to one side and back against the wall.

Both Canning and Howard were thrown down by the force of the explosion. As the roar of Ritter's half-track filled the tunnel, Howard grabbed the general by the arm, hauled him to his feet, and urged him into a stumbling run.

Hesser and his men were firing furiously now, retreating up the steps and back through the door at the foot of the north tower, but continuing to give them covering fire. As Howard and Canning made it to the steps, the half-track emerged from the tunnel across the courtyard and its machine gun tracked them across the cobbles.

Hesser's men were already getting the doors closed when, as Howard urged Canning up the steps, the general stumbled and fell. Hesser and Birr ducked out through the narrowing opening and hurried down the steps to help.

Howard and Birr got Canning between them and dragged him up the steps. Behind them, Hesser turned, firing a Schmeisser one-handed across the courtyard, catching in reply a full burst from the machine gun that drove him across the steps in a crazy dance of death, hurling him over the edge into the snow.

A second later, Howard and Birr staggered in through the narrowing gap with Canning, and the massive doors closed.

■

Gaillard's speed was tremendous as he hurtled down into the gray mist, yet he was entirely without fear. What lay ahead, it was impossible to say. He could be rushing straight to his death, his only consolation the knowledge that his pursuers would follow him.

And what good would that do? he asked himself, suddenly angry, and moved into a parallel swing, changing course, the right-hand edge of his skis biting into the snow.

The mist was thinning now, and he glanced over his shoulder and saw that the lead Finn was perhaps forty yards behind, closely followed by another. Gestrin and the other two were a little farther back.

Gaillard came out of an S-turn and went down vertically again, knees together, and suddenly a gust of wind dissolved the remaining shreds of mist in an instant, and below was the valley, an awesome sight, the present slope vanishing into infinity fifty yards farther on.

Gaillard didn't deviate, but held his course true, skis so close together that they might have been one.

At the last possible moment, that edge which meant certain death rushing to meet him, he hurled himself into a left-hand christie. It came off beautifully, and he had a brief impression of the glacier far below as he skirted the ultimate edge.

His pursuers were not so lucky, for behind him the lead Finn went straight over the edge with a terrible cry, his companion following him.

Gaillard, out of the area of immediate danger, started to traverse the lower slope. Above him, Gestrin and his two remaining comrades changed course and went after him.

■

Canning had a deep cut on his forehead above the right eye, of a kind that would require five or six stitches at least. Howard hastily bound a field dressing around it.

"Is he all right?" Birr asked.

"Sure I'm all right," Canning told him. "How many of us left?"

"Six Germans and us three. Finebaum upstairs, of course."

"Not so good."

He peered out through a spyhole in the door. The remaining half-track had retreated into the tunnel. Nothing moved.

"I'd say they could walk in here anytime they chose," Howard said.

"Then we retreat upstairs, floor by floor, like I told you."

The half-track nosed out of the mouth of the tunnel and stopped. Its heavy machine gun, Hoffer firing, started to spray the door at the rate of 850 rounds per minute. As Canning and the others went

293

down, the door started to shake to pieces above them.

"This is bad," the general cried. "No good staying. Better get up those stairs now, while we still have a choice."

He called to the Germans, and they all started to drop back.

∎

Gaillard was incredibly tired. His body ached, and his knees hurt. The amazing thing was that he hadn't fallen once, but now, as he went into a right-hand christie to make for the cover of some pine trees, he snarled a ski and took a bad tumble.

He slid for some considerable distance before coming to a halt, winded. His skis were still on and apparently undamaged, which was something. No broken bones in evidence. But God, how tired he was. Hardly enough strength to get up. He turned and saw Gestrin and his two comrades traversing the slope above him, terribly close now.

Suddenly the earth shook, there was a tremendous rumbling like an underground explosion, and above the Finns the snow seemed to boil up in a great cloud.

Avalanche. Not surprising, really, fresh snow having fallen so late in the season. But already Gaillard was on his feet and dropping straight down the slope, taking that vertical line again, for the only way to beat an avalanche was to stay in front of it, one of the first lessons he'd learned as a boy in the Vosges.

And the trees were not too far away—some sort of protection there. He moved to the right in a wide curve that took him into their shelter within seconds. He halted, turning to glance back.

The avalanche had almost overtaken the Finns. The enormous cloud of white smoke rolled over the one in the rear, enveloped him completely, but Gestrin and the remaining man rode the very edge, managing to run at the last minute, coming to a halt above the line of trees.

The rumble of the avalanche died away. Gestrin pushed up his goggles, searching for Gaillard, whose red anorak gave him away instantly. The Finns started down the slope at once, and the Frenchman turned and pushed himself forward and through the trees, every bone aching.

■

From the shattered great window of the upper dining room, Finebaum sniped down and across the yard at the half-track.

"What's happening, Mr. Finebaum?" Claudine Chevalier, crouched on the floor, asked him.

"Whatever it is, it ain't good, ma'am. I figure it's time maybe you and me made a move upstairs."

There was a burst of firing, and more of the window shattered above their heads, spraying them with glass. Amazingly, she showed no fear.

"Whatever you say, Mr. Finebaum."

"You're something special," Finebaum said. "You know that?"

He took her arm and helped her toward the door, and below, in the courtyard, the half-track surged forward.

■

For Gaillard, the sight of the road below was like a

shot in the arm, and he dropped toward it with renewed hope, although his pursuers were closer than
ever now, Gestrin trailing his companion, a young
man called Salmi.

Gaillard glanced over his shoulder, aware that
this couldn't go on, that he had been existing on
willpower alone for too long. There was one final,
suicidal chance, and he took it, dropping straight
down through the trees like a bullet to the embankment at the side of the road below.

As he hit, he dug in his sticks at precisely the
right moment, launching himself into space. The
road flashed beneath him, he soared across, landing
perfectly in soft snow on the other side, sliding
broadside on in a spray of snow. At the last moment,
the point of his left ski caught a branch hidden beneath the white blanket. As he crashed heavily to
the ground, the ski splintered.

He lay there, winded, and Salmi soared through
the air across the road, smashing straight into a pine
tree with a terrible cry.

Gaillard sat up. There was no sign of Gestrin. He
tore at the frozen bindings of his skis and got them
off. When he rose to his feet, he was convinced for
a moment that his limbs had ceased to function. He
took a hesitant step forward and fell headlong over
the embankment, sliding down to the road.

He picked himself up and started to walk, putting
one foot in front of the other, a roaring in his ears,
and Gestrin slid down the embankment about fifteen yards in front of him. He'd taken off his skis
and was holding his rifle.

"No!" Gaillard said. "No!"

He turned away, and Gestrin shot him in the right shoulder. Gaillard lay on his back, the roaring in his ears louder, then pushed himself up on one elbow. Gestrin stood holding the rifle across his chest, and now he started to raise it.

The roaring became the sound of an engine, and a Cromwell tank came around the bend in the road. Gestrin swung to face it, raising his rifle. A burst of machine-gun fire hurled him back into a snowdrift at the side of the road.

Gaillard lay there, aware of footsteps approaching, his eyes closed, breathing deeply, hanging onto consciousness. He opened his eyes and saw to his astonishment that the man leaning over him in a tank officer's uniform wore a kepi.

"Oh, my God," Gaillard said in his own language. "Can it be true? You are French?"

"But of course, *monsieur*." The officer dropped to one knee. "My name is Dubois. Captain Henri Dubois of the Second French Tank Division. We are at present pushing toward Berchtesgaden. But who are you?"

"Never mind that now," Gaillard said hoarsely. "You know Arlberg?"

"The next village, two miles along the road from here."

"Only two miles?" Gaillard said in wonder. "I must have been running in circles up there." He pulled himself up and caught hold of Dubois by the front of his uniform. "Listen to me, my friend, and listen well, for lives depend on it."

■

When the half-track started across the courtyard,

Ritter himself was at the wheel, a dozen Finns packed in behind him, Hoffer at the machine gun. The rest followed behind on foot.

In the tower, the defenders had already retreated up the main staircase and taken up position on the first landing, except for Howard, who stayed at the shattered door, peering out.

"Here they come!" he cried and started to fire his Thompson furiously.

Ritter gunned the motor, giving the half-track everything, roaring straight up the steps, hitting those shattered doors at full speed. Howard was already halfway up the marble stairs as the doors disintegrated, the half-track smashing through, sliding to a halt, broadside on.

The defenders immediately started to pour it on from the landing, Canning and Birr firing Schmeissers between the pillars of the balustrade, Howard backing them up with the Thompson.

The Finns were caught badly, three or four of them going down as they scrambled from the half-track. Hoffer took a bullet in the shoulder that knocked him over the side, and Ritter, without hesitation, stood up and grabbed the handles of the machine gun.

He started to spray the landing expertly, shattering the windows behind the rows of marble statues, an awesome figure crouched behind the gun, his face pale beneath the black cap. Howard let loose one burst after another, even standing up on occasion, all to no effect, for it was as if the German bore a charmed life.

The landing had become a charnel house, four of the Germans hit, one of them crying out continuously. Birr had taken a bullet through the right hand, and below, in the hall, at least nine of the Finns were down.

Canning pulled at Howard's sleeve, eyes wild. "This is no good—we'd better get out of here."

"Take Birr with you," Howard said. "I'll cover you."

He rammed another clip into the Thompson, and behind him the two surviving Germans got Birr by the shoulders and dragged him along the landing. Ritter stopped firing. He looked down and found Hoffer leaning against the side of the half-track, stuffing a field dressing inside his uniform blouse.

"All right, Erich?"

Hoffer nodded, his face twisted with pain, and from up above, in the smoke on the landing, Howard called, "What's keeping you, Ritter?"

Something flared in Ritter's eyes. He picked up a Schmeisser and vaulted to the floor. He did not say a word, gave no command, simply went up the stairs into the smoke, and the Finns went after him.

The curtains were on fire now, the wood paneling on the walls, smoke swirling, billowing along the landing, so that it was impossible to see more than a few feet. Howard fired blindly, moving back a step or two, then turned and started up the stone staircase.

He paused at the bend, slinging the Thompson over his shoulder, and took two stick grenades from his belt. He could hear voices below, stumbling steps on the stairs. He tossed the two grenades down into the murk, one after the other, went around the corner, and continued to climb without pause.

There was an explosion below, followed by another. Cries of pain. He could hardly breathe now, smoke everywhere, choking the landing outside the dining hall. He groped his way around the wall, found the entrance to the upper staircase, and started to climb to the top of the tower.

■

Had he but known it, the others had gotten no farther than the upper landing, Birr having collapsed completely, so that the two Germans had been compelled to drag him into the dining hall.

Canning crouched over him, almost overcome by smoke, waiting for the end that seemed inevitable now. He got to his feet, lurched across to the window, and smashed what glass remained in the lower half. The Germans dragged Birr across the floor, choking and coughing.

They all crouched at the window, drawing in deep lungfuls of fresh air. Canning cried, "The table —get it over."

They crouched behind it, waiting for the end.

■

On the landing at the foot of the stairs, Ritter rolled over, pushing a body away from him. There was blood on him—but not his own—and he pulled himself up and leaned against the wall. A hand reached out to steady him—Hoffer.

"Are you all right, *Sturmbannführer*."

"Everything in perfect working order, or so it would seem, Erich." An old, bad joke between them, no longer funny.

A gust of wind blowing in through the shattered doorway below cleared the smoke from the landing. It was a charnel house—bodies everywhere, blood and brains sprayed across the walls.

There were perhaps a dozen Finns left alive and unwounded, crouched at the head of the stairs. Ritter glanced at his watch. It was almost eight-thirty.

"All right, damn you. You're still mine for another thirty minutes. Still soldiers of the *Waffen*-SS. Let's get it done."

They made no move. It was not that there was fear there. Only emptiness, faces drained of all emotion, all feeling.

"It's no good," Hoffer said. "They've had enough."

As smoke swirled back into place again, the Finns retreated, simply melted away.

"So?" Ritter said, and he leaned down and picked up a Schmeisser.

As he turned, Hoffer caught his arm. "This is madness. Where are you going?"

"Why, to the top of the tower, old friend." Ritter smiled and put a hand on his shoulder. "We've come a long way together, but no more orders. It is over. You understand me?"

Hoffer stared at him, horror in his face. Ritter started upstairs.

■

When Howard lurched out of the smoke onto the roof, Finebaum almost shot him. Howard fell on his hands and knees, and Finebaum crouched beside him.

"Is he all right?" Claudine Chevalier demanded.

Howard answered her, struggling for breath. "All I need is a little air." He looked around him. "Where's the general?"

"No sign of him up here," Finebaum said. "What happened below?"

"It was bad," Howard told him. "The worst I've ever known." He got up on his knees. "I'll have to go back. See what's happened to them."

Madame Chevalier, who had gone to the parapet to look down, cried, "There are tanks coming. A whole column."

Finebaum ran to join her in time to see half a dozen Cromwells, several Bren-gun carriers and trucks moving toward the castle at full speed. The surviving Finns had just emerged from the entrance. As they started across the courtyard, the first Cromwell emerged from the tunnel and opened up with its machine gun. Two Finns went down; the rest immediately dropped their weapons and put up their hands.

Finebaum turned and found Howard leaning over the parapet beside him. "Did you ever see a prettier sight?" Finebaum demanded. Howard gazed down blankly, eyes remote, and Finebaum shook him roughly. "Hey, noble Captain, it's over. We survived."

"Did we?" Howard said.

And then Claudine Chevalier cried out sharply.

■

Ritter stood there at the head of the stairs, smoke billowing around him. He wore no cap. There was blood on his face, and the blond hair flashed pale fire in the morning light. The black panzer uniform was covered with dust, but the Knight's Cross with Oak Leaves and Swords still made a brave show at his throat.

"Captain Howard?" he called.

Finebaum turned, unslinging his M1, but Howard knocked it aside. "My affair—stay out of it."

He was smiling, his eyes full of life again. He leaned down slowly and picked up the Thompson.

Ritter said, "A firstrate show. My congratulations."

Howard fired then, a long burst that ripped the Iron Cross First Class from Ritter's tunic, hurling him at the wall. The German rebounded, falling to his knees. He flung up the Schmeisser, arm extended, firing one-handed, driving Howard back against the parapet, killing him instantly. For a moment, the young German hung onto life on his knees there in the snow, and then he fell forward on his face.

Hoffer emerged from the smoke, a Walther in his good hand, and crouched beside him. Finebaum dropped to one knee by Howard. There was a pause, then the American's M1 came up.

It was Claudine Chevalier who ended it, her voice high on the morning air. "No!" she screamed. "Enough! Do you hear me? Enough!"

Finebaum turned to look at her, then back to Hoffer. The German threw down his Walther and sat back on his heels, a hand on Ritter's shoulder. Finebaum, without a word, tossed his M1 out over the parapet to fall through clear air to the courtyard below.

■

It was on the steps outside the main entrance that Canning met Henri Dubois for the first time. The Frenchman, a pistol in one hand, saluted. "My respects, *mon général.* My one regret is that we couldn't get here sooner."

"That you got here at all is one small miracle, son."

"We must thank Doctor Gaillard for that."

"Paul?" Canning caught him by the arm. "You've seen him?"

"He escaped from the village this morning and skied across the mountains, hotly pursued by some of these Finnish gentlemen. It was only by the mercy of God that he came across us when he did. He is in the ambulance now, at the rear of the column."

"Thanks." Canning started down the steps and paused. "There was a man called Strasser in the village. He was in charge of this whole damn business. He had Madame Claire de Beauville with him. Did you get them?"

"We came straight through without stopping, *mon général.* Naturally, Schloss Arlberg was our main objective, but if this man Strasser is there, we'll find him."

"I wouldn't count on it."

He found Gaillard on a stretcher in the ambulance at the rear of the column, as Dubois had indicated. The little Frenchman lay there, a gray army blanket up to his chin, eyes closed, apparently sleeping. A medical orderly sat beside him.

"How is he?" Canning demanded in French.

"He is fine, Hamilton, never better." Gaillard's eyes fluttered open. He smiled.

"You did a great job."

"And the others—they are safe?"

"Claudine is fine. Justin got knocked about a bit,

but he'll be all right. I'm afraid the rest makes quite a casualty report. Max is dead, and Captain Howard. Most of the Finns. Ritter himself. It was quite a shooting match up there."

"And Strasser?"

"We'll get him—and Claire. Only a question of time now."

Gaillard's face was twisted with pain, and yet concern showed through. "Don't let him get away, Hamilton. He is capable of anything, that one. What he did to that girl was a terrible thing."

"I know," Canning said soothingly. "You get some sleep now. I'll see you later."

He jumped down from the ambulance and stood there, thinking of Strasser, wanting only to get his hands on the German's throat. And then there was Claire. Suddenly he knew that she was by far the most important consideration now.

There was an empty jeep standing nearby. Without the slightest hesitation he jumped behind the wheel, gunned the motor, and drove out through the tunnel and across the drawbridge.

■

When he braked to a halt outside the Golden Eagle, the square was silent and deserted, everyone staying out of the way. There was an M1 in the rear seat of the jeep. He checked that it was loaded, then jumped out and kicked open the front door.

"Strasser! Where are you, you bastard?"

It was very quiet in the bar—too quiet. He saw the bullet holes in the wall, the blood on the floor, and the hair rose on the nape of his neck. A stair creaked behind him. He turned and found Meyer standing there.

"Where is he?"

"Gone, *Herr General*. After the Finns left to hunt Herr Gaillard, he moved their field car to the rear courtyard, where it was out of sight. When the French soldiers with the tanks came half an hour ago, they passed straight through without stopping. Herr Strasser drove away shortly afterward in the field car."

"And Madame de Beauville—he took her with him?"

Meyer's face was gray, his voice the merest whisper when he said, "No, *Herr General*. She is still here."

He stumbled along the hall, opened his office door, and stood back. She lay on the floor, covered by a blanket. Canning stood there, staring down, disbelief on his face. He dropped to one knee and pulled back the cover. Her face was unmarked and so pale as to be almost transparent, wiped clean of all pain, all deceit. A child asleep at last.

He covered her again very gently, and when he turned to Meyer, his face was terrible to see. "Do you know where he went?"

"I overheard them speak of it several times, *Herr General*. There is an abandoned airstrip at Arnheim, about ten miles from here. I understand there is an airplane waiting."

"How do I get there?"

"Follow the main road to the top of the hill east of the village. A quarter of a mile on, there is a turning to the left, which will take you all the way to Arnheim."

The door banged. A moment later, the engine of the jeep roared into life. Meyer stood there in the quiet, listening to the sound dwindle into the distance.

■

At Arnheim it was snowing again as the Dakota taxied out of the hangar. Strasser, standing behind Berger in the cockpit, said, "Any problems with the weather?"

"Nothing to worry about. Dirty enough to be entirely to our advantage, that's all."

"Good. I'll get out now and see to the Stork. I don't want to leave that kind of evidence lying around. You get into position for takeoff, and I'll join you in a few moments."

Berger grinned. "Spain next stop, *Reichsleiter*."

Strasser dropped out of the hatch, skirted the port wing, and ran toward the entrance to the hangar as the Dakota moved away. He took a stick grenade from his pocket and tossed it through the entrance, ducking to one side. It exploded beneath the Stork, which started to burn fiercely.

He turned away, aware of the Dakota turning in a circle out there at the end of the runway, and then the jeep swung through the entrance from the road and braked to a halt about thirty yards away.

■

Canning saw the Dakota turning into the wind, thought for one dreadful moment that he was too late, and then the shock of the Stork's tank exploding turned his eyes to the hangar. He saw Strasser in front, crouching as he pulled a Walther from his pocket.

Canning grabbed for the M1, fired three or four shots, and it jammed. He threw it away from him and ducked as Strasser stood up, firing at him coolly, two rounds punching holes through the windshield.

Canning slammed the stick into gear, revving so furiously that his wheels spun in the snow and the jeep shot forward. Strasser continued to fire, dodging to one side only at the very last minute, and Canning slammed his boot on the brake, sending the jeep into a broadside skid.

He jumped for the German while the vehicle was still in motion, and they went over in a tangle of arms and legs. For a moment, Canning had his hands on the German's throat and started to squeeze, and then Strasser swung the Walther with all his force, slamming it against the side of the general's head.

Canning rolled over in agony, almost losing consciousness, aware of Strasser scrambling to his feet, backing away, the Walther pointing. Canning got to his knees, and Strasser took careful aim.

"Good-bye, General," he said and pulled the trigger.

There was an empty click. Strasser threw the Walther at Canning's head, turned, and ran along the runway toward the Dakota.

Canning went after him, forcing himself into a shambling trot, but it was hopeless, of course. Things kept fading, going out of focus, then back again. The one thing he did see clearly—and it was all that mattered—was Strasser scrambling up through the hatch, the Dakota's engine note deepening, and then it was roaring along the runway.

Canning slumped down onto his knees and knelt there in the snow, watching it flee into the gray morning like a departing spirit.

Sixteen

IT was almost dawn in La Huerta when Canning finished talking. Rain still tapped against the window of the bar, more gently now, but when I got up and looked out, the square was quiet and deserted.

Canning threw another log on the fire. "Well, Mr. O'Hagan—what do you think?"

"Such a waste," I said, "of good men."

"I know. They were all that. Not Strasser, of course. He was the Devil walking, but Jack Howard, Ritter, Sorsa, and those Finns. . . ."

"But why?" I asked. "Why did they persist in going through with it? Why didn't they simply tell Strasser—or Bormann or whoever—to go to hell?"

"Well, Sorsa and his Finns are possibly the easiest to understand. As he said, they were fighting for wages. They'd taken the gold—if you like to look at it that way—pledged their word, and stuck to it—until the final carnage, anyway."

"And Ritter?"

"He was like a man in deep water, swept along by the current, able to go only one way. He and Jack

Howard were a lot alike—opposite sides of the same coin. At the end of things, I believe now that they'd both had enough. After what they'd been through, the things they'd done for their separate countries, the future held nothing. Didn't exist, if you like."

"You mean they were looking for death, both of them?"

"I'm certain of it."

"And Strasser, or should I say Bormann?"

"That's the terrible thing—not being sure. Remember Berger, the pilot who brought them out of Berlin? The guy who flew the Dakota out of Arnheim in the end? I found him in Italy fifteen or sixteen years ago. Dying of cancer. He was in the kind of state where a man just doesn't give a damn."

"And?"

"Oh, he thought Strasser was Bormann, all right. Last saw him in Bilbao in June of 'forty-five. In the ensuing years, they gave him plenty of work to do, the *Kameraden*. They looked after him."

"I'm surprised he didn't get a bullet like the rest."

"Well, he was something special. A pilot of genius. He could fly anything anywhere. I suppose that had its uses."

"But all those facts," I said, "about what took place in the bunker. Where did they come from?"

"Erich Hoffer," he said simply. "He's still alive. Runs a hotel in Bad Harzberg, and when a Russian infantry unit checked out Eichmann's hideout, they found one of the assistants still alive, a man called Walter Koenig. He pulled through after hospital treatment and spent twenty years in the Ukraine. When he was finally returned to West Germany he wasn't too strong in the head, so they didn't take much notice of his story at his interrogation. I heard about it from a contact in German Intelligence."

"Did you go to see this Koenig?"

"Tried to, but I was just too late. He'd committed suicide. Drowned himself in the Elbe. But I managed to get a look at the report. The rest, of course, is intelligent guesswork."

"So where does it all leave us?" I asked.

"I don't know. Was it Strasser at Arlberg and Bormann in the bunker, or the other way around? That's what's plagued me all these years. Oh, I told it all to the Intelligence people immediately after the events."

"And what did they say?"

"I think they thought I'd been locked up too long. As far as they were concerned, Bormann was in Berlin right to the bitter end. Strasser was something else again."

"And what did happen to Bormann, then, according to history?"

"He left the bunker at one-thirty A.M. on May second. As far as we know, he didn't attempt to disguise himself. It seems he wore a leather greatcoat over the uniform of a lieutenant general in the SS. He met his secretary, Frau Kruger, by sheer chance on his way out. He told her there wasn't much sense in any of it now, but that he'd try to get through."

"And from that moment the myth began?"

"Exactly. Was he killed on the Weidendammer Bridge as Kempka, the *Führer*'s chauffeur, said . . ."

"Or later, near Lehrter Station, where Axmann said he saw him lying next to Stumpfegger? Those two bodies, as I recall, were buried near the Invalidenstrasse by post-office workers."

"That's right, and in 1972, during the building work, they found a skeleton which the German authorities insist is Bormann's."

"But wasn't that refuted by experts?"

"One of the greatest of them put it perfectly in perspective. He pointed out that Bormann couldn't be in two places at once—dead in Berlin, and alive and well in South America."

There was a long silence. Rain continued to tap at the window. General Canning said, "As we know, that bizarre condition is only too possible. I need hardly point out that it would also explain a great many puzzling features of the Bormann affair over the years."

He went to the bar and poured himself another drink. "So, what now?" I asked him.

"God knows. All of a sudden I feel old. All used up. I thought I was close this time. Thought it would finally be over, but now. . . ." He turned on me, a surprisingly fierce expression on his face. "I never married, did you know that? Never could, you see. Oh, there were women, but I could never really forget her. Strange." He sighed. "I think I'll go home to Maryland for a while and sit by the fire."

"And Strasser—or Bormann?"

"They can go to hell—both of them."

"It would make a beautiful story," I said.

He turned on me, that fierce expression on his face again. "When I'm dead—not before. You understand me?" It was an order, not a request, and I treated it as such.

"Just as you say, General."

I hadn't heard the car draw up, but there was a quick step in the hall and Rafael entered. "They have sent the taxi for you from the airstrip, *Señor* Smith. Your pilot says it would be possible to leave now, but only if you hurry."

"That's for me." Canning emptied his glass and placed it on the bar. "Can I offer you a lift?"

"No, thanks," I said. "Different places to go."

He nodded. "Glad we met, O'Hagan. It passed a lonely night at the tail end of nowhere."

"You should have been a writer, General."

"I should have been a lot of things, son." He walked to the door, paused, and turned. "Remember what I told you. When I'm gone you can do what the hell you like with it, but until then . . ."

His steps echoed on the parquet floor of the hall. A moment later, a door slammed and the taxi drove away across the square.

■

I never saw him again. As the world knows, he was killed flying out of Mexico City three days later, when his plane exploded in midair. There was some wild talk of sabotage in one or two newspapers, but the aviation authority's inspectors turned over the wreckage and soon knocked that little story on the head.

They buried him at Arlington, of course, with full honors, as was only proper for one of his country's greatest sons. They were all there. The President himself, anybody who was anybody at the Pentagon. Even the Chinese sent a full general.

I was still in South America when it happened,

and had a hell of a time arranging a flight out, so that I almost missed it, and when I arrived at Arlington, the high and the mighty had departed.

There were one or two gardeners about, no one else, and the grave and the immediate area were covered with flowers and bouquets and wreaths of every description.

It started to rain, and I moved forward, turning up the collar of my trenchcoat, examining the sentiment on the temporary headstone they'd put up.

"Well, old man, they all remembered," I said softly. "I suppose that should count for a lot."

I started to turn away, and then my eye caught sight of something lying close to the base of the stone, and the blood turned to ice water inside me.

It was a single scarlet rose. What some people would call a winter rose. When I picked it up, the card said simply: *As promised.*

HELEN MacINNES

Helen Macinnes's bestselling suspense novels continue to delight her readers and many have been made into major motion pictures. Here is your chance to enjoy all of her exciting novels, by simply filling out the coupon below.

MATT HELM

"Makes British spy James Bond seem like a powder-puff."—DENVER POST

DONALD HAMILTON

☐ THE AMBUSHERS	13572-1	1.25
☐ THE BETRAYERS	P3291	1.25
☐ DEATH OF A CITIZEN	P3338	1.25
☐ THE DEVASTATORS	Q3512	1.50
☐ THE INTERLOPERS	Q3498	1.50
☐ THE INTIMIDATORS	Q3489	1.50
☐ THE INTRIGUERS	13757-0	1.50
☐ THE MENACERS	P3280	1.25
☐ MURDERERS' ROW	13578-0	1.25
☐ THE POISONERS	13780-5	1.50
☐ THE RAVAGERS	P3339	1.25
☐ THE REMOVERS	P3337	1.25
☐ THE RETALIATORS	13567-5	1.50
☐ THE SHADOWERS	M2995	95¢
☐ THE TERMINATORS	13665-5	1.50
☐ THE WRECKING CREW	13838-0	1.50

Buy them at your local bookstore or use this handy coupon for ordering:

FAWCETT PUBLICATIONS, P.O. Box 1014, Greenwich Conn. 06830

Please send me the books I have checked above. Orders for less than 5 books must include 60¢ for the first book and 25¢ for each additional book to cover mailing and handling. Orders of 5 or more books postage is Free. I enclose $_____ in check or money order.

Name_____

Address_____

City_____ State/Zip_____

Please allow 4 to 5 weeks for delivery. This offer expires 6/78.   A-26